A Cocktail of Secrets

C T Luxon

A Cocktail of Secrets

Copyright 2014 – The Creative Peak

First paperback edition printed in 2014 in the United Kingdom
The author asserts the moral right to be identified as the author of this work

A catalogue record for this book is available from the British Library

ISBN 978-1-910236-03-1

No part of this book shall be reproduced or transmitted in any form or by any means, electronic or mechanical, including photocopying, recording, or by any information retrieval system without written permission of the publisher. All rights are reserved by the publisher.

Published by The Creative Peak
www.thecreativepeak.com

For more copies of this book, please email: info@thecreativepeak.com

Book Design: Terry Goble
Cover Image: Copyright Shutterstock/zzveillust

For further information about this book please visit:
www.thecreativepeak.com

Printed and Bound in Great Britain by
imprintdigitial Printers
www. imprint.co.uk

This is a work of fiction. Names, characters, businesses, events and incidents are either the products of the author's imagination or used in a fictitious manner. Any resemblance to actual persons, living or dead, or actual events is purely coincidental.

Dedication

To the people and village of Wentworth, near Sheffield.

It was an early spring morning when we walked through this village, which was shrouded in fog. It became the inspiration for the setting of this novel.

The Creative Peak
Fiction

Model for Murder - Mel Cope
(Paperback and e-book)
Will He Come Back? - T A Cherry
(Paperback and e-book)
Cocktail of Secrets - C T Luxon
(Paperback and e-book)
The Elusive Quest - T M Elvey
(Paperback and e-book)
Weaving a Tangled Web - Terry Melvin
(Paperback and e-book)

Non-Fiction

The Literary Way - Terry Goble
(Paperback and e-book)
Food for Countryside Moods - Terry Goble
(Paperback and e-book)

For all books please visit the website
www.thecreativepeak.com

Chapter One

'How long does this journey take?' asked Amy to no one in particular, as she sat alone in the rickety one carriage train. She was on her way to stay with her brother, the local vicar, in the small South Yorkshire village of Nether Crimpton. It had been a long journey from Brighton on the south coast. She was feeling hot and bothered. Despite several heavy hints about a quiet journey, the Yorkshire sheep farmer, who sat opposite her on the journey from St Pancras to Sheffield, had talked all the way. At this moment in her life, whatever men did, they seemed to annoy her.

She looked out over the gentle rolling countryside as the train slowly ground to a halt at yet another signal. There was no air conditioning in this old carriage, which she thought was a left over from a bygone age. The seats were uncomfortable and looked like they had been taken from an old bus. She remembered sitting on seats like this nearly thirty years ago, when she first went to school with her governess.

Amy's discomfort was made worse as it was a blazing hot summer's afternoon and her feet ached. It hadn't been a good decision to wear new shoes on such a long journey. She looked down at her feet and admired the sleek, pink and blue, high-heeled shoes. The delicate bow on the front of them, had captured her attention yesterday, as she had moped around the shops in Brighton.

After the emotional traumas of Scotland, she had gone home to her parents in the seaside resort. Both were very busy GP doctors and could spare her little time. She had only been there for about a month, when they suggested that she should go to stay with her brother Augustus. While she didn't want to leave Brighton, she was looking forward to seeing Gus again. It had been eighteen months, since they had been together in Africa.

Amy looked at her two heavy cases and hoped there would be a porter to meet her. If not, she was sure that Gus would carry them for her. She sighed as she just wanted the journey to be over, then she could have a long bath and pamper herself a little. As the train slowly rattled into the next station, she glanced out of the window to see the old wooden sign, *Nether Crimpton Halt*. She was relieved to have finally arrived. The guard, who had been in talking to the driver in his cab, since they had left Sheffield, reappeared to shout down the carriage, 'Nether Crimpton'.

He looked at Amy struggling with her two large cases, and promptly closed the door, to carry on talking to the driver. Amy's long legs easily made it down the large step onto the concrete platform. It was much harder to drag the suitcases down the step. As soon as the second one reached the platform, the doors closed and the train began to pull away.

She stood to her full height and looked around. The station, if it could be called that, was two concrete platforms on either side of the track. Near to where she got off was a tin hut, on which the faded writing said, *'Waiting Room'*. There was nothing else in sight. It was hard to even pick out a building in the distance. The halt was in the middle of some lush, yellow fields. The pungent aroma of the fields of rape, wafted over her and she screwed up her nose at the smell. She wondered why Augustus wasn't here to meet her? She looked at her cases and sighed. Her irritation was growing because she had no idea where to go. It was now obvious that this decrepit old station didn't have a porter.

At the end of the platform a slight movement caught her eye. She hoped it was her brother. Amy soon realised her expectations were dashed. A small figure in a heavy black, gabardine coat gradually came up the slope at the end of the platform. As the person walked towards Amy, she could see it was a women, who was wrapped up tightly in the coat, despite the high afternoon temperature. The coat almost touched the ground. She wore a black peaked cap, that completely covered her small head, and came down to just above her eyes. To Amy she looked a very strange lady as she approached. She had glanced over the woman's shoulder to see that there was no one else on the platform. It was then that she realised that the little old lady was coming up to her. As she got closer, the features under the peak cap became evident.

on its hinges and groaned as she bashed the suitcase against it.

'I haven't got a key,' said Amy.

'It's never locked,' said Mavis as she pushed opened the huge front door and went in. She put the cases on the floor under the stag's head, which was just inside the oak panelled hall. Mavis hung her cap on the lowest part of the huge antlers that hung out from the wall.

Amy walked into the hall in amazement and came eye to eye with the stag. Its glass eyes seemed to move to examine her. She jumped initially, but then just put it down to the tricks of the light. Mavis had now walked down the length of the hall. 'This way dear, I expect you will want a cup of tea, after your long journey,' said Mavis as she went into the kitchen. She filled the kettle, placed it on the gas stove, and lit the flame underneath it.

Amy just looked around in astonishment. The kitchen didn't look like it had changed since the 1930s. It was dark in the room, and so she peered through the small window to the outside. Amy stepped back in astonishment. She could clearly read the gravestone, which was only about two feet from the window. The view from the kitchen was over the graveyard. She wanted to pinch herself to make sure it wasn't a dream. She said to herself, 'What have I let myself into? She knew that Gus would take all these things in his stride, but it was surreal to be picked up by a taxi driver, who just walks into a house and makes the tea.

'Where's the milk,' said Amy coming back to her senses. She saw that Mavis already had a tray and the cups organised. She was warming the pot, and waiting for the kettle to boil. Amy looked around, but couldn't see a fridge.

'In the dairy, my dear,' replied Mavis. Amy looked confused as she tried to work out what she meant. Mavis continued, 'Through that door, down the steps, and the door on the left.' Amy opened the huge wooden door and stepped into a well-stocked and precisely organised pantry. She immediately spotted several jars of Gus's favourite jam. She looked around. At the end of the pantry, about ten feet away, were some steps. It was cold in here. The air became chillier and the atmosphere more eerie, as she went down the steps. The small door opened with a slight creak. She had to duck to get into the very small room. She shivered as it was very cold and damp. The milk, butter and other things normally in a fridge were all laid out on the stone slabs. There was no chiller down here, it was just the natural coldness of being below ground. At the top of the wall, that faced her, was a very small grating, which she could just see through. It was at grass level, and she could just see the bottom of a gravestone. She hurriedly took the milk and returned to the kitchen. The teapot was already on a tray, which now had a lace cover. Next to the single cup and saucer was a scone, butter and jam. 'Are you not going to have a cup. Mrs Rudd.'

'No thank you, my dear, the Reverend won't be long. I must go and pick up Mrs Braithwaite.' Amy remembered that Mavis had said, that was where Augustus had gone. She was now far too confused, about what was happening, to ask anything else. She studied Mavis, why would a taxi-driver be going to a person who had died. Amy shook her head and decided to ask Gus for an explanation.

'This way,' said Mavis, who walked back into the hall and went into the first room on the left. It was the old library. Immediately, Amy caught the smell of the musty books, which lined the walls. As she got fully into the room, she smiled as she saw the desk and chair. The familiarity of Gus's briefcase, pens and personal books, gave her a sense of relief.

Within a few minutes, Mavis had left. Amy was sat alone in the huge wing backed chair, in the creaking house, waiting for her brother. There were no other sounds apart from a dog barking somewhere nearby. She was feeling tired after her journey, but was definitely not going to fall asleep in this house on her own. Amy stirred herself to walk around the room and glance at the books and desk, but her heart wasn't in it. She aimlessly drifted, as she had done since her man had let her down so badly in Scotland. She still shuddered every time she thought about it. It was such a calamity after expecting to become Mrs McDougall. She had been so close, but had suddenly found out that the marriage was not going to take place. Shock had replaced surprise when the man, she adored, said that he was leaving her. It had been so close to her wedding day.

In the eerie quietness of Gus's study, a tear gently rolled down her cheek, but a steely glint came into her eye, as she said to herself, 'Snap out of it, it's gone, it's past! You've got to do something positive.'

Amy wanted to stick by the resolution that she had told her parents. She would absorb herself in something that caught her imagination. There definitely wouldn't be any more men for the foreseeable future. She again looked around the room. So this is what my parents and Gus came up with to make me positive. She knew they were trying to do the best for her, but she shook her head in disbelief.

She went back to the chair and sat down to eat her scone. Before the first mouthful, she froze in her chair. There was a very distinctive creak of the floor in the hall. Someone was there, she wasn't in any doubt. Her stomach tightened as she worked out that the noise was coming towards the library. It was now a very clear sound. There was no chance it was just the old building groaning.

Amy stared intently at the door. Her eyes got wider, and she got ready to scream, as it gradually creaked open. She was full of tension but she waited. The first signs made her jump. A long nose on a black face appeared. The deep, doleful black eyes peered at her. She laughed. 'Come here boy,' she said in a gentle tone, but the head quickly disappeared. By the time she had opened the door fully, the dog was gone. A quick thought suddenly crossed her mind. Was it a ghost? No, no it was a real dog. Why does Augustus have a dog?

Her slight shake of the head stopped, as she looked out of the window. Coming along the track was the flowing black cassock of her brother Augustus. His huge frame was striding out, creating a swirl of dust behind him. She could immediately see that his thinning black hair hadn't changed and it stuck out at eccentric angles. A warm smile crossed her face. Quickly she left the library and went to meet him. She got along the hall just as he came in the front door. She ran towards him and flung her arms around his neck. 'Gus, it's so wonderful to see you. I've missed you,' and she promptly burst into tears.

"Hello, sis,' he said in his calm manner, as he hugged her back. He slid his solid strong arms around her and lifted her off the floor. He carried her backwards so that he could shut the front door. He had picked her up like this ever since she was little. Although she was now tall, with even more height given to her by her four inch heels, she still had to look up to him. He took no notice of the tears and gently put her down. 'Let me look at you,' he said in his deep gentle voice. He held her at arm's length. 'You look pale, but I expected that after what you have been through.'

He still took no notice of the tears and led her back into the study. He continued, 'But what I have got planned for you will soon get your cheeks glowing and your wonderful smile back.' Amy gave a little sigh, as she just hoped that Gus was right.

'So what do you think of it all?' said Gus waving his hand around, 'The village? The church? The vicarage?'

'This house is so spooky,' she said. They both laughed together.

'Is my little sis going to be frightened of all the ghosts?'

Amy laughed, 'No, of course not, but it's like something from a horror movie.'

'I think any estate agent would say that it had character.'

'It certainly has that,' said Amy. They chatted for a while about the joy of seeing each other. They had not been together since they were in Africa. Then Augustus said, 'Do you want the first part of your recuperation?'

'I'm perfectly OK, I don't need looking after.'

Augustus gave a gentle smile and said, 'I'll always look after my little sister.' At which point Amy promptly burst into tears again and hugged her brother.

'Stay there,' he said and left the room. He soon returned, put his head round the door and said, 'He's a bit wary of new people.' Brightness shone on Amy's face as that same black nose appeared again. Augustus opened the door fully and came into the library. The large dog stayed very close behind him. Amy called to him, as he stayed half hidden by the door and her brother. She got down on her knees and called him again. Augustus patted him on the head and the dog, taking it as a sign of approval, came out from behind the door and slowly came across to Amy who exclaimed, 'He's only got three legs, poor thing!'

'He has had a bad time, but he's really obedient and he can run the same as a normal dog.' By now Amy was making a fuss of him and his tail began to wag enthusiastically.

'What's his name?'

'Desmond,' replied Augustus, and added, 'The rescue centre said that they called him 'Des', but I thought that naming him after Desmond Tutu was much more appropriate.' Amy laughed for the first time in a long while as she followed her brother into the hall, followed very closely by the padding of three paws.

Augustus said, 'Let me show you around, it's a grand old house.' Amy made a face at which Augustus laughed. Augustus spotted the suitcases and, with one in each hand, bounded up the stairs. 'I'll show you to your room.'

Amy didn't know what to expect. Augustus opened the door and then stood aside so she could go in first. As Amy stepped into the room, she took in the magnificent view of the huge four-poster bed. It had crisp clean sheets that immediately caught her attention. She looked around. A wide bay window made this one of the brightest rooms in the house. It was a huge room. Even the eight-foot bed seemed to be lost against one of the cream walls. 'It's delightful,' said Amy, 'it's so clean.'

The old furniture was highly polished. As she opened one of the old oak wardrobes, the fragrance from the fluffy towels wafted over her. 'You didn't do all this, did you?' said Amy turning to her brother and grinning at him.

'No, I must own up, it wasn't me. It was Mrs Battersby.'

'Oh!' said Amy, teasing her brother, 'It's a pity it's not Miss Battersby.'

'She is a widow,' said Augustus.

'So there's hope for you yet!'

'But she is nearly eighty,' replied Augustus with a smile.

'You certainly work them hard in the village, the taxi driver was in her seventies.'

'I spoke to her when she came to Mrs Braithwaite's. She

thought the world of you. She said that there would be plenty of men, in the village, that would turn their cap to you.'

'I've finished with men,' replied Amy with finality. She knew Augustus wouldn't rise to the bait. He just smiled, put his arm round her shoulder, and gave her a hug. Amy carried on, 'How did she come to such a conclusion about me so quickly?'

'Respect,' said Augustus.

'Respect?' queried Amy looking confused.

'Yes, you called her Mrs Rudd. Most people in the village call her Mavis, because she is the taxi driver. She doesn't like it at all. She says it's a lack of respect to call an old woman by her first name.' Augustus went on, 'Local village lore is that anyone older than you, you call Mr or Mrs, but anyone younger, you can call them by their first name.'

'That's a bit old-fashioned isn't?'

'This is an old and traditional village, as you are going to find out.'

'Anyway why was she at Mrs Braithwaite's? I thought that was the poor old lady who had died.'

'She'd come to collect the body.'

'In a taxi!'

Augustus laughed, 'No, of course not! The Rudds are the village undertakers, as well as the taxi drivers.'

'And while we are on that subject of this village, why did you want me to come here, you said on the phone it needed my skills?'

'Yes, exactly right.'

Amy said, while grinning at her brother, 'You want a fully qualified outdoor instructor, who is good at skiing, rock climbing and canoeing?'

'You have other skills as well.'

'Hmm... dare I ask?'

'I really do want your organisational skills. Both of the church wardens sadly died a few months ago. I'm struggling to cope with all that is expected of me.'

She couldn't hide the surprise in her voice, 'You want me to be a church warden?'

'Only if you want to be, but I rather you just helped out. The village festival week starts tomorrow.'

'Yes,' said Amy warily.

'Could you do the home-made jam stall at the visitor's centre tomorrow, also can you help me judge the best garden in the village at the weekend?'

Amy laughed and repeated, 'A jam stall and garden competition?'

Augustus wasn't daunted by her teasing and added, 'I could do with some help in church on Saturday, as there is a big wedding.'

With that word, wedding, Amy turned to look out of the window, so that Augustus couldn't see the expression on her face.

Chapter Two

Amy pulled back the big heavy curtains. The sun streamed into the bedroom. She had slept well on her first night in this creaking old house. It had been after midnight, she had just been dropping off, when there was a dull scratching noise at the door. The noise had made her wide awake again. It took a few moments to realise it was nothing sinister. It was Desmond at her bedroom door, wanting to come in. As soon as she had opened the door, he had come in, flopped down by the side of her bed, and promptly went to sleep. He was still there now.

She looked out of the window. The only part of the church grounds that she could see was part of the cemetery. Her bedroom overlooked the burial ground of the aristocracy from the old hall. It was surrounded by a rusty old railing, to differentiate it from the rest of the cemetery.

The tall trees, which overshadowed the elaborate and rather Gothic memorials, blocked out the view across the countryside. It was a sombre sight to wait up to in the morning.

The weather forecast for today was good and she was looking forward, in a strange sort of way, to exploring the village. She wouldn't let her brother down. She had to remember that she was manning the jam stall later on.

'A jam stall!' she muttered to herself. 'I thought it was only old spinsters, who did them.' She looked in the mirror. No she wasn't an old spinster. Yet! She finished dressing by pulling on her purple trainers and trotted down the stairs. Desmond, who was now awake and lively, followed her. 'Coming for a run?' she said to him as she went to put his lead on, but he backed away. As she went to leave he came up to her again. 'OK, I give in, no lead.'

Amy turned right onto the track and began to run. She decided to explore the village on her first jog, and so she ran along the track towards Crimpton Manor. She crossed the road. Then she followed the footpath along the drive towards the stately home. She was surprised at the immense size of the building. Gus had told her it had been built for the aristocracy, but she had pictured something small and refined. She had to revise her opinions as she ran towards the house. It was very large and had a very long frontage, with large columns in the centre. There were extensive wings on both sides of the main building. She guessed it must have several hundred rooms and be one of the biggest houses in the country.

As she approached the gate, so there were several large signs which said *Private, Trespassers will be Prosecuted* and *Beware of the Dogs*. Amy had been enjoying her run, but suddenly realised that she had forgotten that she had Gus's dog with her. But she was relieved when she looked round to see Desmond trotting along behind her. There was a footpath to the left and she continued her jog. It went round the back of the old stable block, which had now been transformed into a visitors' centre. She smiled as she realised it was where her afternoon was going to be spent.

The path led her out onto the main road through the village. She crossed the road and carried on along the path past the *Marquis* pub. The route took her across the fields to the railway station. A footbridge took her onto the lane. It was the road along which she'd had her frightening taxi ride of yesterday. As she increased her speed down the lane, she suddenly noticed that Desmond was no longer with her. Her guess was that he would catch up. She kept looking round to see if he was coming. She was running in one direction and looking back for Desmond, which led to the calamity.

She hadn't seen that there was a drive that opened onto the lane. As she ran on, she turned to look for the dog and didn't see the car that came out of the drive. Fortunately, the car driver saw her and stopped. By the time she had turned and had seen the car, she was too close to stop. Her trainers skidded on the loose gravel on the roadside. She fell head first across the bonnet of the large Mercedes. Her water bottle jumped out of her hand and the top of it came off. The water from the bottle splashed down the front of the windscreen. As she spiralled across the front of the car so her purple headband fell onto the car.

The water was trickling down the windscreen, and set off the automatic wipers. As they moved for the first time, so her headband was caught by one of the wipers and became entangled.

The driver leapt out of the car, 'Are you all right? Have you hurt yourself?'

Amy managed to pull herself back to her feet from being sprawled over the bonnet and said. 'No harm done, I just scared myself a little.' She was very conscious that she had turned bright red with embarrassment. Amy looked at the driver, who she guessed was in his early forties. He was slightly balding, with thin grey hair, and wore a very sleek grey Armani suit. In the few seconds of their meeting, she recognised a very handsome man. He looked her up and down, but kept a bland face when he said, 'Well, if you're not hurt, I'm in a hurry and I'll be on my way.'

'That's a pity,' thought Amy, before she remembered that she wasn't have anything to do with men. Then she caught sight of her self in the darkened windows of the car. Her hair was a mess, and her tracksuit was dishevelled. In the collision, one of her trainers had come off. Also, she knew that she would be glowing pink from her jog, which would have been made worse by her embarrassment. He had been standing close to her and she knew she didn't smell too good, as she had been sweating a lot in the hot morning sunshine. When she had dressed she hadn't bothered with perfume as she hardly expected to meet a good-looking man.

With some embarrassment she said, 'Can I have my headband back?' This made her go even redder, as she blushed at asking for such a silly object. The bright purple band was now assiduously wiping the windscreen as it was firmly trapped under the wiper. The man sighed, reached into the car and turned off the wipers.

He went to stretch across, but Amy said, 'I'll do it,' and they both collided. He smoothed down his suit, while Amy extracted the headband. She muttered, 'Sorry', as he got back into the car and sped away down the lane.

She sat on the verge to put her trainer back on. Even though there was no one around, she blushed at the fool she had made of herself. Whilst all this had been happening, Desmond had caught her up and had taken advantage of stopping, by laying down on the grass verge.

Finally, she was ready again and she started to jog at a more moderate pace down the lane. She made sure that Desmond was nearby. When she got to the main road through the village, she glanced around to see which way to go.

She was just near a building, which had peeling paint and grass growing out of the cracks in the front step. The old broken sign read, *Brace of Pheasants*. It was an old pub. The sign on the opposite side of the road, then caught her attention. It indicated a footpath and it seemed to go between the farm buildings opposite. She crossed the road and jogged up the concrete yard between the two barns.

A tall thin wiry man of about Amy's age came out from one of the small doors at the side of the barn. He's not bad-looking, thought Amy, before remembering her resolution. But she knew she could easily dismiss him, as his hair was unkempt and he was quite scruffy. He was wearing dirty jeans and an old tee-shirt, which was partly covered by a torn red check shirt.

'Morning,' he said cheerfully, 'do you want me?'

'No,' said Amy as she stopped running. Desmond went straight past her and up to man, who made a fuss of him.

'I'm Ged,' he said, 'you must be Amy, Augustus's sister?

'Yes,' said Amy a little surprised, but then realised that it was Desmond, who he recognised.

'The footpath goes around the other side of this barn.'

'Oh, sorry,' and she turned to go.

'While you're here. I could do with a lift. It's not heavy, but I can't pick it up on my own.'

'OK,' said Amy and followed him. She crossed the yard and went in through the door and gasped under her breath, 'Oh my God.' Ged was standing at one end of a coffin and was expecting her to take the other end.

'It's just through here, into the Chapel of Rest.'

Amy put it down as quickly as she could, turned, shouted goodbye and ran out of the barn. She glanced up and didn't know how she had missed the sign which read, *Rudds, Funeral Direc-*

tors. She shivered and shuddered all the way back to the vicarage.

*****

She hadn't been sure what to wear for serving on a jam stall. In the end she had opted for an embroidered tee-shirt, summer trousers, and flat strappy red sandals. She was already regretting the shoes as she walked along the track to the visitor's centre. Not only were they getting covered in dust, but the sand was getting under her toes. Also she could feel every sharp stone through the thin soles.

The visitor centre was a large square seventeenth century building, with ornate stone work, and elaborate arched entrances. In the olden days they were capable of taking a coach and four.

In the middle of the building, there was a large square courtyard, with what was, originally, a covered riding area. The old stables had been converted into a restaurant, an information centre and a bar. There were also a number of other gift and tourist shops, with several small craft outlets in the Craft Centre, at one end of the courtyard.

It was just outside here, that the local parish sold its produce, which was mainly jam. Amy walked through the main arch and immediately spotted the jam stall. So this was going to be her life for the next few hours. At least this shouldn't be too troublesome. She might even have a bit of time to think through what she was going to do after she left Nether Crimpton.

As she approached the stall an old lady, who had been sitting knitting behind one of the tables, stood up.

'Mrs Battersby?'

'Yes, and you must be Amy. Such a pretty name. Aren't you tall, just like the Reverend.' Amy looked at the little old lady, who typified the picture of the kindly old aunt. It was hard to believe that she was Gus's housekeeper. 'I'm glad you've come to take over, it gets so busy here.' Amy looked around at the one or two people browsing holiday gifts, but chose not to say anything.

After Mrs Battersby had explained everything about running

the stall, she left Amy to it. Before she could sit down, and open the book she had brought to read, she saw a man striding purposefully towards the stall.

He doesn't want any jam, she said to herself. He was tanned, had a large beer gut, and his open shirt revealed tattoos and several medallions. The large gold watch on his wrist glinted in the sun. He boomed a large, 'Hello' from the far side of courtyard. Amy knew it was directed at her, she gave a weak grin and waited for him to reach her.

As he shook hands he said, 'I'm Damien Smith, the owner of the visitor centre.'

Amy tried to pull her hand away, but he had it in a firm grip. 'I'm Amy, the vicar's sister.'

'Yes, I know, I've heard a lot about you,' he said finally releasing her hand.

'From Augustus?' she couldn't believe that Gus would have said very much.

'No from the villagers. Did you enjoy your run this morning?' Amy sighed, it was obviously going to be one of those places, where nothing was secret.

'Yes, thank you, I did,' but she blushed at the thought of how embarrassed she had been.

A woman in a white summer suit, with short dark hair, approached from the bar. Her jewellery bouncing slightly, as she struggled to walk on very high heels, across the cobbled courtyard. As she got close, Amy could see that she wore a lot of make up.

'What's this stall doing here? I said that I wanted it over there in that corner, out of the way.'

She looked with a scowl at Damien who said, 'I thought it was all right here.'

'No it isn't, it doesn't make any profit for us, all the proceeds go to that crumpling old church,' she replied as she scornfully looked Amy up and down.

'I'm Amy.'

'And I'm the owner of this centre, so perhaps you will make sure it's in the right place next time.' And with that parting remark, she turned as quickly as she could in her heels and went back towards the bar.

Amy could see that even Damien was embarrassed as he quietly said, 'That's Lorraine, my wife, she's under a bit of stress at the moment. It's the pressure of the business.'

Lorraine turned before she went into the bar and shouted across the courtyard, 'Damien, there's a barrel that needs changing.' Before he turned to go, he said quietly to Amy, 'Perhaps I might see you, in the *Marquis*, for a drink.' Amy gave the faintest of smiles and didn't reply, but she thought, absolutely no chance whatsoever, and she transferred her attention to re-organising the jams on the table.

Having assured herself that Damien and Lorraine had finally gone, she went to settle down when a soft Irish voice behind her said, 'They are having a bad time at the moment and take it out on the rest of us.'

She turned to see a pretty round faced woman, with long black hair, and a delightful smile. Amy guessed that she was in her early forties, but she had a good figure and was dressed in a neatly pressed white blouse and straight black trousers.

They chatted for a few minutes and Amy found out that her name was Bernadette. She had only lived in the village for a few years, and she was just on her way to work as a waitress in the restaurant. Bernadette said that most of the staff tried to avoid Lorraine, but that Damien was all right, despite the first impression he made.

A pretty dark teenager walked across the courtyard. She was dressed in a white blouse and black trousers. Bernadette said that she was Mary, Damien and Lorraine's daughter. She was also a waitress and that she was really nice. She added that they also had a son, Clint, who never worked in the centre, even though he didn't have a job.

Bernadette looked towards the arch, 'Here they come,' she said pointing to the coach coming into the car park. 'There's another three coaches, plus a load of cars, who are booked into the children's activities around the back of the centre. It's going to be a busy afternoon.'

Within twenty minutes the visitor's centre was thronging with people and Amy was busy. It stayed like that all through the afternoon. By five o'clock her feet ached and she wanted to go. There were still a lot of people around and she wanted to take as much money as possible. She was hot, bothered and fed up with people being so picky. There were lots of badly behaved children running around and their constant shrieking had given her a headache.

She was just getting ready to finish, when a short overweight man, with thinning hair, approached the stall. He was sweating profusely in the hot afternoon sun. His tee-shirt and shorts looked like they had been bought, when he was a smaller size. A girl of about five was holding his hand and screaming with a temper. He was clearly immune to the noise that was being generated from those little lungs.

He looked at the stall, and then picked up a couple of jars of jam and scowled at them. He put them down again and pushed some others around. Amy wanted to get rid of him as soon as possible so she said, 'Are you looking for any flavour in particular?'

'How do I know they have been hygienically made and packed?'

Amy ignored his question, picked up the most professional looking jam, and said, 'The strawberry jam is very popular.'

'It might have come from a dodgy kitchen.'

Amy looked at the label, which said that it was made by Mrs Battersby. 'I personally know Mrs Battersby and can assure you that she is very thorough and clean in everything she does.'

'But there's no Health and Safety certificate, saying it was packed in a controlled environment.'

The hot afternoon sun and her aching feet got the better of Amy and she snapped, 'Look at the sign above this stall. It says *Home-Made*. So common sense should tell you there won't be any official certification. If you were so particular, why did you come to such a stall in the first place.'

He glared at her and said, 'You are dammed rude. I shall report you to the manager.'

By now he had passed Amy's tolerance threshold. 'Don't be so ridiculous, this is a charity stall for the local church. If you don't want the jam, you could just give me a donation for the grand old parish church.'

He turned and stormed away dragging the screaming five-year old with him.

Amy assumed that her other duties in the parish might be slightly less stressful and she began to pack up the stall. Finally, she thought that she ought to say goodbye to at least someone, but certainly wasn't going to approach Damien or Lorraine. She went to the restaurant to say goodbye to Bernadette, who had been the only other person from the centre she had really spoken to that afternoon. As she walked into the restaurant, she changed her mind as she saw that the awkward man, that she had just dealt with, was now in an argument with Bernadette. He was waving a bill at her. Amy had had enough and so she turned, and took her aching feet, back to the vicarage.

******

Amy walked slowly into the vicarage. She noticed on the hall table, a letter from her friend, Jane, in Scotland. She kicked off her shoes, went into Augustus's office, and sat to read it. Her brother wasn't expected back until later.

Amy had spent several years in various parts of Africa with Augustus, who was working for a charity that built schools. She had really enjoyed her time there, but one day in one of the British newspapers, which her parents had sent through, there was an advert for an Outdoor Pursuits Instructor at Pitlochry in Scotland.

She was late in applying, but they wanted to interview her and she flew to Scotland and got the job. Jane was appointed at the same time and they became good friends. They worked together on canoeing, rock climbing and orienteering. She hadn't heard from Jane since she had left Scotland, which she had done so very quickly after she was jilted. Amy smiled and had a good feeling inside, as it was really good to get a note from Jane.

She got herself comfortable, and opened what was a long letter, and settled down to read it. It started brightly enough, but then came the bit where Jane said that it was very difficult to write. Bad news would be better coming from a friend, rather then her finding out from a rumour. Amy paused and looked up from the letter. It was going to be something about the wedding. As far as she was concerned everything, that could have gone wrong, had already happened. So what else could there be?

While working in Pitlochry, she had been swept off her feet by Duncan, the owner of a small distillery. Within a year, he had proposed and she had been over-the-moon to accept. She was looking forward to a grand Scottish marriage, developing the best job she had every had, and settling down in a wonderful house in the highlands. All was going well, and the wedding date had been set, and she had chosen her dress. They were just about to send out the invitations, when Duncan suddenly said that perhaps they were being too hasty, and should postpone the wedding to the following year.

Amy was very concerned, but put it down to the nervousness of her fiancé about commitment. She seemed to re-assure him that it should all go ahead as planned. He had returned to being his bright and bubbly self for a few weeks and Amy had suggested it was about time to send out the invitations, as the planned date was only a month away. Again Duncan had seemed a little edgy, but Amy was keen and he agreed. They wrote them out together and he said that he would post them the following day.

In the evening of the following day, he picked Amy up from work, which was the normal pattern. Instead of going home, he drove to a quiet place near the lake. He said that it was all over between them and that he was leaving her.

Despite being very upset she had pleaded for a reason, and finally it had all come out. One of the directors of his company, was a wealthy lady who owned a castle and large estate. She had found out that Duncan was going to marry Amy and said that she would have been very happy to be his wife. It was at that point Duncan decided to change his mind.

Once Amy could see that he was determined to go through with it, she decided that she couldn't possibly stay living in the same village, and she resigned her job. She then had fled back to her parents in Brighton, She had been there trying to recover from the upset, when she got the invitation to come to join Augustus.

Amy looked again at the letter. If she hadn't been shocked enough at Duncan's behaviour, had he done something else to hurt her? The tears started to flow as she read on. By the end of the letter she was sobbing and had thrown the letter onto the floor. She lost all sense of time as she cried.

It was only Augustus walking in that made her look up. His quick eyes saw the letter and the tear-stained face of his sister. He went straight over to her and, kneeling beside her chair, took her hands into his. He didn't say anything, but just held her hands. Finally Amy took a deep breath and gasped through the tears, 'I hate him.'

Very gently Augustus said, 'You know I don't like such talk. Take your time, you have obviously had a shock.'

Amy snatched up the letter and handed it to her brother, 'Read this!'

Augustus glance down both sides of the letter and the fine handwriting and said, 'Are you sure? Would you prefer to leave it to later? Then see whether you want to offer it to me again?'

'No,' she said, 'I'm sure, please read it.'

Augustus slowly read it, as he still held his sister's hand. By the time he had finished it, he looked up to see that Amy was watching him. He had shown no reaction to the contents. He knew that Amy was expecting him to speak, 'Avarice is a terrible thing. It doesn't matter whether it is for money or position.'

'How could he be so cruel to me, when he knew how much I loved him.'

'The actions of some men are very difficult for many of us to understand. I would have dearly shielded you from such a man, if it was in my power.'

'I know you would. Dear Gus, you have always been such a support to me. But he couldn't have been more cruel. Why did he have to keep all the same wedding arrangements and then marry someone else.'

Gus said, 'It is the action of an unthinking and self-centred man. Such behaviour never leaves the mind of people who know him. Your friend says that she and many others refused to go.'

'But...'

'Hush, my little sister. You have done nothing wrong, and as I would always expect of you, you have behaved in an extremely dignified manner, despite the severe provocation.'

'Oh, Gus, I feel so betrayed.'

With his gentle smile he said, 'I can tell what you're thinking. Do not let such an idea as revenge or retaliation enter your mind. I know after it first happened, you were thinking of legally investigating breach of promise. Please I beg of you, show courage, and move forwards not backwards.'

They sat for a long time in silence with the love of a brother for his sister, who had been so badly wronged. Amy knew that her Gus would not move from her side, until she had regained her composure. He would sit there in their sibling silence all night if necessary.

Finally Amy said, 'Gus?' He just looked up at her and gave her a gentle smile. 'I don't think I can go through with helping you at the wedding tomorrow.'

'Of course. I can understand why. It's your decision entirely.'

Chapter Three

Amy stood in front of the mirror in a matching grey jacket and skirt. It was a hot afternoon, and as her legs were reasonably tanned, she had decided to go without tights. She didn't have a hat, but that was only a little concern as she wasn't really going to the wedding. She sniffed, but said to herself, 'I can't burst out crying, every time someone mentions a wedding.' She was trying to be strong, but it was very difficult and she felt completely devastated by Jane's letter. She had wandered around the vicarage all morning constantly telling Augustus she couldn't go through with it. He didn't argue or take her to task, he just kept saying it was her decision.

I can't let him down, I know I can't, however difficult it is going to be. She turned her thoughts again to the mirror. Which pair of shoes to wear, was her final decision. Weddings called for dressy shoes, but she tried to remember that she wasn't actually going to the wedding, I'm a churchwarden. What type of shoes do they wear?

She looked along the line of the six pairs that she had decided matched the grey suit. Perhaps the ones with little bows at the front and tassels at the back would be a little over the top for her role. Amy decided, while she might not be really going to the wedding, she couldn't wear flat shoes, it just wouldn't seem right. She finally chose her faux grey snakeskin high heels. She took a deep breath, checked her make-up, and set off for the church, full of trepidation.

Augustus was welcoming the very first of the guests at the church door as she walked up the path. She saw that kind and benevolent smile that she so loved. She knew that if she hadn't turned up there would be no comment or even the slightest difficulty from Augustus. She was soon briefed as to what was expected of her, but inside she wasn't confident that she would last the afternoon, particularly when she saw the bride. But she settled down to giving out the Order of Service pamphlet and making sure the guests knew where to sit.

Bernadette, who she had met yesterday, came up the path with Mary, the daughter of the owners of the visitors' centre.

'Hello,' said Amy, 'are you not working this afternoon?'

'No, we both have Saturdays off. So we've been into town this morning and have been looking forward to the wedding on such a nice afternoon.'

'Hello,' said Amy to the man behind. 'You're Ged aren't you, we met yesterday.'

'Yes, that's right,' he said with a slight smirk. Amy turned away to get another Order of Service, so he didn't see her blush.' As she turned back she looked him up and down. He was tall and quite handsome, but in a wiry sort of way, and he looked much smarter today than when they had met yesterday. Then the thought came to her. His black suit. Of course he would have a smart suit, he was an undertaker. She didn't know why, but she shivered at the thought. It was a pity, because he had bright brown eyes and a nice smile.

'Are you a relation? said Amy.

'The bride is my cousin.'

'Everyone in the valley is his cousin, or so he claims,' said the man following. He wore an open neck shirt and chino trousers. He didn't smile at Amy and refused the Order of Service that she offered.'

Ged said, 'This is Amy, she is the vicar's sister.'

'Oh, aye,' was the reply, 'not going to be much business from you then.' Both he and Ged laughed.

'Do you have a business in the village?' asked Amy as both men showed no inclination of moving on.

'I'm the landlord of the *Brace of Pheasants*. Come in sometime, the rabbit stew is delicious.' And then they walked down the aisle to take up their seats. Amy thought, it doesn't even look like its open. I've now had invitations to the two pubs and there is absolutely no way I'm going to either.

Having got one of her embarrassments from yesterday out-of-the-way, she hoped the man in the Mercedes might turn up to see her looking a little better than she was yesterday. As far as she could remember from their encounter, he was an extremely good-looking man. But the sight of the bridegroom getting out of the car brought her back to her thoughts about men.

She had resolved, while getting ready for this afternoon, that she needed something to distract her from her gloomy thoughts. It would need to be something she could really get her teeth into. She hoped there were no good looking men around this afternoon.

*****

After the coach had arrived at the church for the wedding, Amy had been too busy to think of her problems. She had guessed that Augustus would know that she would be busy and therefore would have to stop dwelling on her past. After the ceremony she had helped her brother tidy the church and they had a quiet evening, where they enjoyed each other's company. What had happened in Scotland wasn't going to go away, but Gus was doing his best to keep her occupied, so she didn't have time to think about it.

As they came to the end of their chat, Augustus said with a meek smile, 'You did such a good job as a churchwarden this afternoon for the wedding. Could you do the same for the Sunday service tomorrow?'

'Yes, of course,' she said and kissed him on the forehead as she got up.

'And you haven't forgotten that we are judging the best garden in the village tomorrow afternoon.'

'Are you sure you really want me? I don't know much about gardening.'

Augustus gave a hearty laugh, 'Judging gardens has nothing to do with it.'

'I don't see what you mean.'

'There was a parish meeting at the beginning of the week. I said that you were coming up to stay for a short while. If it was all right with everyone then you would help me judge the competition.'

'And so?' said Amy, not seeing any connection.

'We've had five extra entries since then. They all want to meet you.'

A frown came over her face, 'Of course, I don't mind doing it, but I'm worried, I'll make the wrong decision.'

'Don't worry about that. There are three judges. You, me and a consultant doctor, who lives in the village. He's very knowledgeable about gardening but, to be frank, he is not that popular. He keeps himself apart from the village most of time and lives in the large gentleman's residence near the station.'

'Ah,' said Amy, 'I think I might have met him.'

'That's good,' said Augustus.

'No it's not, it's totally embarrassing. Are you really sure, I cannot get out of it?'

Augustus shook his head. "You can talk to all the people. I will stand there doing nothing. Theodore will inspect the garden. He's very good at making the right decisions.'

'I remain unconvinced,' said Amy but she smiled and said, 'and now I'm going for a run.'

She looked down at Desmond and said, 'Walkies.' But it was only greeted with a snore. 'It doesn't matter we had a good walk after the wedding.' Amy left Augustus writing his sermon for the service and went to get changed.

In a few minutes she was coming down the stairs, in her purple lycra leggings with a bright purple tee-shirt, over her black leotard. On her feet she had her usual purple running trainers. It was getting dark, so she decided to head out into the country, while she could still see. It was good to loosen up after the day. The moon came out and there was enough light to be able to see quite well. She went around the back of Crimpton Manor and saw that there were only a couple of room lights on at one end.

Most of the building was in total darkness. The run through the countryside was exhilarating and it was completely dark by the time she came back to the lane by the station. With only half a mile to go she quickened her pace. As she approached the backs of the cottages, which lined the high street, some strange movement caught her attention. She slowed, and her trainers made no noise on the grass path. There was someone in the garden that was near the lane and the person was thrashing around. As she quickened her pace in that direction, she could see a figure kicking out at the plants and flowers. As far as she could tell it was the figure and movement of a young man. She immediately guessed that it wasn't the owner so she shouted, 'Hey! What are you doing?'

As soon as the figure had heard Amy's shout, he stopped thrashing and made a run for it. He went out through the gate and took the lane towards the high street. Amy shouted, 'You're not getting away with that,' and sprinted to catch up with him. But the figure was quite a long way ahead. It was when Amy turned on to the high street that she could finally see that it looked like a teenage boy. Whilst he could run, Amy was quicker and fitter. As they covered the length of the high street, so she gradually gained on him.

She knew that he was flagging, and although she had already done five miles, it wouldn't be long before she caught up with him. They were now getting near the *Marquis* pub, which was opposite the visitor's centre. He looked round and realised he was going to be caught, he turned quickly down a ginnel. Amy turned into the same gap between two cottages. He couldn't get any further and turned to face her. She could see his face, which was snarling at her, and wondered if he had a knife.

'Be careful,' she said to herself, but her adrenalin was flowing and she wasn't giving up that easily. 'You've got some explaining to do young man,' as she sized him up. He was shorter than her and a bit over weight. He was also breathing very heavily from the running.

'Piss off!' and he took a step forward and swung his fist at her head. Amy adroitly stepped back and his punch flailed in the air, nearly knocking himself off of his feet.

'Stop that!' she shouted, but it had no effect and he came at her again, this time trying to kick her with his big boots. Again she jumped out-of-the-way. At his third attempt to hit her his fist caught her shoulder. 'That's it, I've had enough of you,' and she stepped towards him.

The next kick was aimed at her knee, but before its landed, she stepped to one side, and used his own weight to tip him on to his face on the ground. She hadn't meant him to hit the gravel that hard, but he yelped in pain as his face hit the hard surface.

Before he could recover, she twisted his arm up his back, grabbed him by his hair and hauled him to his feet. 'And now I'm going to find out who you are,' she said dragging him back on to the high street. He struggled, but she entwined his fingers, with hers and squeezed. He yelped in pain. 'Stop struggling or I shall hurt you even more. Who are you?'

'Piss off!'

She frogmarched him into the street light, where she could see him better. They were now just outside the *Marquis* pub, when the door opened and a man came out. Amy couldn't believe it. He was the same man who was driving the Mercedes.

'What the matter?' said the man with a degree of impatience.

'This young man has been trampling some of the gardens. Then he's tried to attack me, when I caught up with him.'

'I didn't do anything!'

Amy noticed the man was as smart as before, but it was a different suit. She gave her captive an extra little twist and he yelped. By now other people had been drawn out of their cottages by the noise and one of them said, 'Good on you miss, it was my garden he was trampling.'

The man in the suit looked Amy up and down and said, 'His name is Clint,' and he called back into the open door of the pub, 'Damien you'd better come out here, I think your son has got some explaining to do.'

There was obviously a muttered comment from inside the pub and the man said, 'I would suggest sooner rather than later. Otherwise, the purple avenging angel, who is holding him, might do him a serious mischief.' And with that he said good night and walked up the road.

Chapter Four

Amy was standing in a little brown summer dress on the track that went past the church. She had elected for the brown high-heeled shoes, despite the need to stand for most of the time. Augustus was already inside preparing for the service. There was little else to do so she had been ready early. The precincts of the church for some reason attracted her as she wanted a few quiet minutes to herself. She had wandered round the old and newer graveyards idly looking at the names. What was she was going to do when she left Nether Crimpton?

None of her thoughts had inspired her, but she knew she would only be here for a few weeks. There was plenty of time for more thought, as it was such a quiet little village. It was a glorious Sunday morning and she enjoyed the solitude, as for the last twenty-minutes, she hadn't seen a living soul. Desmond was with her to start with, but the heat became too much for him, and he elected for the coolness of the vicarage.

She had seen Ged walk down the track towards Crimpton Manor. She stood on the track watching where he was going, because she expected him to be at the morning service, which started in about five minutes. She saw him unlock the padlock on the gate at the end of the track and open it.

He went over the road, up the drive of the Manor, and unlocked and opened the gate on to the front of the house. Within a minute, a battered old Morris Minor car came down the drive. Ged stopped the traffic on the lane so that it could pass across. It then made its stately, but stuttering, progress along the track. It went so slow, that Ged could walk behind and keep up with the progress of the car. It pulled up directly outside the church by the *No Parking* sign. By that time Ged had arrived by the passenger door, which he duly opened.

'Good morning, sir, ma'am,' he said as he helped a lady in her seventies from the car. A man who was in his sixties, got out of the driver's door in a sprightly manner. The clothes, of both of them, were from a time long since passed. If Amy hadn't known any better, she would have assumed they had come from a 1950s fancy dress party.

Augustus had appeared at Amy's elbow and said, 'Good morning, Lady Crimpton. Good Morning Colonel.' They both nodded their replies. 'Please allow me to introduce my sister, Amy.' She immediately got the impression that she was supposed to curtsy, but just nodded her head towards the old couple. The old woman looked her up and down and then said, 'Will you both take tea with us this afternoon?' and then added while looking at Augustus, 'church affairs permitting, of course.'

Amy was somewhat surprised by Augustus's swift reply. He said, 'We will be delighted, shall we come round after we have judged the garden competition?'

'Oh that!' said Lady Crimpton.

Colonel Crimpton added, 'Come on, vicar, it's time for the service.' With that he strolled in a military manner to the door. Amy followed everyone else's lead and went into the church. She made sure that the twenty or so worshippers had their hymn books.

As she stood at the back for the service she reflected on those that she had met so far in Nether Crimpton. She knew it would try her patience, if she stayed too long with Augustus, but it was an ideal time to do some serious thinking.

Perhaps she could find another Outdoor pursuits post in Wales, or even in Europe. This seemed to be her best thought so far. She would have to remember to get some of the papers and magazines, which would advertise the jobs. Yes, she felt much happier at that thought. She would start on a serious quest to getaway tomorrow.

At the end of the service she took the collection. She noticed that neither Lady Crimpton or the Colonel put anything in the collecting dish. She wondered why and would ask her brother later.

After the service they returned to the vicarage, where Augustus changed into light chinos and a white shirt, but he still wore his clerical collar. This was the first time that Amy had seen him out of his black cassock. She knew him to be a tall, well built, handsome man and it clearly showed this afternoon.

Since her second encounter last night with the man, who drove the Mercedes, she was apprehensive about meeting him. Her concern had now lifted, a little, as she was determined to leave the village as soon as possible. So as not to let her brother down, she would see if there was anyone she met this afternoon, who would make a good church warden.

Amy decided not to change, but yet again brushed the dust from her tan shoes. It hadn't rained for several weeks and the grass was quite firm everywhere. Therefore she was pleased to be able to wear the high heels that matched her dress. As Augustus decided he was ready, so there was a knock at the door. Amy braced herself and took a deep breath. She hadn't moved since checking that her clothes and make-up were as they were supposed to be.

Augustus opened the door, 'Come in Theodore. This is Amy, my sister.'

He smiled at Amy. She had to admit it was a charming and genuine smile.

'We have met on a couple of occasions around the village,' he said to Augustus, 'but I'm looking forward to her company this afternoon.' He shook hands and added, 'May I say that is a most charming dress.'

'Thank you,' said Amy, who was both surprised and pleased by his reaction. His short-sleeved slightly patterned shirt and his immaculately pressed summer trousers impressed Amy. He's a handsome and charming man, she said to herself. What she thought was going to be a difficult meeting, full of embarrassment, went without a hitch. What Amy didn't realise was that the series of embarrassing moments would accompany her throughout the trip round the village gardens.

It started at the first garden, which was one of the larger houses in the village. As far as she knew she had never even seen, let alone met, the husband and wife, but they seemed to know all about her. It had started badly for her when the husband met her at the gate, stood aside, and said, 'Please enter, our Avenging Angel.' Amy blushed, took a deep breath, and walked through to the back garden.

Theodore whispered to her as they went, 'Amy, my sincere apologies, I think I might have started that name for you. I should have realised there were a lot of people in earshot.' She gave him her best smile, and couldn't hold him to blame for the spread of the remark. As the three judges walked around the immaculate garden, the wife said to Amy, 'That was truly wonderful what you did to that thug last night. He has been a nuisance in the village ever since he arrived, which was about three years ago. And while I've got your attention. Will you come round to tea one afternoon? There are some friends I would like you to meet.'

Amy didn't particularly want to. Afternoon tea and chats wasn't really her style, but she nodded. Finally, she managed to turn her attention to the garden, which she thought was magnificent and even though she didn't know much about gardening, it would be a worthy winner.

The next garden on the route was a surprise. They went around the back of the *Brace of Pheasants* to find a meticulously laid out herb garden that was fully labelled. There were many herbs that she didn't even recognise. The landlord of the pub, who she had met at the wedding, took her to one side and said, 'Good job last night with the hooligan from the visitor's centre. The invitation I gave you yesterday was meant in earnest. Both the rabbit stew and the beer will be free for you.' Again she nodded. The afternoon wasn't going well.

One of the last gardens that they visited was the one in which she had seen Clint kicking at the plants. Amy was embarrassed by the compliments she received but was pleased to see that little actual damage had been done.

The only part she enjoyed, as it was without any comments or embarrassment, was when they visited the small cottage garden belonging to Bernadette. She had taken an hour out of work at the visitor's centre for the judging. It was a traditional country cottage wild flower garden that Amy really liked, in comparison with the other much more formal gardens. She had a happy chat with

Bernadette, as did Theodore and Augustus, who both seemed to know her quite well.

At the end of the tour of the gardens, they went to the visitor's centre, where a room had been booked to announce the results. Amy had more invitations to tea than she could count, and a similar number to join people for a drink, at the *Marquis*. And that did not include the invitations to join the Women's Institute and the village knitting circle.

After this afternoon's exposure to the village, she was adamant it was not a lifestyle that she was going to choose. Theodore had been meticulous in making notes, which he quickly wrote up, so that Augustus could make the speech for the awards. Amy was surprised at the number that had crammed into the room. There were about fifty people, who had come to listen to her brother name the winners of the different categories.

It was about to start, when the loud tones of Damien shouting at his wife echoed around the entrance to the room, 'I know he is your dear little boy.' It was said with a sneer, 'But he's going to apologise.'

He burst into the room marching Clint forward with a strong grip on his arm. 'Now...' he said loudly as he plonked his son straight in front of Amy. 'Go on....' Amy stood there open-mouthed and fully blushing as fifty or more people turned to look at them. Clint wriggled. 'Remember what I said, and I meant it,' boomed Damien.

'Leave him,' said Lorraine quietly. From when they had first met it was clear to Amy that Lorraine ran the show. It was different now as Damien was in such a fury. He was bright red with anger, so even Lorraine had to curtail what she would have normally said.

Damien gave another shake of Clint's arm, and he finally muttered, 'I'm sorry about attacking you last night.'

Amy had no idea what to say and just stood there looking at Clint, who was staring at his own shoes. Much to Amy's relief Augustus intervened. 'Damien, Damien, the lad's said sorry. I'm sure Amy accepts the apology and as far as she is concerned the matter is closed.' Amy just nodded gratefully.

Damien looked at Augustus and said, 'Yes, well... it needed saying..' and seeing that he was the centre of attention, now that his temper seemed to be subsiding, he caught Clint's arm. They both speedily left the room. Lorraine with a face like thunder followed her husband and son.

Augustus presented the awards from the notes that Theodore had made. Amy admired the skilful way in which Augustus managed to praise even the poorest garden. It amused her that Augustus got all the praise for the good speech, and while he kept saying it was Theodore's skills. No one wanted to believe it, as no one seemed to like Theodore.

Amy was hoping that she now could quietly drift away from the spotlight of the village. She just yearned for some time, when she didn't have to talk to any one. What an afternoon! It was almost a total embarrassment. As she thought that, she caught sight of Theodore coming towards her. 'I'm sorry you've had a difficult time.'

Amy thought that he was perceptive as well as good-looking. There hadn't been any difficult moments with him, which was at least a highlight of the afternoon. Theodore added, 'Perhaps you would like to have dinner sometime.'

Amy suddenly felt wonderful, perhaps it hadn't been such a bad afternoon after all. Then the memories that were haunting her came flooding back. She was then just going to say no, when she thought that she really ought to be alone with him. She needed to apologise about their first meetings and to thank him for not making an exhibition of her this afternoon, 'Yes, I'd be delighted, but...'

'Yes?' he said with a gorgeous smile.

'Can we go away from the village?'

'Yes, there's a very nice restaurant near Sheffield, I think it will be far enough away from here. Shall I call you?'

'Yes, please do, I shall look forward to it.'

She was just going to make her excuses to leave, when Augustus caught her eye. It was then that she remembered that she had yet another ordeal to endure. It was afternoon tea at Crimpton Manor. But at least she only had to chat and there would be no more commitments to make. It was only a short walk from the visitor's centre. In the grand days of the manor and its estate, the centre had been the extensive stables.

'Gus, you've not said much about the old couple from the Manor. I'm sure you need to tell me plenty before we arrive, do you want to sit on this bench, so you can explain?'

'They will explain everything, they like talking. The only minor point is she is not really Lady Crimpton, but thinks she ought to be. Most of the village just humour her. Come on. They will be waiting.'

Amy and Augustus walked up the drive and climbed the curved steps that led to the front door.

'It's huge when you get close to it,' said Amy as they walked between two of the columns that made the front of the house look like something from a Roman temple. Augustus ignored the large door knockers and pressed the tiny bell push, which was hard to see in the ornate woodwork that surrounded the door.

'It will take some time, they have quite a way to come.' Amy looked out from the raised balcony, near the front door, across the lawns and distant estate. It was easy to pick out several of the follies that had been built by some of the more eccentric inhabitants over the centuries. The closely cropped grass stretched up to the woods on the hill. The groan of the huge front door got their attention.

'Good afternoon and come in,' said the Colonel. Augustus gave him a hand to swing the heavy door closed. They then walked down a long corridor with dirty windows, shabby curtains and peeling plaster. 'The house is too big just for the two of us. Since we have come from India, we live in a few rooms at end of the west wing.' Amy just walked in amazement, at the number of doors, the length of the corridors, and the extent of the dilapidation of what was once a magnificent house.

Tea, of cucumber sandwiches and scones, was ready when they reached the large high ceilinged drawing room. The room was quite cold, despite the heat of summer. It bore the same level of upkeep as the rest of the house. The only difference was the furniture, which had been restored, and was in a good condition.

Amy settled to a quiet time doing what she needed to support her brother. As the conversation developed, she found that she didn't particularly like either of them, as they both seemed to have delusions of grandeur. All traces of that in the house had long gone.

The Colonel kept staring at her, which made her uncomfortable, while his wife talked down to her. She learned that many years ago the house had passed into a branch of the family, which Lady Crimpton described as profligates. They had squandered their inheritance and let the house turn into a ruin. The house was rented out, as the owners lived in the South of France with the jet set, but that still did not bring in enough money. Finally, after the death of the last of that line, the Government took the stable block in lieu of taxes and sold it on the open market.

The question then arose as to who should inherit the house. After much legal wrangling, it was passed to the current Lady Crimpton. At the time they were living in India, where the Colonel's family had resided since the days of the Empire. As was the tradition in his family, the senior male returned to England, from their home in India, to be commissioned into the Army. They said it had come as a surprise to Lady Crimpton to inherit the estate. She felt family obligations to return and live in the house.

Both of them moaned about the village and its people. The only one that came in for praise was Ged, the undertaker, which quite surprised Amy and she asked why. The Colonel took the opportunity to stare at her again. He said that Ged was in his regiment, when he was in the army. That would explain the elaborate gate opening on the way to church thought Amy.

They all seemed to be getting restless and Amy was hoping it was time to go when Lady Crimpton said, 'The reason we asked you to tea, young lady, was so that we could ask you to do us a little favour.' Amy tried to catch Gus's eye, but he wouldn't look at her.

Amy took a deep breath and shuddered to think of what was coming. Lady Crimpton said, 'There is a meeting next Thursday to discuss the proposal that a new National Path & Cycleway comes through the village.' Amy was just about to say that it seemed a really good idea, when Lady Crimpton continued, 'It crosses our land and we are totally opposed to it.'

'I'm not sure what I can do about it,' said Amy.

'I would have thought that it was obvious young lady. We want you to represent us at the meeting and to speak up very clearly and say that we totally oppose it in any form.'

Amy was just about to stand her ground and say no, when Lady Crimpton added, 'Of course, we know the Vicar supports us. If we are successful in keeping this a quiet estate village, then we will ensure there is a firm donation to the church fund.' Amy tried to show no reaction in her face, but she thought it was plain and simple blackmail.

She became very restless. Augustus picked up her unease and drew the afternoon tea to a close. Amy and her brother then walked down the drive in silence. She was waiting until they were well clear of the house, before she said anything. Her brother kept his usual silence on matters, where there might be some disagreement. They had just come out of the main gate, which was near the footpath when Lorraine and Clint appeared. She stared at the vicar and Amy, looked them up and down, and then seemed to make a decision. She smiled. It didn't impress Amy.

Lorraine came up to them, with Clint quite subdued beside her. She looked directly at Augustus, but didn't even glance at Amy. 'Ah, vicar, I'm glad I bumped into you. I'm going around the village canvassing a bit of support for Thursday's meeting about the footpath. If we all support it, I'm sure it will bring great benefits to the village. Think of all the extra business for the village shop and the pubs.'

'And the profits for your visitors' centre,' said Amy to herself.

But Lorraine wasn't daunted by them not replying and added, 'There will be lots of extra visitors to the church, who I'm sure will donate to the restoration fund.' Augustus just gave her his comely smile. Amy showed no reaction so Lorraine carried on, 'Of course we would make more money at the centre, so its only right that we put some back into the village and we would be very prepared to look at what we could sponsor for the church.'

Seeing that there was no reaction from Augustus, Lorraine added, 'I'm sure, in your position, you will not want to stand up at a meeting supporting us but, as it's open to resident and visitors, perhaps Amy could speak on your behalf. Especially now, that we are the best of friends again, following that unfortunate incident.' Lorraine looked at them and then back at the big house, 'I'm sure they have asked for your support, but they always want to live in the past, whereas we are keen to take the village forward.'

Amy intended to try to make a neutral remark, she was fed up with all this in-fighting, so she said, 'I do think this is a wonderful unspoilt village and that it should attempt to keep its heritage.'

Lorraine snapped, 'So you're going to support them are you. I might have known. Come on Clint, I knew there was no point in talking to them. But I can assure you both, this village will have a National Footpath and Cycle way going through it.' And with that she spun on her heels and stormed off towards the centre. Clint snarled at Amy and then followed his mother.

Amy turned to Augustus, who gently shook his head and said in his slow kind voice, 'Don't say a word please. I've had enough of all this today. Let's go home and have a glass of sherry.' Augustus had yet again defused Amy's indignation. She had to laugh at her brother and his suggestion of the remedy, for he would only have the smallest of drinks about once a year.

*****

Amy and her brother spent a pleasant and amiable evening in each other's company. The talk was almost exclusively about Africa. They re-lived some of the time they had spent there and talked about the subsequent letters they had received from the people they knew. A violent thunderstorm had passed over while they were talking and the torrential rain had brought an end to the long dry spell.

She left Augustus to write the funeral address for Mrs Braithwaite, and went and changed into her purple trainers and tracksuit to have a jog to finish off a frustrating day. Now the heat of the day had long since passed, Desmond was very keen to join her.

'OK, come on then.' Amy shut the door with a crash and they both ran down the path. She turned left to go along the track between the church and the ruins of the ancient church. As they got level with the old church yard, a rabbit ran across the track.

This was a temptation too far for Desmond, who shot after it into the old grave yard. Despite Amy's calling, Desmond didn't come. She resolved to wait, but changed her mind as she heard him yelp and then whine with pain. She followed the direction in which he had gone and the noise he was now creating. The dog had crossed the graveyard and had tried to follow the rabbit through a hole in a hawthorn hedge. The hole wasn't big enough and he had got struck. He was whining because the thorns were sticking into him. It was black in the graveyard and it was now raining hard again.

A flash of lightning illuminated the whole scene for Amy. She worked it out that it was Bernadette's garden. There were no lights on, in the house, so she guessed that Bernadette would not mind her going into the garden to free Desmond. She remembered from her visit there during the garden competition, that there was a gate directly into graveyard. She tried the hasp, but it was padlocked and too difficult to climb over. She returned to Desmond to see that his harness was caught on a branch on the far side of the hole in the hedge. She tried to get close enough, without scratching herself, and put her foot right under the hedge to try to get the leverage to lift Desmond off of the branch.

She hadn't realised that the thick bush had been planted in a small ditch, which was now overgrown. Her foot went straight through the loose grass, with its friable top soil, and into the ditch. She lurched forward into the hedge and was now caught the same as Desmond. Her foot had become trapped in the ditch under the root system of the hedge. The rain fell torrentially as she struggled to free herself. The lightning flashed and the thundered crashed. Amy was getting frightened, and she made one final attempt to drag and twist her foot from under the root. Despite the rain, she heard her shoe rip as her foot was suddenly released. The roots tore at her foot as she pulled it back from the ditch. Her eyes had now become accustomed to the light.

The trainer had ripped down the side by the lace holes and was lying torn and wet in the bottom of the shallow ditch. She couldn't reach it with scratching herself again and decided to leave it there. In the commotion of her pulling and yanking at the bush to get herself free, it was enough to release Desmond, who had gone through the hedge into the garden and had turned and come back through without getting caught.

Amy was cold, very wet, and bleeding, so she hobbled back to the house, crept quietly in and went upstairs to bath and go to bed. As she lay in her bath her immediate thoughts were for her brother. How could he remain so calm and pleasant in this village. It wasn't in her nature to dislike people but she would make every effort to avoid the Colonel and Lady Crimpton.

Chapter Five

It was a grey, chilly and foggy morning when Amy woke early after a restless night. As she couldn't hear the rain, she assumed it was just a misty start to the day. She decided to shake off her weariness and frustration, about not getting a run last night, by going for a jog before breakfast. She had already taken from the wardrobe, the orange leggings and black top. She completed her outfit with her second pair of trainers, which were orange.

As she got near the front door, she picked up the single mud covered and wet purple trainer, having left the other one at the bottom of the ditch. As she left the house on her run, she threw her remaining purple trainer into the wheelie bin. She would retrieve the other one from the ditch later in the day. Desmond appeared none the worse for his ordeal and bounced along at her side. She turned to the right on the track, it would prevent Desmond chasing the rabbit if it reappeared. But within fifty yards he had dived into another hedge and wouldn't come out. She was getting frustrated, but had to go back to see what the problem with him was.

His head was firmly in the bush and she couldn't see, but from his action she guessed he had something in his mouth. She put her hand down the side of his head and felt a piece of cold metal. She prised it from his mouth and it dropped through the hedge as she pulled him back. She had cut her hand and it was bleeding quite a lot, so she had to go back to the house.

Ten minutes later having cleaned the cut, which seemed to have bled a lot, she went for her run, but this time without the disappointed Desmond. There was no sign of the weather improving and the damp, foggy cold air clung to her clothes and hair. She had blood down her front, from the cut, but decided to live with it for the run and wash out the orange outfit afterwards. No one was likely to see her, as it was a cold, wet and damp morning, before most people were even up.

It was nearly an hour before she returned. It had been her first trip up through the woods that she could see from the Manor. She felt much more relaxed and ready to face the day, whatever happened in Nether Crimpton.

She took the long way round and didn't see anyone, although she did hear a few footsteps in the fog. As she came down the lane, past Theodore's drive, she remembered the disaster before and checked that his car was not emerging. She had had enough of running and decided to nip through the old ruins to get back to the vicarage. She jogged along the gravel path, near the cottage gardens, when something caught her eye. Bernadette's gate was swinging in the swirling fog. 'That's strange,' she said to herself, 'it was locked late last night. Why would Bernadette have opened it during the night?' Even though the garden was small, the fog was thick and Amy couldn't see whether there were any lights or movement in the house.

She rounded a large memorial just near the gate and gasped in horror. She went weak at the knees and nearly collapsed at the sight of the bloodied naked body of Bernadette, which was lying over a gravestone plinth. The dead face, with open eyes, faced the sky and Amy couldn't fail to notice the blood all across Bernadette's chest.

Amy screamed as she never had before. She closed her eyes just hoping that it was a bad dream. When she re-opened them the poor woman's body was still there and she screamed again. But no one came.

It took a few moments to regain some semblance of composure and she sprinted to the vicarage, which wasn't far. As she burst in the front door, she collided with Augustus, who could immediately tell that something bad had happened to his ghostly white and near collapsing sister. 'What is it?' he said with alarm.

Amy couldn't manage more that to gasp, 'Come, come,' and she mustered all her energy and ran down the path. Augustus followed as quickly as he could. In a very short time, they had reached poor Bernadette. Augustus momentarily closed his eyes in silent prayer. While they had both seen dead bodies, during their time in Africa, the shock of discovering one was traumatic for both. Augustus said, 'Can you stay here, while I ring the police?'

'Yes,' she gasped and clutched at Desmond, who had bounded along with them, thinking it was a game. He became subdued as he approached the body, but at Augustus's word, he lay down next to Bernadette. Augustus went to vicarage and made the call. He then returned as quickly as he could. He was so worried about Amy. He had grabbed the first covering he could find, which was an old horse blanket. He place it over the body, said a short prayer and then turned to Amy, who collapsed in his arms.

With the words, 'Stay. Guard!' to Desmond he carried his fainted sister back to the vicarage. He wasn't sure whether Desmond understood him, but he had to look after Amy. She had come to, by the time they had reached the house. He laid her on the couch and fetched her a glass of water. She managed to sit up to drink it.

After a few minutes she slowly said, 'I'm OK, Augustus, it was just the shock of finding her.'

He was re-assured as the colour had come back to her face and her voice had returned to normal. The phone rang. He answered it and mouthed to Amy that it was the police. While he was on the phone, the front door bell rang. Amy gathered up her strength and went to answer it. She opened the door and recognised the man immediately, who vaguely waved his arm at her. He was the one with whom she had argued on the jam stall. He looked her up and down, with his stare hovering over the blood stains, which were down her front. He said, 'Who is it that found a body, and where is it?'

'And exactly who do you think you are?' said Amy remembering her dislike for the man. She wished the police would get here and take control of everything.'

The man snapped back, 'I'm Detective Inspector Harrison,' and thrust his warrant card right in front of her face, 'and now answer my questions.'

'It was me that found poor Bernadette, and she is in the graveyard.' His piercing eyes stared at her face. He was trying to detect if there was anything not quite right about what she said or how she said it.

'Is Constable Bright here yet?'

'You are the first policeman that has come to the house.'

'Who's guarding the body, is it the vicar?'

'No, it's Desmond, the vicar is in there on the phone to the police.' She knew she should have said more, but chose not to, as she didn't like him one little bit.

'Stay in the house. I want to talk to you in a minute,' and with that he turned back down the path. Amy went in and watched him out of the window. The irritable conversation had brought her back to reality and she no longer felt faint, but she was trembling from the shock. She saw him look from the track at the church and then the old ruin. He was looking around and, with graveyards all around him, he couldn't decide which way to go.

'That serves you right,' thought Amy, but her conscience got the better of her and knew she should really help the police. So she went to the front door, opened it, and called out, 'Do you want me to show you the way?'

'Yes,' came the snapped rely.

Amy walked past him in the gloomy fog and turned into the old cemetery. 'Who's there?' came a voice from the fog.

'Police,' snapped the Inspector, who walked forward and could now see the young constable.

'What's that dog doing here? Why have you let him sit next to the body? Constable Bright you will be in trouble for this.'

Amy could see that the young policeman looked terrified. He kept looking at the graves and the swirling fog. He was as white as a sheet. But Amy admired his spirit when he said, 'You try and move it.'

Before Amy could intervene the Inspector stepped forward and waving his arms shouted, 'Get out of here!'

Desmond stood up, showed his teeth and let out the most ferocious growl. Even Amy was surprised, as he had seemed so placid.

'Good boy, Desmond, come here.' The dog keeping a careful eye on the inspector, went and sat at heel next to Amy.

'I don't believe it. You left a bloody dog to look after a body that you found.'

Amy wasn't going to be lambasted by the inspector and said, 'He seems to have done a good job, no one could have got near her.'

'And what the bloody hell is that covering the body?'

Amy went to answer when Augustus's voice said, as he appeared through the mist, behind the policemen, 'Inspector, I would appreciate it, if you would modify your language. And to answer your question, it is an old horse blanket, which was the first thing to hand. I used it to give poor Bernadette some dignity in death, as she was naked, when my sister found her.'

As the Inspector spun round and began to shout, 'And who the...' He stopped clearly shaken. Augustus towered over the two policemen. He was very close to them and they had spun round to see this large figure in a flowing cassock, with wild black hair peering down at them. Constable Bright jumped and quivered at the sight of Augustus.

The inspector regained his composure much more quickly, 'I'm very much concerned at the contamination of the site,' and added as an afterthought the word, 'vicar.'

Before the inspector could say what he wanted to happen next, there was a rumbling noise that suddenly got very much closer. The noise became so loud it would have been impossible to hear anyone speak. Suddenly out of the swirling mist came this gigantic structure. Constable Bright whelped and jumped to the other side of the path. His big eyes looked in horror as this twelve foot tall apparition appeared through the fog with a noise, which was now deafening. The brightness of its lights meant it was difficult to discern the exact structure of this monster.

'Stop, stop, stop!' shouted Augustus. The structure lurched, and the noise suddenly died, and at the same time the lights went out. It was all too much for Constable Bright, who by this time had sunk to the ground in fear.

Out of the mist, and from high up behind the structure came a voice, 'Good morning, Vicar, it's a strange time for a meeting, I thought I'd have the place to myself.'

The inspector having regained his equilibrium said, 'Who are you, and what are you doing here? Come over here.'

Amy had already recognised the voice, as Ged appeared through the mist. 'Well?' said the inspector impatiently. Ged had a quick look around and saw the constable in uniform, who had just managed to regain his feet and was leaning against the tree. 'I'm Ged Rudd, and I've brought my JCB to dig a grave.'

'I though all burials took place in the graveyard over there?'

'Old Mrs Braithwaite wanted to be with her ancestors, and as the vicar agreed, I've come to dig the hole.'

Ged's eyes flashed around the group and he soon saw the body, which was only partly covered by a blanket.

'Oh!' he muttered and then asked, 'who is it?' looking at Augustus

'It's poor Bernadette,' replied Amy.

'That's no way for a good woman to go.'

'Did you know the deceased?' asked the inspector having suddenly realised that he hadn't actually checked for himself that she was dead. He had no faith that Constable Bright had done anything.

'Yes of course, we all knew her, she lives in that cottage there.'

*****

The day had passed in a blur for Amy. She had been asked by the police to stay at the vicarage all day. They had taken the clothes that she had been wearing, when she had found Bernadette, including the orange trainers. A woman police sergeant had come and taken her statement. She had been surprised how brief the whole process was and that there were very few questions about details.

She guessed that they must take everyone's statement, look over them, and come back and ask more questions. But it wasn't the tedium of the day that got to her, but the image of Bernadette that kept coming back into her mind. Amy found it unbelievable that anyone would want to kill such a lovely woman.

It was nearly time for bed and Augustus was still out. He had been going round the village, since mid afternoon, to console and reassure people. He knew that many of those, who lived on their own, would be frightened by what had happened on their doorstep. Amy had tried reading, but couldn't concentrate. She finally decided that she wouldn't wait up for Augustus. She would go to bed and try to sleep, but she knew that it would be very hard as she would keep seeing the image of poor Bernadette laying naked on that gravestone.

Chapter Six

Amy came down to breakfast the next morning feeling frightened and weak. She had struggled to sleep. It was the fear that there had been a murder so close to her. Between her fractured sleep, her mind, not only thought of Bernadette, but she realised how close she must have been to seeing or even meeting the murderer. She shivered again at the thought. The only bright spot, amongst the harrowing images and the fear, was a voice message left by Theodore offering his sympathies. He said he would come round to see whether there was any thing he could do. It was the one good thought that managed to work its way into the cascade of her frightening memories.

Breakfast with Augustus helped her to settle to the day, he was his usual kind and sympathetic self. How such traumatic matters affected him, Amy never knew. In times of crisis, he totally devoted himself to others. His quiet manner, that never changed, gave Amy support for the day ahead. They had just finished breakfast, when the door bell was rung impatiently. Augustus answered it and returned with Inspector Harrison and a woman police sergeant.

'How may we help you, Inspector?' said Augustus, but he ignored the remark and walked up to Amy, who was still sat at the breakfast table.

'Amy Andrews I am arresting you for the murder of Bernadette Murphy. You do not have to say anything, but it may harm your defence if you do not mention when questioned, something which you later rely on in court. Anything you say may be given in evidence.'

Amy was stunned, but the words said directly to her dashed away all of the weariness and fright that she had felt a few moments ago. 'Don't be so ridiculous!'

'I'm sure there must be some mistake,' said Augustus seeing

the fire in his sister's eyes.

But Amy hadn't finished, 'I assume that you have cobbled together some facts about me. As it has been very evident that you do not like me, you think you can arrest me for murder?'

Augustus added, 'It's a shock, Amy, let the inspector explain his reason.'

'Kindly stay out of this matter, sir,' snapped the policeman, 'I have made an arrest and will question your sister at the police station. That is the end of the matter. I have no intention of making any further explanation at this point.'

'You really are an odious little man,' added Amy, who ignored Augustus. Her brother had put up his hand to try to quell her temper. But Amy hadn't finished yet, and she continued, 'And you are a very poor detective, if you think I did the murder,' she said standing over him and looking down.

His only reply was, 'Put the handcuffs on, as she is resisting arrest.' Even the woman police officer looked surprised, but he said, 'Get on with it, I'm not taking her out of here without handcuffs.' Augustus could see Amy's fury in her eyes, but she was too shocked to say anything else.

As the police woman was putting on the handcuffs, she whispered, 'Sorry about this, ma'am.' The police inspector led the way out of the house. Augustus asked, 'Shall I will come with you?'

'Yes, please, Augustus. I'm frightened.' After her initial outburst against the inspector, the reality of the whole situation had hit Amy now that she had handcuffs on. A police car was waiting on the track outside the vicarage. As she was led down the path, so Theodore came along the track, intending to call to check if Amy was all right. He saw Amy in handcuffs, with tears streaming down her face, being placed in the back of the police car. Amy focused on him as he turned around and walked back the way, he had just come.

Within thirty minutes, she had been placed in front of the custody sergeant, who had read the arrest out to her again. She had managed to stop crying, but was very shaky. Augustus stood next to her and answered any questions with the utmost brevity. Amy kept glancing at him, but his face was emotionless. She knew he would wait until it was the right time, before he spoke. The custody sergeant advised her to have a solicitor, but Amy said she did not need one, provided her brother could be with her.

She was led to an interview room where the inspector and the woman police sergeant were waiting. He immediately switched on the recorder. After stating the time, date and those present, he looked up and straight at Amy, who sat on the other side of the table.

'As the case against you is very strong, I expect to take you to the Magistrate's court later today, where I will state the charge and you will be remanded in custody. I would strongly recommend, that you ask for a delay in this questioning, so you may have a solicitor present.'

Amy had now conquered her emotions and glared back at the inspector. 'I have done nothing wrong, I did not murder Bernadette. Her voice croaked a little, as she said Bernadette's name, 'I do not require a solicitor.' She could feel her confidence returning, she said to herself, 'How dare they accuse me of the murder'. She paused and then said, 'Inspector?'

'Yes, Miss Andrews,' Amy could tell that the look on his face meant that he was hoping for a confession.

'I would be grateful, if you would ask your questions, as I do not like being here under this scrutiny, and then I may return home.'

The inspector frowned, 'At the moment, we do not have a clear motive, but we are continuing enquiries and I am sure we will find what we are looking for. We have your footprints at the murder scene. Also there are your fingerprints on the murder weapon. I can also confirm to you that the blood on your running top was not your own, as you stated, but was that of the deceased.'

Amy was shocked, and speechless. She gently shook her head and tears began to roll down her face. From the drawer of the table where they were sitting, he produced a large thick clear plastic bag. The outside was transparent. It was the trainer that she had left in the ditch, on the edge of Bernadette's garden.

'Is this your trainer?'

'Yes,' said Amy.

'Where is the other one?'

'I threw it in the bin yesterday morning, as I knew that one was damaged.'

'At what time did you go for a run in these trainers.'

'About ten o'clock,' said Amy very quietly.

'And what time did you get back from your run?'

'I didn't go very far, as I lost my trainer.'

'Answer the question please.'

'At about fifteen minutes past ten.'

'The police pathologist believes that the murder took place sometime between ten and eleven o'clock on Sunday evening.

Amy did not know what to say.

Augustus said, 'Inspector, may my sister explain, for your recording, exactly how she came to lose her trainer.'

'Very well,' was the impatient reply.

Amy gathered her strength and gave a detailed account of how Desmond followed a rabbit and she came to lose her trainer.

At the end of the account the inspector said, 'It changes nothing. It only confirms that your sister was at the murder location, near to the time of the attack.'

'My sister has never denied being there near the time. Inspector, may I ask if your forensic team have collected the evidence to show that my sister's story to be true?'

'What evidence?' said the inspector, who was clearly getting annoyed at this development.

Augustus replied, 'Desmond's hair and blood on the hawthorn bush. Slivers of the material from Amy's trainer and her blood on the root of the hawthorn.'

'No, we have not collected it, as it was not relevant.'

Augustus deepened his voice and said, 'Then you leave us no alternative, but to call in a private forensic team. So will you ensure the area remains cordoned off to avoid any contamination.'

The inspector ignored what Augustus said, but Amy saw a gleam from the eyes of the woman police sergeant. It was at that point, that Amy knew that the sergeant did not think she was involved.

'The trainer was not found in the ditch as you stated.'

Amy went to speak, but Augustus touched her on the arm and said, 'Shall we move on to the murder weapon inspector?' Amy didn't know how her fingerprints could possibly be on the murder weapon, unless it was stolen from the vicarage.

Augustus then added, 'Before you speak inspector may my sister state, for the recorder, what happened when she set out for her run the following morning.'

As Amy started to explain that Desmond had gone into the bush and she had prised something from his mouth. It then dawned on her what Augustus was thinking. Augustus said at the end, 'I am sure your forensic team will find the dog's saliva on the metal, which I assume was a knife, and fragments of material that snagged from Amy's clothes on the bushes.'

There was a silence from the inspector. 'May we assume,' said Augustus, 'that the murder weapon was found in the bush along the track from the vicarage.'

'Yes,' said the inspector, 'the defendant's blood was found on the knife as well.'

'That would be likely from the description my sister has just given. But how do you account for the dog's saliva being on the knife?'

The police sergeant searched through her papers and said, 'The pathologist says there is unidentified saliva on the knife and it is not human.'

Augustus nodded in acknowledgement. Amy wanted to speak, but she knew that she must leave it to Augustus.

The police inspector was working out his next move when Augustus said, 'My sister has clearly stated that she was at both places and has given her account, which can be verified with evidence. As far as I see it your conjecture in charging my sister is that she would commit a murder and leave her trainer at the scene and discard the murder weapon close to her own house.'

The police sergeant asked the inspector, 'Shall I arrange for the custody officer to release Miss Andrews?'

'No,' snapped the Inspector.

Augustus said, 'If I give you my word that Amy will return with me to Nether Crimpton, where she will remain until you have finished your enquiries, may she now go.'

The sergeant had packed up all of her papers, but the inspector clearly wasn't giving up yet. He went to speak but Augustus added, 'Just in case you think that I am in some way involved, then the Bishop will, I am sure, give you his word, which will cover both myself and my sister.'

The sergeant gave the slightest of smiles, because she knew that the inspector would not want the Bishop involved. The inspector snapped, 'Neither of you leave Nether Crimpton,' and with that he stormed out of the door of the interview room.

'I will ensure you are checked out correctly,' said the sergeant as she led them back to the custody desk.

'Are we letting them go?' asked the custody officer with a smile.

'Yes,' replied the sergeant, 'I'm not sure why we arrested her in the first place.'

The sergeant replied, 'Perhaps the inspector was hoping to wrap up the case, so he could get away on his golf weekend.'

They both smiled at each other and completed the paperwork. Amy was relieved that ordeal was over, but it did clearly pose the question as to who had killed poor Bernadette.

Amy and Augustus were just about to leave, when he turned to the sergeant and said, 'Bernadette lived on her own, and I just want to be assured that you have traced her next of kin. And then I would be content in the knowledge that someone would deal with the funeral arrangements. Otherwise, I would normally make any arrangements, as the death occurred in my parish.'

'It is strange you should mention that Reverend, as we cannot find anything about Bernadette, and certainly we have had no contact with the next of kin. There was nothing in the paperwork that was in her house, so we will continue to make enquiries. If you have any information from the village, it would be very helpful.'

Amy was very relieved to finally leave the police station and they travelled back home in the back of the police car in silence. They went into Augustus's study. Amy breathed deeply and said, 'I feel that we ought to help Bernadette in some way.'

She very much expected her brother to say that they should leave it to the police but he replied, 'I'm sure the truth lies somewhere in this village. I'm afraid that certain police officers may easily antagonise the villagers and get nowhere.'

Amy liked the thought of helping poor Bernadette, but she wasn't sure how she could go about it. However, she could tell that Augustus was thinking and she waited until he said, 'Judging by her name, she is likely to be of Irish descent and may have been in the Catholic faith. I think I shall drive over and talk to Father O'Connor to see whether he knows her.'

'Augustus! The police said not to leave Nether Crimpton.'

'And I shall not,' he replied with a smile, 'as Father O'Connor lives within the parish of Nether Crimpton, even if it is about fifteen miles away.'

'What shall I do?' sighed Amy, who was expecting him to tell her to stay at home. Surprisingly he answered briskly, 'Go to the visitor's centre and speak with Damien. He employed her and so may know about her background, which seems to be a mystery. He is likely to know a little because of the documentation necessary when she worked for him.'

'Why?' said Amy, who was now intrigued by Augustus's thoughts.

'Bernadette arrived in the village a couple of years ago. She didn't know anyone when she came here. Why would a single woman in her thirties, move to a small country village with neither contacts nor a job?'

They both set off on the agreed tasks and Amy arrived in the visitor's centre. She immediately bumped into Damien, who was just leaving. She had planned what to say to try to get the information, but he said, 'I'm just off for a late lunch at the *Marquis*, can I tempt you?'

She had been adamant that she wouldn't go for a drink with him, but it was a really good opportunity to find out more. He wouldn't think anything unusual as they could chat. Also, Amy was very aware that she hadn't eaten since breakfast and was hungry.

He brought her a sandwich and orange juice. They sat in the

garden at the rear of the pub. Amy had chosen a table away from the rest of the customers. She just hoped that he didn't read anything into her choice. He wasn't his usual flamboyant self. To her surprise he was quiet and polite. He certainly seemed to have changed from when she had first met him, but she guessed that a murder, in the village, would affect everyone in different ways.

'The police didn't keep you then?' was his opening line as they settled to their lunch.

'No, thankfully.'

'It seemed pretty ridiculous to me that they even wanted to question you.' It was all said in a distant manner and nothing like the intense and loud way in which he normally spoke. He continued, 'It must have been a shock for you discovering the body.'

'Yes, it was, and it was made worse because I knew her. She was such as lovely woman. I'm sure that if I stayed in the village for very long, then we would have become very close friends.'

'I really liked her, she was so gentle and caring,' said Damien. Amy studied his face and could see that he was holding back emotion. Something didn't seem right about this reaction, but she couldn't tell what it was. She waited, but he didn't say anything else, he just stared at his sandwich.

'How long had you known her?'

He brightened slightly and replied, 'About two years. She arrived in the village just after we took over the centre. She didn't have a job, and we were looking for staff, so she started straight away. Bernadette was very good with the customers and became very friendly with Mary, my daughter.'

'Yes, I noticed that,' added Amy

'They got on very well and even went into town together. It was good for Mary to find someone she liked. We are so busy with the centre we haven't given Mary some of the time that she deserves.'

'Where did Bernadette come from?' Amy hoped that he wouldn't think anything unusual in the question.

'I don't really know. Whenever she was asked, she used to say Ireland. She would then add that she had been living in London, but had generally moved around a lot.'

Amy decided to make a guess based on Damien's accent, 'Did you know her in London?'

'No. It was only when we moved here that we first met.'

'What made you come here?'

'We lived in Lewisham and got fed up with the commuting grind and city life. We packed in our jobs, and took a chance by buying the centre.'

'Damien, I want to help Augustus.' He nodded, but he was distant and in a world of his own. 'He is concerned that there has been no contact with the next of kin, and wants to trace her relatives for any funeral arrangements.'

'Yes, that would make sense, but I don't know them.'

Amy could tell he was in a helpful mood and so she added, 'You paid her, so she must have a National Insurance number.'

'That was the strange thing about Bernadette.'

'What was?' asked Amy, becoming very interested in the background.

'She wanted to be paid as a sub-contractor, which is really unusual for a waitress. I told the police and gave them the details of the agency, for which she worked, and where we paid the money. If we walk back to the centre, I will give you the same information.' He paused and then added, 'It's important she has a proper burial with her friends and family.'

As they slowly walked back to the centre, Amy had an idea as to what was troubling Damien. She wondered whether he thought Clint might have done it. 'How have the rest of your family taken it?'

'They are all quite distressed about it, even Clint.' That came as a surprise to Amy. Damien had glanced at her and must have seen the surprise on her face. 'Bernadette seemed to be the only adult that Clint got on well with. He's not too bad with his mother, but you've already seen that Clint and I clash. He doesn't argue with Mary, his sister, but he avoids her. He liked Bernadette.'

'Mary must be upset,' said Amy.

'Yes, its been all we can do to console her. She has been with her mother ever since.'

Amy knew she had to ask, 'What about Lorraine?'

'She has gone extremely quiet and won't talk to me. I don't think she has said a word to me since it happened.' And with that, he let out a deep sigh and turned into his office at the centre. He gave Amy a copy of the agency details and said, 'I'd better get on, Lorraine and Mary aren't doing anything at the moment, so it is down to me to run the centre.'

Amy had just left and was on her way back to the vicarage, where she would log on to the internet to find out something about the agency. As she walked along the path, she remembered that Bernadette said that she had a part-time job at the manor. She might have talked to them, about where she came from.

She wasn't keen to get involved again with the owners of the stately home, but she was doing this for Bernadette, so she turned along the path. In a few minutes she walked up to the front door, and rang the bell. There was a long delay, before the Colonel answered. A smile lit up his face, as he saw Amy.

If she went into the house, she would have to endure his leering at her, but she'd put up with it to try to get some information. He beckoned her in with his usual staring look.

'Is your wife in?' asked Amy, as she followed the Colonel down the long corridor.

'No,' he said with a smile. Amy shivered a little with nervousness. He then added, 'She has gone around the estate houses to collect the rent.'

They reached the drawing-room and the Colonel invited her to sit, which allowed him to sit opposite, so he could leer at her. She took a deep breath and prepared to ignore his eyes. Suddenly an idea struck her, and she snapped rather bluntly, 'Did Bernadette rent one of your cottages?'

The Colonel moved uncomfortably in his chair. He continued to stare at Amy and eyed her up and down, 'Why do you ask?' he replied with a calm voice.

'The police have not traced a next-of-kin yet. So if no one is found, then the responsibility for her funeral would fall to Augustus, because it is in his parish.' She had started along this line and so she continued with confidence, 'If she rented her cottage from you, then you will have details about her. Perhaps even where her bank was, or a cheque from her.'

He ignored the question and added, 'The police broke into the cottage and damaged the door.'

'I expect you can claim it,' answered Amy dismissively.

The stare never wavered away from her. Amy was feeling very uncomfortable and lonely in this big house with this lecherous old man, but she wasn't going to give up easily.

'She was a lovely woman,' said the Colonel.

Amy let the questions about the cottage drop, for a moment, as she thought things through. Bernadette was an attractive woman and Amy guessed that the Colonel would have stared at her. So how did Bernadette put up with it every time she came to clean?

'How often did she do your cleaning?'

'Every week day.'

'That's a lot for the two of you.' He was getting agitated again, but Amy didn't know why.

'She would come early and cook our breakfast as well. She normally prepared us something for tea and then did the cleaning.'

'And all that before she went to work at eleven o'clock at the visitor's centre,' thought Amy to herself.

Amy needed to have one last try as she didn't appear to be getting anywhere, 'Could I see her rent book, and any papers of employment, I might notice something that could help Augustus trace her next-of-kin,' She finished by staring back at him and added, 'You do want to help the Reverend don't you?'

'Yes, yes, of course. Come with me,' he replied, as he led the way to the door, but Amy could tell he was nervous.

He went down a corridor and into a very small room. There was only enough room for a desk, chair and a lot of files. It was completely disorganised with pieces of papers piled up on the desk. She guessed that at one time this room had been a cupboard. 'There are a few things in that file on the top of there, you can look through it if you like.'

Amy had to squeeze past him. He came up behind her as she picked up the file and took out the contents. There wasn't much there, but she opened the rent book as the Colonel came near her.

He stood very close and put his hand on her waist.

'That's the rent book,' he said peering past her shoulder and getting ever closer.

'Yes, I can see, but there are no other details in the documents,' she said, as she flicked through the scraps of papers.

His hand began to slide down on to her bottom. She turned quickly, grabbed his wrist, and twisted his arm. He yelped in pain, 'Now we don't want a disagreement do we?'

He turned and left the little office in a hurry, whilst still rubbing his wrist. Amy said goodbye and let herself out of the house and walked back through the village as she tried to gather her thoughts. Why would Bernadette go there every day with that awful man? He must have preyed on her.

As she had left the house, she had rung a local estate agent, who confirmed that a similar cottage to where Bernadette lived would be about £400 a month, which is what the rent book showed.

Amy thought to herself that it was a lot for someone, who lives on her own, and is a domestic and waitress. Also there was something strange about the rent book, but she couldn't put her finger on it. She walked along the village High Street immersed in her thoughts, when Ged made her jump as he came out from one of his barns. Amy wondered what Ged would know about Bernadette. He was about the same age and single. Amy wondered whether he had tried to chat her up and he might have even been out with her.

'Hello, Amy, I'm pleased they let you go.'

'Thanks,' said Amy.

'Fancy of cup of tea? I'm just going to brew up'

Amy nodded and within a few minutes she was sitting on a wooden chair in the joinery workshop. On the main bench, Ged was in the middle of making a coffin.'

Amy gulped air as she looked at it and the realisation hit her, 'Is that for Bernadette?'

'Yes, it will be if she is buried here, but if one of her relatives come for her, then it's a spare.'

Amy felt a shiver run down her spine. It was said in such a matter of fact way. But she surmised that if you work as a funeral director, it was the way you normally deal with death and burials.

'Did she say anything to you about any relatives?'

'No, she never talked about her past. We had some Irish people staying in the *Brace* at one time, but she always seemed to avoid talking about Ireland herself.'

'She was a good looking woman,' said Amy, 'she must have had a lot of men chasing after her in the village.'

'To be honest, she wasn't interested. I asked her out, but she always refused.'

'Any reason? You're a good looking man and single.'

'Thanks,' he said, clearly pleased with the comment and then added, 'I really liked her and I told her so. She said she just wanted to be friends and that she didn't want to go out with anyone for the moment. When I asked if I had a chance in the future she just smiled.'

'Did you see much of her?'

'She came into the *Brace* quite a few times during the week and would sometimes have some supper there. She would always buy a round and said she didn't want to be obliging to anyone.'

Amy was getting more and more confused about Bernadette. Where did she get her money from? She sighed. Perhaps all this was beyond her and that she should leave it to the police. Ged wanted her to stay and chat, but the nervous tension and tiredness of the day had caught up with her, and she returned to the vicarage.

Augustus wasn't home so she went up to her room and lay down. Sleep quickly overcame her and she didn't move for several hours. It was dark by the time she awoke, but she did feel much better. Augustus had left a message on the answer phone to say he wouldn't be back until late. But there was no message from Theodore. She had hoped there might be, but when he had seen her in handcuffs this morning she wondered what he had thought. She didn't want to ring him, so she walked Desmond on the paths and lanes near his house on the chance of meeting him, but it was a fruitless exercise.

She was now resolved to leave the whole matter to the police, and would leave Nether Crimpton. Augustus would need to agree to her leaving. But she didn't think that would take long. He wouldn't want her to stay unless she was happy.

Her third pair of trainers were past their best, but would do for an evening run. She could burn away all the frustrations and unpleasantness that surrounded her. She ran up to, and then through, the woods beyond the manor and promptly got lost along the maze of paths and tracks. It didn't worry her, so she decided to keep running until she came out somewhere she recognised.

Finally the manor appeared in the distance, but she knew she was not near a public footpath. She couldn't be bothered about formalities and would run across the estate land. It would take her around the back of the house and out on to the road near the visitor's centre car park. It was dark and as she was wearing all black, so she doubted whether she could be seen. She approached the end of the east wing of the manor. The old couple lived at the far end of the west wing. So she was out of sight from the rooms at that end.

As she came silently along the grass track, she caught site of a figure creeping around the side of the manor. 'Someone is up to something,' she said to herself, but couldn't think why anyone would break into the old and dilapidated house, especially the east wing.

She slowed to a trot and then stopped behind a large tree to watch what was happening. There was chink of light from behind some curtains. The dark figure climbed in through the window. She couldn't tell in the darkness whether it was a man or woman. There was no one else around, so she slowly crept up to the house and then along the side of the building to the window, into which the shadowy figure had disappeared.

There was light in the room, which she could just see around the edge of the curtains. The window was still open and she could hear voices. They were young people. It took a few minutes, but she thought she recognised two of them. She guessed there were four voices. What should she do? It really wasn't her business and they might have permission to be in there, but she thought that highly unlikely.

It was then that a waft of warm air came from the room, accompanied by a little smoke. It was a sweet, aromatic smell and she guessed they were smoking cannabis. Then there was another sound as someone crushed a drinks can. 'Alcohol and drugs,' she said to herself. What should she do? One voice came through really clearly from the room and this time she was sure. It was Mary.

Amy knew she couldn't just pass by. Although she did think she could meet with Mary tomorrow, to tell her what she knew. The voice fell into place. It was Clint, but the other two voices she didn't recognise. What to do? She could just ignore it. After all, she tried to reason with herself, it was just another group of young people taking drugs. But it wasn't in her nature to ignore such matters. Ring the police? That was just too complicated. She would have to explain why she was on someone's land in the dark. No, definitely not the police. 'What would Gus do?' she said to herself.

There was nothing else for it, she had to go in and sort it whatever was happening. That's what Augustus would want her to do and that is exactly what he would do himself. She took a few moments to plan her approach. The window ledge was low. There was a join in the middle of the curtains. She decided to take her chance and step through and take the consequences, if she collided with anything.

'Time to go,' she said to herself. She took a deep breath and with one large step, burst through the curtains. She landed in the middle of the four teenagers,who were sitting in a circle on the floor. They were passing a joint around. She was prepared. They might attack her and she also didn't know if they had any weapons.

'And what do we have here?' she said, seeing that they were slow to move.

Mary said, 'Oh, shit!'

'Who is she?' said one of the others.

'I know who she is,' said Clint springing to his feet, 'and this time I'm going to deal with her.' The others hadn't moved from the floor, so Amy focused her attention on Clint, whose face was full of aggression. The drugs and alcohol had slowed him down, but his angry stare went straight to Amy. Very slowly he pulled a long bladed knife from his pocket.

Mary shouted, 'No Clint, no!'

But he took no notice of his sister, 'I'm going to do for her, this time. She isn't going to make a fool of me twice. I'll make her beg for mercy.'

'No!' screamed the other girl.

The other lad, who was nearly as tall as Amy stood up, but a quick glance at his face, showed he had no stomach for a fight. He was deathly white.'

Amy pointed at the other lad, as she concentrated on Clint, who was in front of her, she shouted, 'You, sit down.'

'I'll sort her out on my own,' said Clint, as his friend half sat and half collapsed on the floor.

'Give me the knife,' said Amy, in as calm a voice as she could manage.

'No way, I'm going to get my own back on you,'

Mary pleaded, 'Clint, don't make it any worse. Do it for me. Give Amy the knife.'

'No, not until she begs and says sorry,'

'Please, please Clint!' The other girl stammered, 'Give up your knife, it's all so horrible,' and she burst into tears.

'Come on,' said Amy facing up to Clint, 'take the sensible option and give me the knife and we will say nothing more about any of this. Come on, give it to me.'

Amy was worried about the others. They were all too close together, and if Clint tried to attack her, someone could get hurt. She knew she had taken the wrong approach, but focused on how she could get out of this situation with no-one getting injured.

'Clint you can't attack a defenceless woman,' said Mary rising to her feet, 'I'm going to stand in your way.'

That was exactly what Amy didn't want, and she said with as much force as she could, 'Stay out of the way, Mary, Clint is dangerous with a knife. He's under drugs and drink. Stay out of the way and no one will get hurt.'

Amy half looked to ensure that Mary was going to move away again. Clint saw a moment of weakness and decided to attack her with the knife. The girls both screamed, but Amy was a few steps away and saw him coming. He missed with his first lunge. Amy wanted to make sure she could get the knife from him, so that no one, including him, got hurt.

He lunged again. She could easily throw him, but it would be towards Mary. Amy would have to get the knife first, so she tried to block him with her body, but the blade caught her arm. Mary screamed and sobbed, 'No! Clint, no!'

Amy could see the knife flashing again, but this time she saw her chance. She went straight for it and grabbed his knife wrist, with both hands. As he tried to lunge, she used his own body weight and was confident that she could disarm him. She threw him so that her grip on his wrist remained uppermost. Before he even landed, she knew he wasn't going to have a good fall. The impact of him hitting the ground from a height, as she manoeuvred him over her hip, meant he released the knife, which fell away harmlessly on the floor. But it was the arm that he was landing on, that concerned Amy. She heard the faintest of cracks. Her mind raced, the injury could be dealt with later, but her total effort now was to get the knife. She sprang across the room and picked it up.

She was relieved that Clint was only moaning from hitting the floor and hoped the sound hadn't been his wrist. He was too disorientated with the drink and drugs to really know what had happened to him. Mary squealed as she looked at Amy's arm, who glanced down and said gently as the adrenalin subsided, 'It's only a scratch.'

Amy looked around the room, which was lit with a low hurricane lamp and saw three very frightened faces. She thought that she probably didn't look too good either, as she shivered with the fright of what had just taken place. Clint was lying on the floor not really sure what had happened. She already had the knife and so she said, 'Give me the grass.' There was a little hesitancy from the faces that looked at her. 'What happens if they won't?' she thought.

There was no time to lose, so she bluffed, 'I'll strip each of you, until I find it.' It had the desired effect and several small packets landed on the floor. 'Has he got any?' said Amy pointing at Clint. All three shook their heads. Amy would have to believe them. She scooped up the small packages and put them into the pocket of her tracksuit jacket, along with the knife. There was stony silence as she did this.

Clint was lying on the floor shaken, but conscious, and he was well under the drinks and drugs by now. The other three were white as sheets. They began to shake as reality hit the drugs and drink in their systems, but they undoubtedly knew what was going on. The silence lingered as Amy tried to work out what to do next. It was then that she heard the shaky voice of the Colonel, 'Who's there! Show yourself. I'm armed.'

That was all Amy needed at this point. She had to think quickly. She doused the light and said quietly, 'Don't make a single noise.' She eased back the curtain so at least there was a little of the night sky in the room. Clint groaned. In the outline of the window, she saw Mary go down to him and whisper, 'Clint, Clint, it's me, you must be quiet. Just for me, you must be quiet.'

The Colonel's voice became more distant as he moved past the room they were in, but he still held a great deal of fear for Amy. She had no doubt that he had his officer's pistol with him. If he heard, or saw, any movement he would fire. She thought that he might be old these days, but years of training with a pistol meant that he was not likely to miss. She shivered at the thought. Another thought struck her. If he didn't find anyone he might ring the police. She corrected herself. Lady Crimpton had probably had rung the police, while her husband went to investigate.

Whilst normally they might not respond very quickly. When there had just been a murder in the village, then she thought they would respond with a lot of police. Her heart sank. She was now carrying drugs and a knife, which had followed on from trespassing and climbing uninvited into a house. She was now a burglar in the eyes of the law. How do I get out of this?

She thought for a few moments and then said, 'Come on, all of you, this way.' She opened the curtain and climbed out, 'Bring him with you,' she said.

Clint moaned, 'My wrist hurts.' They all got through the window safely and skirted the edge of the building going round the back of the manor. There was a small patch of trees between the house and the visitor centre. She stopped there and turned to the four teenagers. She said to the two that she didn't know, 'What are your names?' As she said it she realised that their only hope was to lie, even though Amy had seen their faces.

They mumbled two names, but Mary's voice cut across them, 'Don't be so stupid we're in a bloody mess. Amy isn't going to turn us into the police.'

She got the names she required and then Amy said to Mary, 'Go in the back way to the centre, you must know how to get in.' She nodded in response. 'See if you can get Clint to go to sleep, it wouldn't be a good idea to take him to hospital tonight.'

'Why what's wrong with him?' said Mary with an agitated voice.

'He's probably broken his wrist, but it will be OK until the morning.' They all froze as they heard the distant sounds of sirens. 'Go, go!' said Amy, 'Try to stay out of the way until everything quietens down. And I want to see you three tomorrow.'

'We'll leave Clint out of our meeting, I will be in contact. Now go!' Amy had decided what to do, as she had been speaking. She stayed in the woods a little longer and watched the four of them creep to a small door at the back of the visitor centre. Amy was now convinced they were safe. Even if Damien or Lorraine caught them, they would no doubt have a story ready, as they must have done this before.

It was now time for her to get away, so that she didn't have any explaining to do. The road near the woods, and the back of the visitor's centre, was still quiet as the police sirens were in the distance, but getting closer. She ran away from the village for about four hundred metres and then took a footpath across the fields. She knew it would eventually lead to the station and from there she could get back to the vicarage easily.

The house was in darkness as she reached it, with a sigh of relief. She guessed that Augustus had gone to bed. She very quietly went to the bathroom and flushed away the drugs. At least that was one problem solved. As she started to undress so the immensity of her problems hit her. It was the police inspector's face that she saw looming over her when she had her interview.

He had been badly embarrassed in front of his colleagues this morning and judging by his general irritable nature, he would blame Amy. There was no doubt in her mind that he would attend the manor to see what had happened in a quiet village, just after a murder.

It was her arm she thought about the most. Had she dripped blood on the floor. They would match it straight away because they already had her blood sample and DNA. She looked at her arm, which she had bathed as soon as she got in. It was only a scratch, but it had bled. But whether it dripped onto the floor, she didn't know.

She looked down at the floor and began to cry. Her old trainers were there and their imprints would be in the mud outside of the manor. She hadn't done the murder, so she was justified in her outrage at being arrested.

What she had done tonight was different. She had illegally entered the building and was for some time in possession of drugs. The knife that she had taken from Clint was wrapped in a plastic bag and lay on her dressing table. What if the murderer was Clint? He had a nasty temper and if he was under the influence of drugs at the time. The knife could be one of a pair and the other had been used to kill Bernadette. Her mind was racing through all the possibilities and she just got more and more confused.

She needed to tell Augustus, but she knew his advice would be to go to the police, or would it? He was keen enough to try to find out more about Bernadette. Perhaps he's not impressed with the police, but it is something that he would never directly admit. Amy was confused and the more she tried to think about everything the worse it got. She was very tired and decided to go to bed and to see if she could sleep.

Chapter Seven

Amy had been awake by five o'clock and her mind had cleared during her sleep. She found what she was looking for in her handbag. It was a train timetable. She left a note for Augustus, saying she would be back for a late breakfast. She delved into her wardrobe and found her largest handbag, which took both the knife and the old trainers. If the police came for her then she would have to tell the truth. The only way they would connect her with the manor would be the blood and she didn't think that she had dropped any. The cut was grazed and, while it was quite long, it hadn't bled that much. She had got rid of the drugs, but she still had to deal with the knife. The only other connection was the trainers.

Amy felt much better this morning and began to see the whole village situation in perspective. It was a bright and sunny day. She almost enjoyed the walk to the station and the journey on the old rickety train into Sheffield. She was going to buy some new trainers, that were similar to the ones she wore last night, but with a different tread. If anyone had seen her in her black outfit they would not be able to match the trainers, she would show them, to the prints at the manor.

Last night's pair were old and she rarely used them anyway. As she made her way through Sheffield town centre, she looked around at the old steel town. One noticeboard caught her eye and she smiled, as she was in luck. She'd intended just getting rid of the knife somewhere in town, but the notice said there was currently a police amnesty on knives. She popped into the foyer of the police station and dropped the knife into the large bin that had been provided. That cheered her up and she set off in a hearty spirit to the shops to buy trainers.

It only took an hour and she had bought two new pairs of trainers, one black and the other pink. A multicoloured pair of fine sandals had caught her attention and they were added to her purchases. She explained in the shop, that she had brought her old trainers as she wanted a similar pair, which is what she bought and the shop kindly agreed to dispose of her old ones.

During her walk back to the station she felt pleased. All her problems had been solved, and not only that, but there was nothing suspicious about the way in which she had acted. She had given the knife to the police and bought new trainers to replace the old. There was nothing doubtful in that.

The morning got even better as she walked into the station foyer. Theodore was coming the other way as he had obviously caught the next train into Sheffield. She bit her lip as she wondered what his reaction would be when he looked up. When he did, he immediately saw Amy and smiled. They met in the middle of the concourse.

'Good morning, Amy, I'm pleased to see you looking so bright and smiling.'

'Good morning, Theodore, I am glad I bumped into you as I wanted to tell you about yesterday's misunderstanding with the police. I'm afraid that a rather over zealous police inspector misinterpreted some circumstantial evidence.'

She thought what she had said was a bit over the top, but she had planned it carefully in case they met. She just hoped he would understand and mention something about the date again

'I'd love to hear all the details,' he said with a broad smile, 'but I've got to be at the hospital shortly.' Amy feared that he would use an excuse to get out of the date.

'Never mind,' she said forcing a smile to hide her disappointment.

'But I am free this evening, if you would like to have dinner?'

'I'd like that very much,' said Amy and this time she didn't have to force the smile.

They quickly arranged the time and Amy skipped along the platform to wait for her train. The whole world felt so much better this morning and her mind was now entirely focused on her date and what to wear. As she got off the train so her mind switched back to Bernadette. It would be good to come to a resolution on that today, but she wasn't hopeful.

She planned to go back to the vicarage to ask Augustus's advice about dealing with Mary and the others. After that she would go and find Mary to have a chat with her.

It was going to be a good day. That was until she turned the corner onto the track to see the police car outside of the vicarage. She gulped, but at the back of her mind, she had expected it. They had found the blood and made the connections. She took a deep breath. There was no alternative. She had to face whatever it was. She was convinced that it would be about last night.

She breezed up the path, even though her stomach was tightening and went into the house. Augustus opened the door to his study and said that they were all in there. She studied his face and relaxed a little as he was smiling.

'Good morning, inspector, good morning, sergeant,' she said in the most confident manner.

The inspector didn't reply and the sergeant only smiled.

'They have only just arrived,' said Augustus. He turned to the police officers and said, 'Ask away.'

'First of all, I called around at about nine o'clock last night. Neither of you were in. Where were you?'

Augustus said immediately, 'I went over to visit Father O'Connor.'

The inspector snapped, 'I told you not to leave the village.'

Augustus carefully studied the inspector. Amy glanced at the sergeant, who looked surprised at her superior officer's outburst. Augustus said in a slow and measured tone, 'You said to not to leave Nether Crimpton. All day yesterday, I remained in the parish of Nether Crimpton.'

The inspector scowled and turned his attention to focus on Amy.

'I went for a run, which as you know, I do most evenings.'

'Where did you go?'

'If you are asking did I leave the village. The answer was no as I was in sight of the village all the time. That is apart from the fact that by the end of my run it was dark.' Amy had planned what to say next.

He repeated his question and Amy said, 'I went up to the woods, through them, and came down around the back of the manor and the long way around to the station.'

She knew it would be the next few questions that were going to be difficult. So she would try to disrupt his thought process and she said with a smile, 'Oh, I've just realised, I'm so sorry inspector.'

'What about?' he answered with a bemused look

'I've been into Sheffield this morning. I forgot to contact you and ask permission.' The police sergeant looked away and out of the window to hide the smile on her face. Amy dramatically rummaged in her bag. She produced the receipts which she handed to the sergeant, 'I needed to buy some new trainers, for obvious reasons, and just went without thinking.'

The sergeant nodded that the receipts were valid and handed them back to Amy.

'Did you see anything?' said the inspector abruptly.

Amy was on her guard and concentrating hard on what was likely to be said. 'When?'

'On the night of the murder. You were very close to the scene. No, in fact you were in the middle of it, near the time it happened. Can you think back? Did you see anything unusual or anyone?'

'No,' said Amy thoughtfully, 'There was nothing unusual in the churchyard and I didn't see anyone. My whole attention was focused on Desmond, when he got stuck.'

'What about you, sir?' asked the sergeant, 'only I noticed I can see the graveyard from this room. Upstairs you must have a better view.'

'Yes, there is. But I'm afraid I didn't see anyone coming or going. I was in here, with the curtains drawn.' There was a slight pause in the conversation before Augustus added, 'What was it that you came to talk to us about last night?'

'We had a call last night to the manor about a break-in. We decided to come too as we were in the area at the time, so we came round to find that both of you were not in.' Amy thought that he obviously wants to make a point.

The sergeant said to Amy, 'We wanted to ask you about the

young lad.'

'What young lad?' said Amy warily.

The inspector studied her for a few minutes and said, 'On Saturday evening.'

Amy was now focused on what he meant. 'Oh, you mean Clint.'

'Did you know him?'

'Not at the time. I saw him kicking at flowers in one of the gardens. As we were judging the gardens the following day I shouted at him.'

'But you chased him, we have witness statements.'

'Yes, I did through the village.'

'He was a young man causing vandalism and you ran after him. He might have had a knife,' said the inspector.

'It was a very brave and commendable act, ma'am,' said the sergeant, 'but we would strongly advise you to call the police and let us deal with it.'

Amy smiled and said, 'I'm sure you've much better things to do with your time. I was only taking a lad back to his parents.'

The sergeant said with a serious tone, 'Was the lad, as you called him, Clint Smith, who lives at the visitor's centre.'

'Yes, that's him.'

'Last year he was cautioned for possession of a knife.'

Amy smiled weakly back and gently rubbed her arm where the wound was stinging slightly. She wanted to bring this conversation to a close so she said, 'I caught him, and one of the villagers recognised him. By coincidence his father came out from the pub at the time, so I handed him over.'

The inspector said, 'We will pick him up later and talk to him, but I think he is just a young thug and not a murderer.'

The sergeant said, 'While we are on the topic of safety, we would advise against jogging in the dark in isolated places, especially now a murder has been committed, although we do not think it is a random attack.' She turned to Augustus and said, 'I'm sure you would agree with us, sir, and perhaps you could ask your sister to think twice about her late runs.'

To the definite surprise of the police officers, Augustus

laughed and said, 'I can assure you that I have advised Amy many times about personal safety. However, we spent many years in Africa together, where life was much more dangerous than Nether Crimpton. And if you haven't yet gathered my sister is a very competent athlete and is especially proficient in judo and karate. So I think my advice will fall on deaf ears,' but the words were delivered with a smile.

The inspector looked at Amy and Augustus. He then seemed to make a decision, and said, 'I have consulted my superiors over the murder of Bernadette Murphy. We are following up various leads and are confident of making an arrest.' Amy glanced at the sergeant whose eyes told a different story. The inspector continued, 'We have come across a difficulty which I believe you,' looking at Augustus, 'raised with the custody sergeant yesterday, namely the next-of-kin.' Augustus nodded, 'My superiors decided that we should take you into our confidence and ask a favour of you.'

'Please ask away,' said Augustus, 'we will do anything to help if we can.'

'We have not traced Bernadette's next of kin and we are about to release her cottage from police control. The cottage is rented from the couple, who live in the manor. When we were there last night they indicated they will return it to the market, for new tenants, as soon as we release it. At the moment all Bernadette's possessions are still there. Whilst we could package them up, the sergeant said yesterday, that you volunteered to help with the next-of-kin.'

'Yes, we did,' said Augustus, 'and we will be happy to package up her possessions and keep them, until the next-of-kin is known.' Amy nodded her agreement.

The inspector continued, 'It is not only her next-of-kin that is proving difficult to trace. We have been very unsuccessful in finding anything about Bernadette, before she came to this village. It's as though she didn't exist. Everything we follow up is a dead-end, even the agency that employed her. It went out of business about three years ago.' Amy thought that at least it answers one question that she had after talking to Damien, but it raises many more.

'Sergeant, why don't you take Miss Andrews down to the manor and explain to the old couple that she will be clearing the cottage, and I will talk to the vicar about some of the people in the village.'

It was with some relief that Amy left the vicarage and walked down the track with the sergeant towards the manor. Amy then saw the next problem. The Colonel might say something about yesterday and how Amy was trying to find out some information. It was all getting to complicated. Amy knew she couldn't go on with all this tension.

'Am I still considered a suspect?'

The sergeant smiled, 'Well, the inspector thinks you are. The rest of us on the case, as well as his boss, don't think so.'

'Any reason?' said Amy warily.

'Even the most hardened murder doesn't give a blood-stained murder weapon to a dog to play with. And all the rest of what you said panned out. Your description of the events was borne out by the forensics team down to the last detail. You had no motive, and all the witnesses in the village, said you got on well with Bernadette. Even when threatened by the young thug, you didn't lose your temper.' Amy could see behind that stern face were sparkling eyes and a genuine smile. She liked the sergeant.

Amy said, 'I think I can guess what amuses you.'

'Go on, then,' she said lightly.

'The last person to lose their temper with Bernadette was the inspector.'

'Yes, that's right you must have been at the centre as a witness.'

'Yes, I was, in charge of the jam stall.'

'That's sad!'

The two women strolled amiably through the bright sunlight of the summer's morning

'How do you get on with the inspector?' said Amy, but she expected a guarded reply, although she might be able to read something into it.

'Why he doesn't like you. I don't know, unless, of course, it

79

was the jam stall,' she said with a chuckle. 'Normally he's OK, in fact, he is a good detective, but he is fiercely ambitious.'

'Does that make a difference to the murder of Bernadette then?'

'Oh, yes. These local murders, despite Agatha Christie, are normally wrapped up quickly, which is what he would have expected. He doesn't like being questioned by his senior officers about the lack of progress. It will be a black mark on his promotion campaign.'

'He sounds terribly dedicated to the police.'

'He is. He followed in his father's footsteps and wants to get to Chief Superintendent at an earlier age.'

'He must be difficult to work for?'

'It's not his ambition that's difficult, it's his golf. Any spare minute he plays golf, often with the senior officers who knew his father. But, from the accounts at the station, he's useless at it.'

Amy enjoyed the jibe at him, but very much took into her thoughts the other comment that he was a very good detective. The sergeant said, 'By the way, my name's Sharon. I think we are going to get to know each other as this is going to be a long case.' Amy was surprised by her openness and was even more surprised when she said, 'What happened in Scotland?' Amy's smiling face turned quickly to a frown. Is she trying to trick me, by lulling me into a false sense of security? Hey, it's no big deal for me. There are no tricks.'

'How do you know? asked Amy.

'For a short time you were the prime murder suspect. So we checked up on you. It's now a vast machine that normally produces more information than we can handle, but we wanted to track your movements. We can tell from addresses and, of course, the most useful to us, your bank withdrawals and mobile phone use. All of a sudden you left Scotland and went back to your parents. It often means a bust up.'

'Can you just do that?' said Amy and then qualified it, 'I don't mean, I've got anything to hide.'

'Only with some court warrants, but they are not difficult, if we have you as a prime suspect in a murder.'

Amy said sadly, 'I was due to be married and someone came along with a better offer. Not only that, but he used the same wedding day.'

'Nasty man, you were better off without him. You were saved.'

Amy had never looked at it like that, but it did give her some food for thought. They walked on a bit further in silence and stopped to gaze at a farmer cutting the hay.

Amy said, 'There is something I need to tell you. It's not about the murder, but I realise it might get me into trouble.'

'Let's sit on the bench,' said Sharon in a casual manner. Amy couldn't tell whether Sharon was just stringing her along or it was genuine casualness. They sat down. 'Before you start,' said Sharon.

'Yes,' said Amy somewhat annoyed at the delay, now she had decided to tell all.

'There are some things that if I am told as a police officer I am obliged, by my job and the law, to take action. But I can give advice on hypothetical situations.'

Amy immediately picked up on the idea. 'Supposing a normal person came across a group of teenagers taking drugs for personal use.'

'Does this normal person know these kids?'

'Only two of them, but they are all friends.'

'What drugs?'

'Cannabis and alcohol.'

'How old are they?'

'Seventeen or eighteen.'

'It makes a lot of difference,' said Sharon, 'but let's assume they are all seventeen.'

'What should that normal person do in those circumstances?'

'The police would always advise to notify them, because we can track the supply and see if any of them have previously been caught.' Amy was disappointed with the answer, she expected more help from Sharon, who added, 'The police would check them out, but if it was a first offence.' She paused. 'Shall we assume it is the first time?'

'Yes,' said Amy finally picking up the drift.

'If they were seventeen, from relatively stable homes in a middle class area, we would inform the parents. That must always be done and then it is their responsibility. Most of the time it works. The parents anger is enough in most cases to stop the experiments.'

'Thanks,' said Amy, although she didn't know how she was going to do it.

'And now,' said Sharon standing up from the bench, 'let's go and see this old pervert.'

Amy giggled, 'You mean the Colonel.'

'When I met him for the first time, he wouldn't take his eyes off my boobs. The inspector was the one who wanted to lead the questions and he didn't notice him staring, so I'm looking forward to meeting him. We're both quite well endowed, so I wonder which one he will look at.' It was said with a laugh. Amy concluded she must meet people like the Colonel all the time.

Amy was determined to be clear with Sharon, 'I went to the manor yesterday to try to find out about the next-of-kin and whether he had any papers about Amy.'

'Did you find anything?'

'No, the only thing was the rent book, did you see it?'

Sharon said, 'Yes, an obvious forgery, not unusual.'

'You don't think it had anything to do with the death of Bernadette?'

'No, I'm sure it's not. The ink had hardly dried in it and the silly sod had used the same pen throughout. It will be just the normal scam.'

'I'm naïve,' said Amy, 'what's the normal scam?'

'If they have a formal rent book, then they have an income and the tax people are interested. So you do a deal with the tenant. A lower cost rent and no rent book. Cash in hand, both sides benefit, and only the tax man loses out.'

*****

As the left they house Amy was amazed at how Sharon had conducted the interview. Lady Crimpton and the Colonel were their usual selves, and hinted at complaints that it was all too slow and they were losing rent and had influence in high circles. Sharon had been compliant are first as she told them that Amy and the vicar would be taking charge of Bernadette's possessions.

The staring started and Lady Crimpton made some bland remark about Bernadette. From then on Sharon had transformed herself. She had said directly to the Colonel, I find you behaviour offensive. You know what I mean. I shall start making enquiries with young women in the village about your attitude to them and whether any of them want to make a complaint.

Before they could say anything, she had added aggressively that she was going to take the rent book and pass it to the Inland Revenue. The transformation was amazing and they offered any help to Amy, the vicar or the police. They immediately produced a key to Bernadette's cottage and said to take as long as necessary.

Sharon and Amy walked back down the drive and Sharon said, 'I don't think you will have any more problems with them, but if there is just let me know.'

'Yes, thanks,' replied Amy.

Sharon asked, 'Before I go?'

'Yes,' said Amy a little hesitantly.

'You know the hypothetical advice?'

'Yes,' replied Amy beginning to worry.

'It would be good for the normal person, who found the teenager to meet one of them, whilst coincidentally in the company of a police officer. Of course, the police officer would have no idea, who they were being introduced to.'

She wants to check one of them over, thought Amy. She returned Sharon's smile and said, 'Perhaps a cup of tea at the visitor's centre, before you go.'

Amy saw a slight nod of the head. And she knew that Sharon understood that was why they hadn't caught any intruders, although they had a lot of police in the area. They had all gone into the back of the visitor's centre.

It was still quiet in the visitor's centre and only one waitress was working, it was Mary. They sat down and Mary had no option, but to come over. Amy could see she looked very worried.

Amy tried to be as normal as possible as she said, 'Mary, this is Sergeant Dawkins from the police, she is...' The colour drained completely from Mary's face.

Sharon looked Mary up and down and finally said, 'Nice to meet you. I'll have a tea with two sugars.' Mary with great relief left the table and Sharon said, 'She looks OK to me. The meeting frightened her witless. It won't do her any harm. There's no obvious signs of drug use. She's the daughter of the owner isn't she? And the brother of the thug you had a run in with.'

'Yes,' said Amy.

Amy enjoyed Sharon's company over the drink, and after she had gone Amy arranged a meeting with Mary. She told her that the ones from last night should all be at the folly in the woods at four o'clock this afternoon. Mary tried to ask if the police were involved, but Amy would only say to make sure they were there.

It was getting very warm, so she decided to go home and change. She also wanted to talk with Augustus about Bernadette's cottage. The vicarage was quiet, when she arrived, and Augustus wasn't in his study. She went up to change, as she was particularly keen to wear her new multicoloured sandals. There was a noise from Augustus's room at the top of the stairs. His door was open so she called out, 'Gus, are you there?' Amy was shocked as a good-looking woman, in her thirties, came out of his room. She had a good figure, which was amply shown off by a vest and tight cut-off jeans. Her blonde hair was bunched and stretched down past her shoulders.

The woman said, 'You must be Amy, I'm Katie. the housekeeper.' Amy remembered joking with Augustus about having a good-looking housekeeper. He said it was Mrs Battersby. Amy could see that she wasn't a burglar as she was carrying a duster and some polish. 'You look confused,' said Katie, 'can I help at all?'

'Augustus said that Mrs Battersby was his housekeeper.'

Katie replied perkily, 'That's gran, she's been here for decades and has looked after all the different vicars. She mainly does the kitchen now that she is in her seventies and I do the heavier jobs. Oh and by the way, it's often confusing, because I'm Mrs

Battersby. She's not really my gran, as I married into the family.'

Amy could tell that Katie was the talkative type as she carried on about men not being good in the family. My husband was good to start with, but then it all went wrong. Gran kicked out her own grandson and now there is just the two of us.'

'Does it work well?'

'Yes, really well, we get on fine together.' Amy went towards her room, 'I was just going to do your room, but I'll do it later.'

'Come and do it now, I'm only going to quickly change and go out again.'

They chatted generally as Amy changed. Katie dusted and polished. She also admired the new coloured sandals that Amy put on. Amy was just about to go when Katie said, 'You found poor Bernadette, didn't you?'

'Yes, it wasn't pleasant. Did you know her well?'

'Not really, but I used to see her at the doctor's quite a lot.'

'The doctor's?' said Amy.

'The big house where the doctor lives in the village. The one who judged the gardens, with you.'

'Theodore?'

'Yes, that's right.' Amy was confused again. 'Gran has always had two jobs, the vicarage and the Gentleman's house, as it's called. I help her with both.'

'And you still do both of them?'

'Yes.'

'Did Bernadette come to the house of lot?'

'It started about six weeks ago and she seemed to be there most days. She often arrived, just as I was leaving.' Amy's heart sank. Theodore must have been going out with Bernadette. It would explain why she said to Ged that she wasn't interested. Perhaps she was trying to entice Theodore. 'And I saw him going to her cottage a couple of times.' She paused, looked directly at Amy and said, 'Of course, it's none of my business.'

Amy tried to sound casual as she said, 'You must have spoken to her a day or two before she was killed.'

'That's the strange thing. About a week ago, the visits seem to stop, and I didn't seen her at all.'

The conversation made Amy feel uneasy. She wasn't sure what it was that nagged at the back of her mind, but she wondered who else knew. Theodore wasn't popular in the village and that was obvious in the judging of the gardens on Sunday. He kept himself out of the main life of the community and just occasionally went to the *Marquis* for a drink. Bernadette, in contrast, was known throughout the village, but the only strange thing was that she didn't go out with any of the men. Ged was the obvious pick, but she kept turning him down, but why?

She tried to think through the implications of Theodore and Bernadette. It was certainly going to cast a cloud over dinner with him tonight, unless she could think of a way of bringing it up and finding out the truth. But there again, did she want to know the truth. She would have to wait until this evening, to solve that problem.

Amy was at a loose end because she didn't want to go to Bernadette's cottage on her own, as she wanted Augustus to be there. It was just in case there was something suspicious. So she decided to go back to the visitor's centre and talk to Lorraine. She would have employed Bernadette and might have had more contact with her than Damien. By the time she got there the centre was full of people. The board outside, which showed the daily activities, had in large writing that the main event of the day was a clay pigeon shooting competition, between local villagers and visitors. It's obviously popular, thought Amy as she made her way through the crowds.

She turned a corner to go to the office, when she nearly collided with Clint, who stood there with his arm in a sling and a plaster cast on his wrist. They both looked at each other, she tensed because she wasn't sure of his reaction. Lorraine came up behind him, and said, 'Amy, look at poor Clint, he fell over last night coming back to the centre and broke his wrist. The poor love slept all night without knowing he'd done it. But it was so swollen this morning, I took him straight to hospital.'

Amy looked directly at Clint. The scowl was gone, but there was no other reaction, it was just a deadpan face. Amy said, 'You look a little pale, it's nice and sunny out, why not get some fresh air and take a stroll up to the woods.'

Clint grunted, but then Amy saw the reaction in his eyes. 'I might do later this afternoon.'

At least he is going to come thought Amy, as she looked past him and said to Lorraine, 'I was hoping to have a chat with you, but I didn't realise it would be so busy today.'

Lorraine smiled back at her, which took Amy by surprise who expected a brush off.

'Come through to the office, we have taken on some temps and they seem quite good, so I can leave it to them and Damien for a short while.'

Amy had planned her approach and as soon as they were sat down she said, 'I'm sorry we've got off on the wrong foot. I'll make sure the jam stall is in a different place next time.'

'That's OK,' said Lorraine, 'perhaps I was a little over the top, I've been feeling the strain as its been so busy. If you do it again, let's just agree before it gets set up.' It was a very different Lorraine that now sat in front of her. She seemed the same business woman, but was much more relaxed. Damien came into the office and muttered some words to her, but she showed no reaction to him and completely ignored his presence. He took some papers and left. That was the reaction that Damien described yesterday, I wonder why she is not talking to him?

Amy said, 'There really wasn't any reason for you to take offence with me about the route of the path and cycle way. The Colonel and his wife asked me to help, but I certainly didn't agree. I'm only here for a short time to visit my brother and, like him, I will stay out of the debate.' She could tell Lorraine wasn't happy about it, so she added, 'as far as I see it's just the widening of the existing paths and a better surface, which will suit me as I'm a runner.'

It brought the faintest of smiles from Lorraine. Amy thought that at least she didn't seem to want to argue. Damien was right, she was much more subdued than before. Lorraine wasn't going to start chatting, but on the other hand she didn't seem to want Amy to leave, so Amy said, 'You might already know that Augustus is trying to trace Bernadette's next-of-kin.'

'Yes, I heard, but I don't know anything about her. Damien does all the paperwork.'

'I just wondered if you had had any woman to woman chats with her, during which she talked about her past?'

'No, not really. Whilst she has worked here since we opened, apart from normal and general conversations we've not spoken. To be honest I didn't really like her that much but she was a good employee...' Lorraine looked like she was going to say something else, but changed her mind. 'She got on with her job and that was it really...'

'I believe she used to talk quite a lot with Mary.'

'There was nothing in that, it was just that they worked together and so chatted, nothing more.'

As Amy had arrived at the visitors centre, the rain had started. The forecast was for heavy showers. By the time they had finished their conversation, the rain was torrential. Damien came rushing back into the office. 'We started the shooting competition, but have suspended it because of the rain.'

Lorraine looked him up and down, thought for a moment, but decided not to reply. Amy wondered whether she was only going to answer, because she was there, Lorraine said, 'I didn't think you could get a team from the villagers, so you were going to make it a general competition.'

'That's what I came to say, I managed to get hold of Theodore from the Gentleman's house, and he has arrived, so we are only one short. So if you can manage the centre for a while, I could complete the team.'

Lorraine was spiteful in her reply, 'Don't be so ridiculous we are running a business, no, you can't go.' Amy thought her reply was harsh, as she was happy to sit there with Amy.

Damien said to his wife, 'Why don't you go and join the team then, one of the men will show you what to do, and it will be good for business too.'

The same spitefulness was there as she said to him, 'Are you stupid or something. I'm not going and neither are you.'

Damien looked flustered and in desperation he turned to Amy, looked her up and down, and saw her bare shoulders, with strapped pink summer dress. He focused on her multicoloured delicate sandals and said more in hope than expectation, 'Could I persuade you to join the team?'

Amy stood up, 'Anything I can do to help, but I'm only a visitor though.'

Damien said, 'You are part of the village family as far as I'm concerned. You can't get much closer to the heart of the village than being the vicar's sister. Lorraine didn't look impressed with her husband, but she chose to say nothing.

'Come on,' said Damien enthusiastically, 'one of the men will show you what to do.'

'Thanks for the chat,' said Amy as she left the office. Lorraine gave her a weak smile to say goodbye.

Damien looked her up and down again, 'I don't think it's going to work, you're not really dressed for it, but you won't have time to change. I can hear they have started again.'

'Never mind,' said Amy, who wanted to take the opportunity to talk to Theodore before tonight. She knew if she could have a quick chat about Bernadette, then the matter could be cleared up or, if they couldn't agree, then the date might get cancelled. But it was better to do it before they got to a restaurant. She had thought about not bringing it up at all, but she knew that it would nag at her and spoil her evening.

Damien led the way along the path from the visitor's centre to the lane. The shooting competition was in a field on the opposite side of the lane. They crossed the lane, Damien opened the gate and looked at the muddy, sodden field and then at Amy. The grassed area, where the spectators were standing was damp, but it was easy to walk on providing you didn't mind your shoes getting wet. There was a complete contrast with the shooting area, where most of the shooters were wearing Wellington boots and the area had cut up badly with all the movement of those who had been shooting. It was now a quagmire of mud and water.

She could see that Damien was expecting her to pull out, now that she had seen what was required. Theodore, who was about to shoot, looked at her, then down to her feet, and a quizzical smile crossed his face. Ged was normally the last to shoot for the village, as he was the best shot, and he came over to her.

'Are you joining the team?'

'Yes, that was the plan, she said eyeing up the mud, 'but Damien has only just asked me.'

'Are you going to go through with it?' he said without any confidence in his voice.

Amy said, 'Yes,' They both looked at her feet and the sandals. Amy so far hadn't left the gravel outside of the gate. She slipped off her sandals, picked them up, and put them in her handbag. 'I'm as ready as I will ever be,' she said as she stepped into the mud and walked across to where the shooters were congregated. There was a big scoreboard up and she could see that the visitors were in the lead. They went quiet as the next two shooters were ready to start.

Theodore was on from the village and a middle-aged woman represented the visitors. The woman went first and shouted pull, and the two clays flew across the sky. She missed both by a long way. Then it was Theodore's turn and he missed both, but he was much closer. They had another nine turns each with Theodore winning 10-5.

The announcer called out the next two names and it was the Colonel for the village. This brought a large scowl from Damien, which Ged noticed. 'He's a good shot,' said Ged, 'despite him getting on in years.' The young man from the visitors' team looked confident, when he saw the opposition.

As the shooters got prepared Ged handed Amy an empty shotgun and said, 'I think its going to hurt your shoulder to much, it goes there,' and he showed her how to hold it. 'Do you want a thick sweater to help the impact of the gun, as it has quite a kick.'

She shook her head and continued to listen to Ged's advice. Theodore also came over and said, 'I didn't know you were going to be here.' It was said with a smile, 'Ged's given you good advice, but try to keep it away from your collar-bone as it kicks back.'

Amy just smiled again as Damien said, 'She's a last-minute recruit, but what a good sport to make us up to a full team. It doesn't matter about losing.' Amy looked at the scoreboard and the two columns of names. The last ones for the village read, Theodore, Colonel, Ged and the last space had a question mark. The shooting started and the Colonel narrowed the score again by winning 16-4.

Ged said to Amy, 'Do you want to go next?'

'No, I'm the question mark at the bottom, that's fine by me, it will allow me to practice holding it as you said.'

Amy watched Theodore and Ged chatting. They seem to get on fine together she said to herself. I wonder why?

But then she got cross with herself and dismissed her own inquisitiveness. She was beginning to see something suspicious in everyone and all that happened. As Ged was preparing to shoot, she looked around at the crowd, which was quite substantial, and noticed the two who had just arrived. It was the inspector and the sergeant.

No more guesses she said to herself and turned to watch Ged shoot, who was relaxed and easy with the gun at his side. Before he had even shot for the first time, Amy could tell that he was confident. Damien whispered to her just as they were going to start, 'Ged will get a good score, but it won't be enough.' He was right about the good score, Ged hit 19 clays and his opponent only 8. Ged rejoined Theodore, Amy and Damien, who said, 'That was an excellent score and we have put up a good competition going into the last round. We are only one behind, but the last one of the opposition has his own shotgun and a shooter's jacket. They have put their best one on last.' They watched as the visitor made his way down to the shooting area.

'Your turn,' said Damien, 'thanks for turning out.' The others muttered good luck and Amy picked up her gun and rather precariously went down the grassy slope in her bare feet. She slipped a little on the mud as then went over to her opponent to shake hands. He looked at her pink dress and muddy feet, then gave a little laugh and shook his head.

Amy thought that he was yet another condescending male, so she went close to him and whispered, 'Appearances can be very deceptive.' She could see the look of confusion cross his face.

They each went to their shooting stations. The man started and he directly hit both of the clays from the first pull. Amy steadied her feet in the mud and shouted, 'Pull!' She fired twice and just missed with both. He looked across at her with some surprise on his face. Amy knew she had been much closer that he would have expected, she said to him, 'Just getting used to this gun.'

He turned, called, fired his two shots in rapid succession and hit both clays. Amy didn't delay, 'Pull!' She fired twice and hit both of the clays. This brought the crowd alive, who could see she was the underdog. They reached the halfway stage with Amy still two behind, but he had only just got the last ones. By now the crowd were cheering ever shot she made.

The announcer said, 'Ladies and gentleman the final 12 shots to determine this match and the overall competition. I have been asked to tell you that the lovely lady shooting for the village is Amy.' At this a loud cheer went up. Her opposing shooter looked deadly serious.

Amy waved to the crowd and got another cheer, and she said to her opposing number, 'The pressure is all on you. It would be embarrassing to lose to a woman in a pink dress and no shoes, wouldn't it?' She waited as he took aim and fired. A smile came across her face as one of them missed.

She was relaxed now and thought she could win, but she was still behind so he had to miss again. Amy fired twice and scored two hits. She could see the resolve in his face and he scored the next four. His confidence was back and they matched shots. It was down to the last two shots each. His first just hit the target, but the second missed, which was greeted by a great roar from the crowd.

Amy had to hit the last two just to level the final scores for the match and the competition. She called for the clays and her aim was perfect on both of them. The crowd roared with approval.

'Tremendous shooting,' said her opponent as he congratulated her, 'you handle a gun extremely well.'

'Thank you,' said Amy, 'it was a good competition. I thought I could win it, until I saw you shoot.'

The announcer said, 'Congratulations to both teams a fine competition and now, if the two captains could nominate their choice for the sudden death shoot-out.' Ged, the villagers captain, immediately pointed to Amy, and the visitors' captain gave her the same opponent again. He shot first, but missed one of the clays.

Amy stepped up to the firing position, took her stance and shouted, 'Pull!' She smiled as both of the clays disintegrated in the air.

Amy received congratulations from lots of people as they all returned to the visitor's centre. Her own plan wasn't working as it was too busy to talk to Theodore, so she would have to leave it until this evening. She made a final try to find him, but someone passed on a message, which said that he'd had to go and he would pick her up later.

It was going to make it difficult this evening. She glanced at her watch, it was getting near the time she had arranged to meet the teenagers. She saw Mary slip away as soon as she finished her shift. Clint was nowhere to be seen.

By the time she got to the woods, the four of them were sat on some logs looking anxious. She had remembered the names of the other two, Anna and Justin. She had decided her approach. 'Breaking and entering is a criminal offence and you could all have got a record last night, if the police had caught you, that's, of course, if the colonel hadn't shot you.'

'We really are sorry,' said Mary, who seemed to have been elected the spokesperson. 'We realise it was foolish and we won't do it again.' They all nodded, but Amy was unconvinced about Clint. He was sober now, and in some pain, and just went along with the others, was Amy's guess.

'Thanks for not handing us over to the police,' said Mary.

'It's not that simple,' said Amy and their faces dropped. 'They went to the manor and found the room. It wasn't difficult to work out what had happened.' Amy thought that she would use a bit of exaggeration, 'There was my blood in the room, from my arm.'

Clint looked down at the ground and didn't say anything. 'It would have been easy for them to trace it back to me. They took my blood sample only a few days ago because of the murder. If they had arrested me, I would have had to explain, who you were and how I came to be cut.'

By now Amy had four, young pale serious faces looking at her. 'I spoke to the police and asked if they would leave it to me. They didn't really want to, but on the other hand they wanted to use all their manpower in finding the murderer. I didn't name any of you.'

'Thanks,' said Clint quietly.

'But there was one condition.' The level of worry in their face increased, the girls were close to tears. 'They said that as you are all under eighteen, I must speak with your parents and tell them what happened, about the drink and drugs.' As none of them challenged her on age, she knew that she had guessed right.

Mary began to cry, but Clint looked relieved. Amy watched them carefully for their reaction. Anna also looked relieved, but Amy didn't know why. Justin had gone white and looked like he was going to faint. Lorraine had the best relationship with Clint, so she should tell her. But Amy wasn't sure what reaction she would get. 'Mary, Clint,' I'm going to try to see your parents after this meeting, but I will wait until I can see both of them together, do you want to be there when I tell them?' Mary began to cry, but mumbled, 'Yes.'

'Clint?'

'Are you going to tell them about the knife?'

Amy looked long and hard at him, 'No, I've decided not to, but only if you do what's expected of you.'

He gave the slightest nod, 'I want to be there.'

Amy turned and said, 'Anna, you need to tell me where you live.'

She gulped some air, 'Miss Andrews, thank you for not going to the police. I realise it was wrong and I went home last night and told my parents everything.'

Clint look alarmed and he stared at her, 'No, I didn't tell them about the fight you had with Miss Andrews.' She controlled back the tears and said, 'They have only let me out today, because I said I was meeting you. We live in a cottage not far from here. It is down this track, and is on the lane at the bottom. It is called Intake. My parents have said they would appreciate it if you would see them.' And she began to cry again. That one at least looks like it will be easy thought Amy.

'And now, Justin,' said Amy.

He had hardly lost his paleness, when he said in a quiet voice, 'My parents are in the Army, and I go to boarding school. It is the holidays now and I am staying with my uncle, as my parents are overseas.'

Amy thought that the uncle would do under the circumstances.

'Is there an aunt as well?'

'No, he's not married.'

'What's his name and where do you live.'

'It's Uncle Theodore and he live in the Gentleman's house.'

Amy's heart sank. It was hardly a conversation to have over dinner.

Chapter Eight

Amy walked down through the woods with Anna. Her home was going to be her first stop. Then it was back to the visitor's centre to see Lorraine and Damien, which wasn't going to be easy. But the last one was the most difficult. She saw that her hopes of getting to know Theodore were diminishing very fast. She tried to reason with herself, that it may be for the best. She should stick with her resolution, of only a few days ago, and forget about men for a good period.

Anna was gulping back the tears and couldn't manage to talk. Whilst this wasn't going to be easy, Anna was contrite and her parents already knew. Anna led the way into the smart cottage, and called out tearfully, 'Mum, Dad, I'm home and I've brought Miss Andrews with me.'

Amy's heart sank as she walked into the lounge behind Anna. In one armchair was a women, who was in her early sixties, and she had been crying a lot. Amy thought that she was vaguely familiar. But her attention went to the man in the wheelchair, who was a similar age and looked extremely worried.

The woman jumped up nervously and said, 'Please sit down, Miss Andrews, I'll make some tea.'

'Not for me,' said Amy, 'I can see you are very distressed, please sit down.'

Anna who was still crying went and sat on a little stool near her father. He stroked her hair and said, 'Thank you for coming, Miss Andrews.' Amy heard his voicing cracking as he held back the tears. She had entered a house that was full of emotion. It had been a day that had completely disrupted this gentle family home. All three of them just stared at Amy.

She knew this was going to be difficult, but she had to take control, 'Please do your best to relax. It is over with now and fortunately no one is hurt or harmed in anyway,' she tried to make her voice lighter as she said, 'I prefer to be called Amy.'

The man took a gulp of air and said, 'This is my family, I'm Jack, this is my wife Shirley, and you already know Anna.'

Amy smiled the best she could to defuse the tension, 'Anna tells me that she has explained what happened last night.'

Anna burst out crying and Amy passed her a tissue, 'Miss, I did tell them all that happened and that included about Clint attacking you.'

'Ah,' said Amy, this was getting more difficult by the minute

Anna continued, 'I've pleaded with them not to tell anyone, until they have spoken you.'

Jack said, 'I very much regret that my only daughter is involved, but the law is the law. As as family we will have to accept the punishment that comes to us. We have had good times and bad times, but we must now face the consequences. Young thugs cannot go around attacking defenceless women. It has to be the police.'

This brought howls from both his wife and daughter. Amy waited for them to recover a little before she went to speak. To her surprise the silence was interrupted by Shirley, 'This isn't just Jack's decision. We sat up to the early hours of the morning as a family, and that's what we decided.'

Amy said, 'Anna, tell me what you think, please.'

'Mum and Dad are right. I've done wrong and must accept the punishment. What seemed harmless to start with got out of hand and I didn't walk away. But more important than me is you, miss.'

'Why?' said Amy very quietly.

'I didn't know he was carrying a knife, otherwise I would never have been with him. You can't allow him to attack you and do nothing about it.' Anna was recovering a little of her confidence and she added, 'and I realise that when you go to the police, you will have to name us all.'

Her father stroked her hair and said very gently, 'Good girl, that was the right thing to say.' Amy realised from the father's reaction that these were his daughter own words, and that he hadn't forced her into it.

'We are unanimous,' said Shirley, 'thank goodness, you were

not hurt.'

'Mum, he stabbed her on the arm,' said Anna ensuring that her mother knew the exact facts.

Amy showed her arm to the mother and father, 'Look! It is a minor scratch, nothing more.' They looked at her arm and it had the opposite effect of what Amy hoped.

Jack said, 'That's clear evidence of how close he got to seriously hurting you. It must be the police.'

Amy knew she had to get them off their line of thinking so she said, 'Anna is Justin your boyfriend?'

Jack went to speak, but Anna grabbed his hand and said, 'We started going out last week, but I told him last night I'd never see him today after...'

Amy said, 'It was his suggestion wasn't it?

Anna hesitated, glanced at her mother and father and said, 'Yes.'

'Did he have the cannabis with him?' Shirley shivered as Amy mentioned the drug.

Anna nodded.

'Let me explain,' Amy said to Jack and Shirley, 'I wanted to find out, which one of the four supplied the drugs.'

'Are you sure it wasn't that Clint,' said Shirley looking at both Anna and Amy.

Amy said, 'Clint has no money. He doesn't work, even when he has the opportunity. He lives by cadging off his sister and parents. He couldn't afford the drugs.'

Anna's parents had said their piece and they had calmed down and were listening. Amy used the opportunity to say, 'When I was standing outside of window, I knew there were four of them. I could have rung the police there and then, as I had my mobile with me. It was hearing Mary's voice that made me decide to go in. I also recognised Clint's voice and knew him to be violent, because I had an incident with him last weekend.'

'Yes, everyone who came into the shop talked about how you caught him and took him back to his father.' Amy then remembered where she had seen Shirley before, it was in the village post office.

'I took a risk going into the room, but it was purely to give Mary a chance. I'd met her before and I know that Bernadette really liked Mary and thought she was a super kid. I didn't know either Anna or Justin at the time.' She looked at Shirley and Jack, 'If I had known her then, as I do now, then I would have wanted to give her a chance as well.'

Shirley began to cry again, but Jack said, 'But you knew Clint was violent, and you still took the matter in your own hands and went in.'

'I was more worried about the others getting hurt rather than me. I've been involved in sports and outdoor pursuits all my adult life and have taught numerous women's self defence classes. It is always frightening when it's for real, but I was prepared to take the risk.'

'But Justin might have been violent as well?'

Amy said, 'I'm sure you don't really want to know all my sports, but karate is one of them. I could have knocked him out with one punch. But all this isn't about me, we need to talk about Anna.'

'You said just now you wanted to give Anna a chance.'

'Yes,' said Amy, 'I spoke informally to the police, without any names, and we agreed that if I told their parents, as they were all under seventeen, then the police would not pursue the matter.'

Jack said, with tears running down his face, 'You are a very lucky young lady, Anna.'

'I know,' she said quietly, 'thank you very much Miss Andrews, I promise never to do anything like that again.'

Amy really wanted to leave this family to themselves, but the mention of Bernadette in the conversation meant that she wanted to change the topic and talk with Shirley, 'Perhaps, I will have that cup of tea now if I may.'

Anna went to help her mother with the tea and she was left talking to Jack.

Amy soon found out that Jack and Shirley were into the mid-forties and had given up all hope of children, when Shirley became pregnant. It was a few weeks before the logging accident that crippled Jack. They were given the house as part of the accident settlement, and now lived on his pension and Shirley's wage as a sub-postmistress. He had been a woodsman all his life and had taught many of his skills to Ged.

Amy said, 'Ged, the undertaker?'

'Yes, that's him,' said Jack.

'So it was you who taught him to shoot?'

'Yes, again, and I hear him very regularly in the woods near here. I can recognise his guns.'

'Does he shoot that regularly?' said Amy

This brought a roar of laughter from Jack, who said, 'How do you think the *Brace of Pheasants* gets its venison, game birds and rabbits. Ged took over as the local poacher from his father. In fact, last year Ged broke his ankle and the only meal you could get at the *Brace* was chicken.'

After they had finished their tea Amy managed a few words with Shirley. She explained about finding the next-of-kin and then said, 'I know you cannot divulge details, but did Bernadette receive many letters.'

'I don't think I'm breaking a confidence in saying she received virtually none. There might have been one occasionally, but I don't remember it. Can I just say I thought she was a lovely person. She used to come into the shop quite often, for small things, but she never posted anything in the Post Office.'

Amy left the little cottage a happier place then went she arrived. She walked slowly down the lane. There was little doubt in her mind that Justin was the instigator and the supplier. She would have to tell Theodore. With all her concerns she couldn't just go out for a date and say nothing, for if he found out later, then any potential prospects might be roundly quashed.

She would have to see him beforehand and put all the matters on the table. She was sad as the relationship wasn't even going to get to the starting post. But she also reasoned with herself that it was too soon after Scotland. Whenever she tried to sleep, since she had been in Nether Crimpton, there was a hideous mix of images and among them was the imagined picture of a bride in Pitlochry.

She drifted along the road, her heart wasn't in what she was doing as there was too much going on in her mind. Should she go back and talk to Augustus, he would always be sympathetic, but would never sway away from duty? She knew what her duty was, but she didn't want to do it. Her footsteps took her past the visitor's centre as she was on automatic pilot and she knew where she was going. She went along the high street and past the quiet cottage where Bernadette had lived. It just revived the images and the first issue that she had to tackle Theodore about. She turned into the lane and then up the drive. His car was there and she guessed he was at home. Her footsteps slowed as she approached the front door, she hadn't really decided how she was going to tackle the subject with him, but it was too late now. She rang the bell.

The door was opened by Theodore.

'Hello, this is a surprise. Come in.'

Amy hesitated, 'Is Justin in?'

A confused look came over his face, 'Justin? Do you know him?' Amy didn't reply and waited, 'No, he's out. I haven't seem him for most of the day.' He had a bright and cheerful smile that Amy thought was wonderful, but it soon changed. He studied her face and could see that she was serious and her normal ebullience had gone. 'Something's happened hasn't it.' She could tell he was thinking about the alternatives. It couldn't be an accident, otherwise she wouldn't have asked whether he was in.

He showed her into a large high ceiling lounge that was immaculately decorated and had a perfect selection of furniture, which complemented the house. Through the French doors, which were open, she could see the long stretch of lawn with precise, but very colourful borders. Amy declined to sit and stood by the French doors looking down the garden. Theodore was too much of a gentleman to sit when a lady had not. He stood by the mantelpiece with his back towards the empty grate.

'I didn't want to spoil the evening, which I have been looking forward to.' He waited for her to finish. She took a long pause and then said, 'There are two matters I need to talk to you about, but I fear, one, you will tell me to mind my own business and the other that I'm interfering.'

'If you think that they might have spoiled the evening then it is much better that you have come to see me beforehand.' It was said with good grace and a smile. Amy thought that was one of the reasons she liked him. 'You mentioned Justin?'

Amy explained about the run, who she found, and what they were doing. She continued to stand by the door, but was looking intensely at Theodore as she explained. His first comment was to say, 'That was a very dangerous thing to do, you could easily have been hurt. You should have called the police regardless of who was there.'

His patronising attitude as he delivery his homily on her safety irritated her. With Anna's parents she wanted to explain what she did and why she did it, but with Theodore, an explanation seemed to be worthless. He had made up his mind, as to what she should have done and wouldn't listen to her justifications. She didn't have any option, but to explain about Justin supplying, which she did quickly and succinctly, so that he couldn't interrupt her to point out his opinion. He looked very thoughtful and for a moment turned and stared at the picture over the mantelpiece. He contemplated it for a short while, and then turned back to face her, but he didn't move from in front of the empty grate.

'I apologise. I was a little hasty just now in offering my opinion before you had the chance to explain. I can see that you had the best interest of those teenagers at heart.' Amy smiled. 'Have you seen the other parents yet? I assume you came to me, because Justin explained why he was staying here.'

Amy had relaxed a little, but he still looked severe. Which she had to admit was reasonable as it was brought on by the news she had just given him. She said, 'I've seen Anna's parents.'

'Yes, I have met Anna a couple of times, she seems a pleasant girl.'

'Anna is the only daughter and the family took the whole incident very badly.'

'Did they argue with you?'

'No, no. They were terribly upset, but said that they expected me to go to the police.'

'And are you going to?'

Amy had taken her time explaining to Anna's parents, but Theodore was a different matter entirely. She simply said, 'No.' But Amy did want to say more about Anna and her family. 'It must be difficult for Anna's mother as her husband is in a wheelchair.'

'Ah,' said Theodore, which Amy took to be a sign of recognition, 'Is his name Jack, and he lives down the lane past the manor?'

'Do you know him?'

'A little, I've met him at the shooting competition before. He wasn't there today and I wondered why.' Amy could see the recognition on his face. 'Who else did you say was there?'

'Mary and Clint from the visitor's centre.' He nodded. Amy added, 'There is something else.'

'Go on,' he said with his stern face, now turning to a deep frown.

'It was Justin that supplied the cannabis.'

'It was definitely cannabis?'

Amy knew her weak point was being questioned. She never liked people to doubt her. She said in a sharp tone, 'I'm not an expert, but as far as I could tell it was. They were smoking it, and it had an aromatic scent, which caught on the air.'

Again he nodded and went to say something, but decided not to. She just wondered whether, as he came from the medical profession, he had a more relaxed view about cannabis. She knew from her parents that some doctors did. All of a sudden his frown disappeared and he came over to her. She liked that smile.

'It's pleasant out there, shall we stroll in the garden.' Amy wasn't sure what prompted the change in attitude. For a little while he just talked about the garden and the plants. He then said, 'I'm sorry about my serious face and frown. I'm afraid it comes on, when I am concentrating and working out what to do next. I can assure that it is not directed at you. Amy was at least a little relieved as he didn't seem to want to blame her for coming to him about Justin.

He went silent for a while as he fiddled with the flowers in the border and then said, 'I have had my doubts about Justin for a while now. I'm afraid that his mother and father give him too much money to compensate for them not being here. His last report from school wasn't good. He prefers to spend all his time being a ladies' man. I thought he was going out with Mary, but you tell me it is Anna.'

He now seemed relaxed and back to the best that Amy had seen him. He chatted for a while about the garden, about which he was very knowledgeable. There was now only one problem to go and she could then think about enjoying his company for the evening.

'Justin's parents arrive back in England tomorrow from their tour of duty. He is going very early to pick them up, which means the only opportunity I shall have to speak to him is this evening.'

Amy thought that both his expression and his explanation were genuine and, as much as she regretted it, she said, 'Would you like to put off our dinner tonight?'

'Yes, I'm afraid I shall have to. I really do apologise, but I need to speak to him and let his parents know. I'm glad to say that they will now be in the UK for a long period, so it is unlikely that Justin will visit me any more.'

Amy thought that he accepted her offer very easily. Could he not have spoken to Justin before dinner? There were still several hours to go. He said, 'I must also make my apologies.' Amy wasn't sure who to, but she just smiled, which hid her disappointment. 'I shall go and see Anna parents to make amends for my errant nephew. Also, I will speak with Damien and his wife, after you have given them the news.'

Amy's feelings were mixed. She admired his sense of duty and obligation. Although for a man of his standing, she knew it wouldn't come easy, but on the other hand, he could have tried harder to keep the date. He caught hold of her hand and looked directly at her, 'If that was one of the topics you wanted to discuss, then I hope the other is easier.'

Amy spoke in a low hesitant voice. 'It is delicate.'

'Let's carry on walking,' he replied as he led the way from the garden into a paddock that backed on to the house. There were two horses in the field. He started to walk around the edge.

Amy just had to know. It would be too easy to say nothing, but she knew she would not settle, so she said, 'It's about Bernadette.'

He immediately picked up what she meant and said, 'You mean Bernadette and me.'

'Yes,' said Amy quietly.

'My immediate reaction is that it is none of your business, but I was hasty earlier, so I will give you the benefit of the doubt. Can you explain what you want to know and why you want to know it?' Amy thought that his attitude was pompous and condescending, as well as being aggressive.

Amy bristled, she was trying to help as best she could and Theodore could do more to support her, so she said, 'Have the police been to see you about Bernadette?'

'No,' but she could see that there was a quizzical look in his eyes.

'I didn't think that you would take kindly to being asked about Bernadette and I was clearly right,' but she didn't give him a chance to speak. 'I am helping Augustus to trace the next-of-kin of Bernadette.'

'Why not leave it to the police?'

'The police have asked for help from anyone in the village' They do not, at the moment, seem to be able to find any relations. As poor Bernadette died in his parish, my brother takes responsibility for the funeral arrangements until a next-of-kin can be found. I am merely helping my brother, by asking anyone who knew Bernadette. We simply want to know anything about her background or family.'

'But why come to me?' he answered tersely.

Amy thought that he was being deliberately awkward, so she said in an emphatic manner, 'You did know Bernadette?'

'Why would the police want to talk to me about Bernadette?'

The question took Amy by surprise, but she was getting more and more annoyed with him.

'Why are you being so defensive?' but she didn't wait for an answer and said, 'she's been murdered, so they are interviewing all those in the village that knew her,' snapped Amy. He went to reply, but changed his mind.

The serious frown had returned. This time it didn't lift as he turned to her and said, 'I am afraid that we are getting annoyed with each other, and while we could go on, I think it is better to stop before we argue and I wouldn't want that, as I particularly like you.'

Amy thought it the strangest way to pay a compliment, but realised he wasn't going to help. She took a deep breath because she didn't want to argue with him. 'That might be for the best. I will leave you to sort out Justin.' She took the opportunity of being by the paddock gate that led on to the lane. 'I'll go out this way,' she said as she unlatched the gate.

They muttered good-bye to each other. Amy walked along the lane with tears streaming down her cheeks. She had found it a very frustrating conversation when all that she wanted was Theodore's help.

Chapter Nine

Amy stopped at a gate further along the lane and looked out over the fields. She didn't want anyone to see that she had been crying. Her tasks were not over yet and she still had other people to meet. It took her about ten minutes to compose herself. She had regretted her approach to Theodore, but thought that he was extremely pompous in his attitude. As she went through the conversation with Theodore, in her mind, she could sense that he felt he was being interrogated. If only he had been more cooperative and less critical, then she knew she would have relaxed, and managed the whole meeting a lot differently. He probably thinks I'm being the village Miss Marple. It would have been much better to introduce Bernadette and ask for his help, rather than challenging him. She took a deep breath. The mumbled goodbye from him wasn't his style at all. There's nothing else for it, she would have to wait to see whether he regrets his attitude and wants to take her out to dinner.

She had reached the bottom of the lane where it met the High Street. Ged's cheery voice called out to her, 'Hi, Amy. Come and see what I am doing.' She had to admit that she did like him, but it was in a completely different way to Theodore. At least Ged wasn't complicated and always seemed to be friendly and jovial. She walked across to the barns where he had his business. He must have read the look on her face because he said, 'Don't worry it's not a coffin,' and laughed. Amy thought that he had a nice laugh. He took her through to the workshop. There were no wood working tools out, but on the bench lay two rifles, one of which he was cleaning.

'That was amazing shooting earlier, where did you learn to do that?' asked Ged.

'I had a go at clays when I was young, but I really learnt to shoot in Africa. Augustus and I were there for several years and it becomes quite a necessity out there.'

'Did you shoot for sport?'

'Good grief, no. We were often in very remote places, where it was normal to kill for food. Sometimes it was necessary to shoot aggressive animals that came to close to the compound.'

'So you are more familiar with rifles rather than shotguns.'

Amy said, 'Yes, these look good ones.'

'Here, try it out, its good and has a lovely balance to it.'

Amy took the rifle and placed the stock against her shoulder. She moved it around and then lined up an imaginary target. 'It handles really well,' said Amy.

'Why not come shooting with me, I'm going tomorrow morning early. It's only up in the woods.'

Amy just shook her head. Ged laughed.

Suddenly Lorraine appeared at the workshop door and stepped in. Amy looked down at her shoes. She was wearing high heels. Amy thought it strange that they hadn't heard her approach across the cobbled yard.

'Ah, Ged,' she said, 'I'm glad I caught you. There is a small job we need doing at the visitors' centre. Could you pop in sometime.' It was said with Lorraine's usual stern face that never seemed to relax into a smile.

'OK,' said Ged, 'I'll come in tomorrow morning.'

'I would like to see you and Damien, if that is possible,' said Amy.

Lorraine snapped back, 'There is no need. Mary and Clint came to see me and told me what had happened.' Amy wondered what version they had been told. She had little doubt that Clint would have led the explanation, and many things had been omitted. While Amy was thinking Lorraine added, 'As far as I'm concerned the matter is over.'

In some sense, it was a burden lifted from her, but she felt aggrieved that Lorraine had almost certainly been told a false version. But Lorraine hadn't finished, she came across to Amy and standing squarely in front of her said, 'Damien and I demand that you stop bad-mouthing our children in this village. Since you have come here, you have gone out of your way to humiliate

Clint.' Amy was speechless at the outburst. 'It should have been perfectly obvious that Justin and Anna were to blame. Mary and Clint were not really involved.'

Amy's fury rose and she went red in the face with anger, 'That is completely untrue, they were all involved, and Clint made it far worse than anyone.'

Lorraine screamed, 'You're at it again. It was the little bitch Anna that pinched Mary's boyfriend...'

Ged said in a strong voice, 'Don't be so bloody rude about Anna, she's a lovely girl. And for that matter don't come into my workshop with your loud mouth lies. Now get out! Everyone in the village knows that your darling little Clint is a foul mouthed lazy yob!' Lorraine hadn't moved. Amy was much taller than her and looked down on the face full of anger and contempt.

Ged shouted, 'I said, get out, now, or I'll throw you out!' Lorraine turned and stormed out of the door. Ged went to the doorway to check the receding click of the high-heels went all the way out onto the street.

He returned to Amy, 'Are you all right, you look a little shaken.' He fetched a chair so that she could sit and he perched on the workbench. 'She is the most unpleasant woman I have ever met. I'm sorry she was so rude to you.'

'It's a pity you had to witness that. I wanted to see her and Damien alone. That's where I was going, when I met you.'

'I know what happened.' Amy looked at his face, which had its usual smile, 'I've just got back from seeing Jack and Shirley. They were very appreciative of your help.'

'Are they OK? They were all very shocked and full of tears when I arrived at the cottage.'

'They are much calmer, although it has been a big shock for all of them. I popped down to see them, because Jack wasn't at the shooting, which is very unusual.'

'They are a lovely family,' said Amy, 'and Anna doesn't strike me as scheming.'

'No, she isn't. And to be fair, neither is Mary. I think the fault must lie with the two boys.'

Amy nodded and stood up to go. Ged walked with her across

the yard to the road. Amy was warming to him much more. He seemed kind and happy, with no complications. His clothes seemed to be scruffy, but perhaps that was a result of the job he did, and his other activities, thought Amy with a little smile.

The confrontation with Lorraine had made her weary. It wasn't the quiet little village, that it appeared to be. She was trying to help, but it wasn't working out. Dinner with Theodore might have had some promise, but that was never going to happen now. She was looking forward to an evening with Augustus, who would listen with patience and kindness to her.

She reached the road and was just going to say goodbye to Ged, when she saw her brother coming along the street in his car. He stopped level with them and wound down the window to say, 'Amy, I have been speaking with the Bishop this afternoon and have accepted his invitation to dinner, I hope that is OK with you.'

'Of course, it is Gus, have a good time.' Ged and Amy both waved as he drove off.

'Can I ask you something?' said Ged.

'Yes, of course,' replied Amy.

'Some of the lads, who were shooting today, have agreed to get together for a beer and something to eat at the *Brace*. I'm just going there now. Your brother has just gone out, so why not come and join us?'

Amy was tired, but thought about the empty vicarage. She would just mope around all of the evening feeling sorry for herself. She was still feeling aggrieved that Theodore had cancelled the dinner date at the first opportunity.'

'That sounds a good idea, Ged. I am beginning to feel hungry.'

She would really have liked to change, especially her sandals as the new ones were rubbing quite badly, because she had worn them all day. They were covered in dust from the tracks in the wood and felt uncomfortable. But it wasn't worth going back to the vicarage. Ged popped back to lock away the guns. He was soon back with her and they walked over the road to the *Brace of Pheasants*.

'Welcome!' boomed the landlord as Amy walked into the pub. The large single room had bare floor boards, dark painted walls and heavy oak tables and chairs. The long bar had an array of beer pumps, and behind it were two small fridges and a shelf, which were the only evidence that the pub sold anything but beer. There were large mirrors on the wall behind the bar. Amy guessed this is how the pub would have look in the early 1900s, and it hadn't changed since. She studied it more closely and could see that it was clean and well kept. A hand written chalk board was the only indication that the pub served food. 'It's a pleasure to have you here, what beer would you like?'

Amy gave a little smile and said, 'I don't drink beer.'

Ged emphasised the first word, as he said, 'Ladies don't drink beer.'

The landlord took no notice, and just waited for Amy to speak, 'Can I have an orange juice with ice please?' The landlord had already pulled a pint for Ged, 'Please let me pay,' said Amy.

'When I invited you to my pub, I said drinks were on me, and that's what I meant.'

Amy thought him rather surly, but he was certainly genuine. Several of the others that had been at the shooting competition arrived and she became the centre of attention. Amy tried to deflect the compliments and had to explain about Africa.

In a quieter moment, one of the locals said she was brave in the way she dealt with finding Bernadette. There was a lot of general talk about the murder, most of which Amy already knew. The conversation left her in no doubt, that all thought Bernadette to be a good lass, who was friendly and very much liked.

She looked at the menu on the board and hoped there might be a salad or at least a pasta. It was all game, apart from fish and chips. The people on the next table had already ordered rabbit stew and she chose the same after some deliberation. The landlord again insisted it was his treat. When the meals arrived on the next table, she went immediately up to the bar and whispered to the landlord, 'Could I have about one-third portion, I couldn't possibly eat all that.'

He nodded acceptance and went to the kitchen. One of the locals at the bar said, 'Evening miss.'

Amy smiled back. The man then turned to his friend and said

in a loud voice, 'I know how you can improve your shooting.'

The big man just grunted in reply.

'You should wear a pink dress and go barefoot.'

Amy and everyone else laughed. As she turned away from the bar, so she bumped into Theodore. They both looked hard at each other for a few seconds and then he said quietly, 'I phoned Justin and he is coming home later. So I took up the invitation to join the others from the shoot.'

'I accepted the same invitation,' said Amy trying to make it sound natural, 'are you joining us?'

'Yes.' Amy returned to her seat and Theodore chose a seat on the edge of the group away from the hubbub of noise that surrounded her. He hardly spoke to anyone during the hour in which Amy stayed, while she was the centre of attention. It was a witty and entertaining time and cheered her up by making her laugh. One time, when she looked around, Theodore had gone, without saying goodbye.

She decided that it was time to go. Ged said he was also leaving and that he was going down to the manor to see the Colonel and would walk with her as far as the vicarage.

They stopped and chatted for a while outside of the vicarage and then Ged went on his way. Amy went into to the house, and as she was on her own again, she became sad. It was a pity that nothing had come of it with Theodore, but his pompous attitude was the cause of the failure. She was tired and decided to go for a run in the morning. Perhaps tomorrow will be a better day.

Chapter Ten

Amy was up early in the morning with mixed feelings. She thought the row with Lorraine was unjust. She still had the disappointment of Theodore hanging over her, but it had been good to laugh at the *Brace*. On the answer machine last night was a message from the police to say that they had released Bernadette's cottage. Amy would go there today to begin the sad process of packing up her possessions. She hoped that Augustus would come as well, because she would be nervous doing it all on her own.

It was now time for a run and so she put on her jogging kit and was soon out in the bright early morning sun. She heard the faintest of gunfire in the distance. So she turned to take the path up to the woods. She guessed it was Ged, and if she could easily see him, then she would thank him for the invitation last night.

She criss-crossed the paths several times and gradually got nearer to the sound of shooting. In the end, she spotted him and jogged along the track towards him. He had waved and was waiting for her. While they were chatting, he spotted a pheasant and drew up his rifle, but didn't fire. He said the bird was a bit too far away to be certain of the shot.

He offered her the rifle that he had been cleaning yesterday, but she declined. 'Go on,' he said, 'give a go, its loaded. It's heavier than the one you tried yesterday.' She took it and braced the stock against her shoulder again, and then went to give it back to him but he said, 'Fire it.'

'I'm not shooting at any animals.'

'Look there is a dead tree. Try to hit the knot which is right in the middle of the solid wood about head height.'

'Yes, I can see it.'

'Go on then.' Amy thought there was no harm in it and she fired, hitting the middle of the knot.

'You definitely are good at shooting, we will have to have a competition sometime.'

'Not today though,' she said handing him back the rifle with some relief.

Amy thanked Ged, who was pleased that she had taken the effort to come and find him. She carried on her run and went out of the woods and across the fields. It was early and she hadn't seen anyone at all, apart from Ged, but as she ran along the track from the manor path to the vicarage she spotted Mary, who was sat on one of the benches.

After all that had gone on, Amy wasn't sure what reaction she would get from Mary. She suspected that Lorraine would have had a lot to say to her and it probably involved instructions not to talk to Amy. She hadn't been spotted as she jogged along the track towards Mary, who was looking out thoughtfully past the church and across the fields. As Amy neared her, at a slow jog, the sound of the trainers crunching on the gravel caught Mary's attention and she looked around.

As soon as she saw Amy she smiled and gave a little wave. Amy stopped when she reached Mary, who said, 'Hi, Amy, I guessed you'd go for a run and I've been waiting for you..

'Waiting for me?' echoed Amy.

'Yes, I wanted to have a private chat with you about all that has happened, but mum said not to talk to you.'

'Are you OK? asked Amy.

'Oh, yes, I think so, but I do want to chat. I've no Bernadette to talk to now.' That hit Amy hard. She was now in a quandary. Should she stay and chat or not.

'If you mother has said its best not to talk to me, I won't take offence, because I do not want to upset your family.'

'Mum obviously had a row with you last night and she does have a temper. But later on she will have calmed down and everything will be back to normal. I know she thinks the world of me and wants to protect me from anything unpleasant that might happen.

She must have seen Amy hesitating and she added, 'Let's go round the back of the church to the benches. Mum will never come round there.' Amy made a reluctant face, but Mary said,

'It's not just about what happened at the manor, there is something else. I need some advice and it can't come from my parents.' Amy didn't want to get involved, but found it too hard to refuse. Mary stood up and said, 'Please, just for a short time.'

Amy would have preferred to have changed her clothes, but she saw she had to take the opportunity just to reassure herself that Mary was OK. Mary looked calm and smiling. There were no sign of tears and she didn't have the body movement associated with being vulnerable or unhappy. In fact, Amy noticed that she was humming a tune as she walked on the footpath that took them to the back of the church, where they sat on the bench in the sunshine. Amy had quickly planned out how to get the conversation going, but Mary was eager and said, 'You really have been very kind to me and Clint. We want to thank you for getting us out of the mess we got ourselves into.'

'Even Clint?' said Amy, who was prepared to think that it was genuine from Mary, but she was very sceptical about Clint.

'Yes,' said Mary with a bit of a sigh, 'I know he doesn't show it, but he is a good brother to me and we get on well. Yes, I know he does daft things and is completely lazy, but I still like him. I do try to persuade him to try a bit harder. Sometimes it works and other times he gets morose and loses his temper. He's just like mum.'

'How does he get on with your dad?'

Mary answered, 'Generally OK, but as they both want to be the macho male at times, they clash. "Sorry" isn't a word that either of them find easy.' Amy was quite surprised at the mature perception from Mary. All the family coped with Lorraine and Clint's temper moods.

Mary continued, 'Anna, of course, did the right thing in telling her parents straight away. So after we all met in the woods, when Clint and I were walking back together we decided it would be best if it came from us. Mum and Dad were in the office together so we went in and told them.'

'What was their reaction?'

Mary looked sheepish and looked down to the ground, 'What is it Mary?'

'We left out the bit about the knife. I hope that was all right.'

'Yes, it was better to leave that out,' said Amy who was not sure what the best policy was with Clint, but it was all over and done with now.'

Mary looked up and smiled and came back to the question and said, 'Mum started shouting, but we knew she would. Dad asked a lot of questions. In the end, we had to persuade him not to go round to Justin's house. He said that he wanted words with the doctor.'

'Do you know if he went round in the end?' Amy also wondered whether Theodore went to see them as he said he would.

Mary replied, 'He didn't need to because about an hour later the doctor came to the centre. Dad was spoiling for an argument. I didn't hear what was said, but the doctor calmed him down straight away. They talked for about ten minutes and shook hands at the end.' That's a relief thought Amy. She was pleased the whole incident was now over and she could forget about it.

Mary said, 'I had a long chat with Clint as well.'

'Did you?' asked Amy enquiringly.

'I didn't know he had a knife, otherwise I wouldn't have been with him. I kept asking him where he got it from, but he wouldn't say. It is really unusual for him because he knows I keep his secrets. But he does realise he shouldn't have attacked you. I told him fair and square, that I do not want a brother of mine on a murder charge.'

Amy was impressed with Mary and she was obviously supporting her brother as much as she could. Amy couldn't fault that.

She decided it was time to change the conversation, so she asked Mary 'Did you want to talk to me about something else?'

'Yes, I would like your advice. I had discussed it with Bernadette,' and as she said her name she gave a little gulp, 'who gave me some advice, but I would like yours as well please.'

'OK,' said Amy, 'I will advise if I can?' but she was totally unsure what it was going to be about. It didn't seem to be a matter that was causing Mary any stress. Whatever it was she was totally relaxed about it.

'I don't think you know, but I have been adopted, since I was a baby.'

'No, I didn't know,' said Amy, 'I just assumed you were all one family.'

'And we are,' said Mary, 'Mum and Dad have never treated me and Clint differently.'

'That's good to hear,' said Amy.

'Mum was told nearly nineteen years ago that she would never have children, and so they decided to adopt. Within a year, I had arrived in their home. I was only a few months old at the time. However, just after I arrived, Mum became pregnant with Clint. After that the social services came regularly to check up on me and as I grew up their visits became less and less. When we decided to move up to this village, we all chose not to mention it to anyone. To be honest, it had passed to the back of my mind.'

Amy could tell from the light way in which Mary was talking that none of this seemed to be a concern to her.

'About eleven months ago a lady came from the social services. She said that when I reach my eighteenth birthday, I can be told about my natural mother. It was entirely my choice. Naturally I talked to Mum and Dad about it and even Clint.'

'What did they say?'

'Dad said that at that time, I would become an adult and that brings with it decisions. He knows what advice he would give me, but that it was entirely my decision. As you would expect Clint was the most forthright. He said that I definitely should not. If the mother had abandoned me then, she had no right to even expect her name to be given to me. Mum was terribly upset by it all and wouldn't speak about it.'

'So are you trying to decide what to do?'

'It got more complicated.'

'How?' asked Amy.

'I thought that my natural mother might be dead and that there would be no point in just knowing a name and perhaps having a picture. So I had virtually decided not to ask about her, when the lady from the social services came again a few weeks ago.'

'What did she say this time?' said Amy

'That my natural mother was alive, in good health and wanted to meet me. She would have no idea who I am and where I live so she cannot just turn up. But the local authority is obliged to pass the request on. If I refuse she will be told, and that will be the end of the matter.' She turned to Amy and with wide and open eyes said, 'I don't know what to do?'

Amy said, 'What did Bernadette say?'

'We talked about it on several occasions. She said that I might regret it if I didn't meet her. There was absolutely no reason why it should make any difference to the family, which could just carry on the same as before.'

'Have you had any thoughts on which way you will decide.'

'No not at all. You are a very sensible and practical grown-up woman, so I wondered what you would do?'

Amy wasn't sure about the compliment, but said, 'Are you worried about making the decision?'

'No, I just want to make the right one.'

'I can't decide for you, but I can suggest a way of approaching it.'

'There I knew you would have an idea. I just knew it!'

'If you decide not to meet her then that is the matter over and done with. But you have been thinking about it for a long time and are a little inclined to say yes, but you are concerned about two things.'

'I am, do you know what they are?' said Mary with a grin.

'The first and the most important is that you do not want to upset your family.'

'Yes, that's exactly it.'

'Second, you are worried that you might not like her very much.'

'Yes, exactly right. So what should I do?'

'If you decide yes, then go to meet her without telling your family. It will only cause anguish and distress, if they know when it is going to be. And second, meet her a long way from here and arrange with social services that they give her none of your details. I don't think they will.'

Mary considered very carefully what Amy had said, 'If I do what you say, then I decide whether I want her back in my life. It will then be time to tell my family.'

'Yes,' said Amy, 'that's right, but you must be very sure of yourself, because it will be a very emotional meeting.'

'Yes, I know.'

Mary seemed very happy with the advice and as they stood up she gave Amy a hug and a kiss on the cheek, 'It would be wonderful to discover that it was someone like you who was my natural mother. It was meant as a compliment, but Amy immediately calculated. Seventeen years ago she was seventeen. She let it sink in as she walked back to the vicarage after Mary had gone.

Amy quickly showered, put on some light casual clothes, and joined Augustus, who was just finishing his breakfast. She only picked at a few things on the table as she hadn't got over the conversation with Mary.

Also, she was still full from her small portion of rabbit stew from the night before. They both had a lot to tell each other, but decided that it would be best to make a start at Bernadette's cottage.

She had said that it wasn't that urgent, but Augustus knew that Lady Crimpton and the Colonel would be out all day. He suspected they might use their ownership as an excuse to come and ferret around. Amy agreed. As soon as the breakfast table was cleared they went through the old churchyard, to the high street, and the front door of the cottage.

Amy opened the door with the key that Sharon, the detective sergeant, had got from the Colonel. It was a small cottage where the front door entered straight into the parlour. Amy moved to the centre of the room. Despite the heat of the day outside, the cottage felt cold and damp. She shivered. Augustus was watching her carefully, but suddenly he turned away. Amy knew that he wanted to pray and she stood looking out the front window of the house onto the high street. She wasn't sure how long she thought about Bernadette. Soon Augustus was ready for the task ahead and was full of practicality as usual. He said they should look to clear the lounge and kitchen on to tables. Then they would know how many boxes would be needed. They collected the items from the parlour and put them on the sideboard.

'It's not much,' said Amy.

Augustus looked around the room with concern and said quietly, 'This is worrying.'

'What is?' asked Amy, suddenly attentive to the tone of his voice.

'In this whole room there is only one personal possession and that is a recent picture of her and Mary.'

'But there are several other things,' Amy said as she put an ornament on the sideboard.'

'I go into many houses,' said Augustus and see many lounges, sitting room or parlours, call them what you will. But all of them show an interest in something. They might be items of low value, but every room has a theme. The owner's theme. This room doesn't. All the items cups, saucers and ornaments are a mismatch. The whole room looks like it was bought at a car boot sale as a job lot.'

'That's a very harsh judgement from you, Gus, it's not like you.'

'It's not about money, I've been in some of the most impoverished places.' Amy wasn't convinced, but Gus said, ' Remember in Africa when we went into some of those huts on the hill.'

'I felt so sorry for them,' said Amy.

'Picture yourself there. Look around the hut in your mind.' The light was beginning to dawn with Amy, and Gus went on, 'Did you say that Bernadette was poor?'

'No, she seemed to have had more money than one would have expected.'

'So why didn't she make this a home, given that she had lived here for over two years?'

'I don't know,' answered Amy.

'Go and look at her bedroom, you will see more in it than me.'

It didn't take Amy long and she came back down stairs, 'The best way I can describe it, is that her bedroom is more like a hotel room.'

Augustus said, 'It is only a supposition, but it doesn't look to me that she was intending staying.'

'So why stay for over two years?' asked Amy, but then she

began to think and finally said, 'Gus?'

'I know what you're thinking. Should we be speculating or guessing.'

'Yes.'

'It's not normally what I would do, but the Bishop said last night that he'd had lunch with the Chief Constable.'

'And?' said Amy

'The police have made no progress so far. They cannot trace a Bernadette Murphy, who fits the age and description of the woman we knew.'

'Did the police remove anything from here?' said Amy

'No, the inspector told me that it's as they found it, and that's another point. There was no address book, no notebook and nothing in her handbag to give her identity.'

'What about a driving licence?'

Gus shook his head and then added, 'Go through her clothes and personal effects and see if anything jumps out at you.'

Gus went upstairs with her. It didn't take long as there wasn't that many clothes. Amy was amazed that a woman would only have three pairs of shoes in her wardrobe. She turned to Gus who was sat on the bed and said, 'Everything, without exception, was bought in M&S.'

'So what do you think, little one?'

Amy smiled, it was his term of endearment. It meant so much to her. The bond with her older brother was as strong as it had ever been.

She had a lump in her throat from the sudden affectionate memory but said, 'Bernadette was a woman with no past and it does not look like she had a plan for the future. Yet she was the most normal of women and was liked throughout the village.' Suddenly her mind raced, 'Gus, she was Irish.'

'Yes,' said Gus, 'the police thought that as well, but they can find no link whatsoever. There is no intelligence about sleeper cells or any such like.'

'Gus, if the police can't find her background and why she was here, then we cannot either. They have a vast machine to do these things. For example, they can get mobile phone records.'

'She didn't have a mobile phone nor a phone in this house.'

'But how do you know all this, it couldn't have been the Bishop.'

'As you know the church doesn't like scandal and the Bishop sees potential problems with newspapers. When murder takes place on church property, that is not immediately cleared up, there will be a lot of speculation in the press. So he contacted the Chief Constable.'

'Yes, I can see he would do that, and what happened?'

'Initially they thought it was someone from the village, but when Bernadette's identity couldn't be found, they thought she was in hiding and it was someone from her past.'

'What do they think now?'

'They have no idea, but the Chief Constable thinks the answer will be found in Nether Crimpton.'

'Why? I'm now lost on this.'

'He thinks that however careful someone is they will have to have some link with the past. Perhaps it was a regular meeting, or a regular stranger arriving. Perhaps a message or a journey, or something she said about the past. He knows that people will not be able to answer the police questions, because they don't know the answer themselves. Also, if they are questioned by the police there is a reluctance to suggest what might be a silly idea.'

Amy said, 'I get the drift now. The dinner last night was to get you involved in the quest for that information.'

Gus smiled, 'To get us involved,' and he emphasised the word "us".

There was the noise of the front door opening, and a voice said, 'Amy are you there?'

'Up here, Sharon,' and she added, 'it's Sharon, the detective sergeant, I recognise her voice.'

Sharon explained that she was nearby and thought she'd drop in to find out whether Amy and Augustus had found any further information. They said no and they exchanged their ideas on the type of person that Bernadette was.

'We come across a lot of people,' said Sharon, 'that want a new life and many decide on a change of name as well, especially women if their previous partner was violent. It's not illegal to be called what you like. Sometimes with officialdom it can be fraud, but you have to normally want to do things. Bernadette didn't do anything, as far as we can find out, that breaks the law with the possible exception of tax evasion. She always wanted to be paid in cash, and was sub-contracted from the agency, so that way she never had to have a national insurance number.

Sharon looked around at the possessions, and then said, 'We wonder if she kept her old life going in some way, but we cannot find anything that will give us a link. It's the absence of phones and letters that is the problem. So any help you can give will be welcome. Where are you going to start?'

Amy said, 'It seems to me money is an issue. She regularly ate in the *Brace* and bought her rounds. Also she used to go into town and presumably spent some money there.'

'Why do you think that?' said Augustus.

'She was always very smart, even if she didn't have many clothes, her hair was always very neat and a well kept style.'

'Yes, I would agree with that,' said Augustus

Amy added, 'There are no hair dyes, straighteners, curlers or any hair equipment, except a brush. No one in the village said they cut Bernadette's hair, so I presume she paid for it when she was in town. And that type of style, regularly cut, doesn't come cheap.'

Sharon asked, 'Do you think money is something to do with the manor?'

'Yes,' said Amy, 'I'm sure there is more than just a dodgy rent book.'

Sharon said, 'Remember you're not investigating a murder, just trying to find us a connection. As soon as you have got an idea let me know and we will follow it up.' She said goodbye and that she would be in touch soon.

Augustus left Amy to do the rest of the clearing of the house. By late afternoon she had boxed it all up. They had carried it back to the vicarage. He had arranged for one of the furniture charities to clear the heavy items and keep them in store.

It was late on in the afternoon, when she was just deciding

what to do, when she spotted the Colonel driving slowly through the village in the direction of Sheffield. Amy said to herself, now is the time for a heart-to-heart with Lady Crimpton, and she set off to the manor. She waited the same long time as usual for Lady Crimpton to answer. The first words from the old lady were blurted out, 'I hope you've come about the footpath.' Amy ignored her and followed her down the long corridor. They had just got seated when Lady Crimpton said, 'Now this is what I want you to say about the footpath and cycle way proposal.'

Amy took the sheet of paper, which was covered in shaky handwriting, and read it. Lady Crimpton went to speak, but Amy held up her hand and said, 'I'm afraid I'm too busy helping the police with their enquiries, about poor Bernadette. Oh, don't worry, I'm not investigating the murder or anything dramatic like that. I am only trying to find out about the next-of-kin.'

'You've been here before about that and we told you all we know.'

Amy said, in a loud and clear voice, 'No you didn't you haven't told me anything that is any use.'

'Well I never!'

'Bernadette's household books don't add up. There are too many outgoings and not enough coming in. I think that her financial affairs such as tax, national insurance and employment need a much more thorough investigation, because everyone in the village is being so cagey. I thought I'd come and give you one last chance, before I tell the police and the inland revenue, that I do not know how Bernadette acquired money.'

Lady Crimpton went to stutter a reply, but in the end said nothing. Amy waited and finally she said, 'My husband has gone to Sheffield.'

Amy replied curtly, 'I know he has, I saw him drive through the village. So I thought I would come and see you.'

'Ahh,' she said obviously picking up the message, but she still seemed reluctant to talk.

Amy thought that she would have one last go and said, 'You seem reluctant to talk. In your mind you might call it sordid and unpleasant, but it certainly won't shock me.'

Lady Crimpton was edging round her seat. There was definitely something.

'It would be such a pity,' said Amy

'What would?' snapped Lady Crimpton irritably.

'Once the police machine starts, there is no stopping it and all the dirty washing comes out. Think of the rumours and your reputation in the village. You met the woman sergeant the other day. Did she seem the sympathetic type?'

'Ghastly woman,' and Lady Crimpton, took a deep breath, 'What do you want to know? But I will only tell you, if you keep the police and others away.'

'I can't keep quiet on anything that's illegal.'

'Do you count tax matters as legal?'

'Try me,' said Amy.

'There was no rent book, because she worked for us and we called it quid pro quo.'

'So what you are telling me is that she worked about twenty hours a week, which would make about £400 a month. The rent was about the same, so no money changed hands.'

'That is a quick calculation, but about right. So both sides should be paying tax, but it was our arrangement. Now are you happy?'

Amy gave her a direct smile, 'I'd already worked out that bit, so that's not really news to me. There is still the crucial information you haven't given me.'

'And what might that be? There is nothing else.'

Amy emphasised, 'Oh yes, there is. That is why I've come to see you, why your husband is out. Lady Crimpton just looked away and pretended to ignore Amy. 'Trying to sweep it under the carpet!' There was no reaction. 'You know of your husband's lecherous ways and how he stares at women. Bernadette was very attractive, in her mid-thirties, with a good figure. Why would she come here for hours each day to be stared at and, no doubt, touched up by your husband?'

Lady Crimpton screwed up her face in disgust and finally the words stumbled out, 'He can't do it any more you know. Hasn't been capable for a long time, but his desire has never left him.'

Amy waited silently for her to continue. 'He doesn't think I know of his little arrangement, but I do, it's disgusting.'

She staggered to her feet. 'Come with me.' Amy followed her to the cramped little room that she had been into before with the Colonel. It was still in the same chaotic mess with files and papers everywhere. She opened a drawer, delved into the back of it, and produced a key. With it, she unlocked the filing cabinet and took out a file at the back of the bottom drawer. She handed it to Amy. 'You'd better take it. It's disgusting and immoral, but I don't think it is illegal. More's the pity.'

Amy flicked open the file, it was full of about fifty photos. The first picture was of Bernadette, who was topless. Amy could see from the background that it had been taken in this manor house. She skimmed through the others. A few were nude shots of Bernadette, but most were topless.'

'You do realise the implications of these?'

'Yes,' said Lady Crimpton, as she began to walk towards the door, 'he didn't murder her you know.'

'How can you be so sure? Was she blackmailing your husband?'

'Absolutely not. We had come to an arrangement. On the day that she was murdered she said to me, what a good deal we had. I then made a face at her, but Bernadette carried on, "You get your house nicely cleaned, he gets his pictures and I get my money. What can be better than that? By the way, you are going into Sheffield tomorrow. Only he wants another session and I need a little bonus, as I'm going to London again."'

Amy left Lady Crimpton standing at the front door and walked down the drive. As soon as she was clear of the grounds, she rang Sharon and explained about the conversation.

Sharon said, 'That all figures and puts the money perspective in place, which is good to clear up. We interviewed him. On the night of the murder he was in London, on a regimental reunion. He was with many of the senior brass getting very drunk until the early hours, so we know he is not our murderer. But he does have some nasty habits.'

Amy was quite taken aback, but she did believe what Lady

Crimpton had said about the arrangement.

Sharon said, 'Keep the file, I'll pick it up sometime. I can get him in and give him a hard time. What do you think?'

'Pretty sordid, but I can't think what else we would want from him.'

Amy decided on a walk to clear her head. As she went along the path to the station she saw Damien coming the other way. There was no chance that he could avoid her, as they were in the middle of a field, with a single path.

As she got closer she said, 'Hello Damien.' He just looked at her, and went to walk past. As much as she didn't like the man, she needed to get him on her side, as she wanted to speak to Mary again. She said, 'I was thinking about going into the *Marquis* for a drink.'

He snapped, 'Then you're going the wrong way!'

'I could be persuaded to turn round.' He looked her up and down. Amy had his attention for a short time, but he was in a dilemma and it showed on his face, Amy added, 'I'm really sorry I didn't handle the kids as you would have wanted the other night. I was trying to do my best for them. Sorry I got it wrong.'

'Yeah, well, you upset Lorraine the other night as well.'

Amy had to try very hard to bite back the obvious comment, but smiled and said, 'It hurts to have to say your wrong. Don't you find the word, "sorry", is so difficult to say?'

'I know what you mean,' he gruffly replied.

'Shall I buy you that drink, as a way of apology?' asked Amy.

'Yes,' he said as he turned round, but let's go back to the *Brace*. Lorraine might be in the *Marquis*.

All went well, until they had drinks and Amy got him talking about the plans for the centre. It was when she said that she really wanted to talk to Mary, that things went down hill.

'What about?' he said.

'It's about Bernadette.'

'The answer is no. I've got to agree with Lorraine, since you have come to the village, its made it very difficult for us as a family. Every time you come near us, things get worse. So no you can't speak to the kids. I'm happy to talk to you and now that

Lorraine has calmed down, I expect she will, but there's no budging on the kids.'

Amy was getting irritated with him. 'Don't you want all the turmoil over Bernadette to be cleared up.'

'Stop bringing up Bernadette. I'm sorry she was killed, and I liked her, but just leave it to the police.'

'I heard a rumour that the police were coming back to the village this weekend to interview all the visitors, that wouldn't be good for your business.'

'At the moment I don't care. I just want to get rid of busybodies like you, making it problematic for my family.' And with that he stormed out.

She got up to leave and a voice behind her caught her attention. Because of her focus on Damien she hadn't noticed the man in the corner, who was half-hidden by the propped up newspaper that he was reading. Theodore said, 'Good evening, Amy.'

Amy, despite her current annoyance, managed a cheery, 'Hello, Theodore.'

He said, 'When you came to the village, I welcomed the breath of fresh air you brought to this slow backwater. I really wanted to get to know you better...' Amy knew that there was a big 'but' coming. 'But you seem to want to interfere with everything and then upset everyone. I must say you handled the matter of the kids quite badly in the end. The man you were just with, practically threatened me.'

Amy was speechless, but Theodore continued, 'I've just been up to the manor and Lady Crimpton was upset. When I asked why, she said you had just been visiting.' He paused, but then decided not to let Amy speak, 'Perhaps it might be better for all, if you think about whether you really want to stay in this village. And now good evening.' He turned and left the pub.

Amy let him go and then left the pub. She was fighting back the tears. Ged came around the corner and waved. She really didn't want to talk to him now and turned the other way and waved back. She hoped that was enough. But it wasn't as far as he was concerned. He trotted along the road and caught up with her.

'Hi, Amy, I was going to come round and see you tonight,

have you got a couple of minutes now.'

Her immediate reaction was to say "no", but she was wary of upsetting everyone. She hadn't intended to and so why had it all gone so badly wrong? 'What was it about?' she said in as calm a voice as she could manage.

'It was an enjoyable evening in the *Brace* wasn't it.'

Amy was very much distracted by what had happened and so rather vaguely said, 'Yes, it was fine.'

Ged continued, 'There were a lot of people there.'

'Yes,' said Amy rather absentmindedly.

'Well, I was wondering if you would like to go over to one of the other villages for a quiet drink with me. It would be nice to have your company for an evening. Nothing heavy, just a friendly chat.'

Amy stopped walking, and turned to look directly at Ged. He must have been doing a funeral today thought Amy, as he still had his black suit on. It was a little too tight for him these days and when up close she could see it had been used many times. He had taken off his tie and loosened the top button of his shirt. His hair was fairly awkwardly combed and his black shoes were scuffed and dusty.

'Thanks for the offer, but I don't think so.'

She could see that it hit him hard. As she said it she realised that it would only echo what Bernadette had said to him.

He sighed, 'I thought as much, I'm not good enough for you, I can tell that.' Ged half turned away from her, 'I wasn't expecting much, just a drink and a chat, but you soon put me in my place.'

'Ged, it's not like that at all.'

He snapped, 'It would have been better if you and Bernadette had never come to this village.' Before Amy could say anything else, he had turned his back completely and strode off down the road.

She called, 'Ged! Ged!', but he was now too far away.

Amy walked wearily back to the vicarage. She knew Gus was out at a church meeting. By the time she reached her bedroom she was crying. Amy threw herself on the bed and sobbed. Why was she causing so many problems? She was only trying to help, but no one wanted it. She was tired and fell into a fitful sleep. By the time she awoke it was late, and she felt less emotional. Hunger got the better of her and so she went down and made herself a sandwich. She was pleased that Gus wasn't there as she didn't want to face him. With a sigh she took her food back to her room. After showering and eating her sandwich her face became set with determination. Nothing would dissuade her now, not even Gus. Tomorrow morning, she was leaving Nether Crimpton for good. It wasn't worth sleeping on the matter to see if she changed her mind. Her decision was made. They wanted her out, and they would get their own way. She had no worry about giving in. Because she was so resolved, she slept well and awoke bright and alert in the morning. It was early. She decided that she would have one last run, before she told Gus, and then she would be on her way. She knew that he would understand.

Amy had enjoyed her runs near the village and the woods. There was the distant sound of shots again, but she didn't pay any attention to them. She would go on her route through the woods. If she saw Ged, she would wave and carry on. It was a brilliant sunny morning. There was no need to delay and so she decided to run fast, as though she were in a race. The path was easy, but it got harder as she went up the hill to the woods.

It felt quick and the next section was level. There was no sign of Ged, but she knew that he might have seen her and was keeping out of the way. She glanced at the stop watch on her wrist. It was her fastest time at this checkpoint by a long way. The next section was going to be even quicker. It was down hill through the woods to the road. The surface of the track was heavily compacted by the logging that had gone on, so it was smooth with very little gravel to slip on. She really sprinted down the hill.

She was about halfway down, and going really well, as she cruised at speed around the gentle bend. Suddenly her feet went from beneath her. She fell head first and saw the harsh gravel looming in front of her face. Just in time she managed to get her hands up as she crashed into the solid gravel surface of the track. She screamed with agony, as it dug into her hands, arms and legs.

Her momentum rolled her over towards the side and she

stopped just short of a large rock. The pain from her leg and arms was intense. The world of the trees began to spin round her mind. She groaned and opened her eyes to see what she had tripped over. Glinting in the morning sun, she saw the wire stretched across the track, and then blackness descended as she lost consciousness.

Chapter Eleven

Amy opened her eyes. The first thing she saw as it came into focus was the face of her brother, 'Hello, Sis,' he said as he rubbed her hand, which she realised he was already holding. She went to speak, but he said, 'Hush, be gentle, take your time and come round properly. You're safe and well.'

As she came to, and took in her surroundings, she said, 'My wrist hurts. She gulped as she looked at the lower part of her left arm, which was swathed in bandages.'

Gus said in a quiet and calm manner, 'You've broken your wrist and knocked yourself out, but you're going to be fine.'

Amy came back to reality, a little more, and realised she must be in hospital but said, 'My leg hurts.'

'It's cut and grazed. You hit the track very hard, you must have been running fast.' Amy had now surfaced much more and was trying to work out what had happened and how she had got here.

'Excuse me, Reverend,' said the nurse. Augustus stepped back. 'Let me check you out, now you're awake.'

She peered into Amy's eyes, took her temperature and blood pressure and went to the drip to assure herself it was working properly.

'What's that for?' said Amy quietly.

'You are better off to rest, your body has had a nasty shock, and the drip will help.'

'But I think I feel OK, now I've woken up.'

'You're going to be a stubborn one, I can feel it in my bones. I didn't say that you had a shock, I said that your body had had a shock hitting the gravel and that's what we are treating.' The nurse gave a token fluff at the pillows and turned to Augustus, 'Now don't tire her.' Then she left. Gus caught hold of Amy's good hand and they both smiled as the nurse retreated.

'Why don't you rest, I will stay.'

'You know I won't, tell me what happened, and how I got here?'

'Only if you promise to sleep afterwards.'

Amy matched Gus's smile, 'OK, I promise,' but Gus just loved that cheeky grin, which he had seen from his sister, since she was little.

'You tripped while you were running down through the woods near the lane. You must have been going fast and lost consciousness for a little while. The girl, I say girl, but the young woman who knows you, Anna, heard you scream.'

'She's lovely,' said Amy.

'Not only lovely, but very sensible and practical. She ran down the track to where she knew there was a mobile phone signal and rang for an ambulance. She called out because she had recently seen Ged in the woods. He came, and by that time she had rung home, and her mother brought blankets.'

'They are a lovely family.'

'They certainly are and I shall go and thank them personally, when I leave here.'

Amy said, 'I'm feeling much better now, but I can see how they patched me up. I'm fine, stop worrying.'

'You were in a lot of pain, but Anna's father was out in the lane to direct the ambulance and said that they could drive up to you. They gave you gas. You were conscious, but the drugs and the gas kept you free from pain and very dopey.'

'It's all happened very quickly,' said Amy glancing at the clock. It was still early in the day.

'Yes,' said Gus, 'the ambulance was quick getting there. Anna used her sense again, and while she was waiting with you, she rang me. I was able to follow you to hospital, and then as you know, the hospital machine takes over.'

Amy looked around more carefully. 'This doesn't look like the NHS to me.'

Gus gave a weak smile, and Amy said, 'Is it the NHS? You know very well I'd be happy with that.'

'Yes it is.'

133

'A single bed in a large room to myself, doesn't seem like the NHS.' She paused and then directly looked at Gus, 'Did you ring mum and dad?'

He nodded, 'I wasn't sure how badly hurt you were at the time, so I had to ring them.'

'You know what that will mean don't you?' said Amy, but she had to grin at her brother.

'Yes,' he said, 'and I think here comes the first one.'

They could see through the entrance to the semi-open room. There was a large man, with wild ginger hair, wearing a loud suit, coming towards them. 'Well, well, well,' boomed the strong Scottish accent, 'if it isn't little Amy. You've grown into a fine woman. The last time I saw you, it was pigtails and no front teeth. But there again it was your fifth birthday.' He gave a great roar of laughter. He turned and with equal enthusiasm said, 'You must be Augustus.'

Gus said, 'Hello, Mr Angus.'

'No need for formalities with family friends, call me Angus.'

Amy obviously looked slightly confused and he turned to her, 'I'm Angus Angus and had many a good evening at medical school with your father.' Amy hadn't recognised him, but knew his name. He said, 'I'm the orthopaedic surgeon here, and when your father rang, I said I be delighted to deal with you.'

Amy said, 'Thanks, and its much appreciated, but I want no priorities. There are many more deserving of your time than me. I assume it has been strapped up and will need re-setting.'

'As your parents are both doctors I expected you to know the procedure. I've a little slot on my operating list first thing this afternoon, so, as you say and quite rightly, if there is no higher priority then you will be on the table just after lunch.' With that he said his goodbyes.

'Oh, Gus, it's not fair, people have to wait days to get on to a list.'

'Sorry I had to ring them, but you know as well as I do, that they seem to know everyone in the medical profession.'

The ward sister came and gave Amy a superficial check and put a sign at the bottom of the bed and then went away. Gus was going to suggest rest, when another figure coming towards them caught their attention.

'I didn't bring grapes,' said Sharon as she arrived, looked at the sign, and then came and sat on the bed.

'Thanks for coming Sharon, but it wasn't necessary I only fell over, why did you come?'

'When we have a major incident like a murder, we always monitor 999 calls in the area. Judging by the description, it had to be you. I spoke to the ambulance crew, who confirmed it.' She paused for a while, looked Amy up and down and did the same with Augustus. 'I don't like accidents happening during a murder investigation, so I went to look at the track where you fell, just to make sure.'

'Yes,' said Amy and then the memory of the wire came back to her.

'Are you alright? You've gone pale.'

'Sorry, I'm fine and did you find anything?'

'No. Nothing suspicious.' Amy thought about it, but decided not to mention the wire at this time. Sharon added, 'By the way, that young lass Anna, she was spot on. She'd seen me walk up the track and followed. When I stopped where you fell she asked me, what I was doing.' Sharon stopped speaking and laughed.

'What was so funny?' said Amy.

'I flashed my warrant card at her and she said, "I presume you must be a police officer, but the show of your card was too quick for me to read." I gave it to her and after she had read it thoroughly, she asked me how she could help. She was absolutely wonderful and a future police woman, if ever I saw one.'

The sister reappeared and said, 'The sign says that this patient should not be disturbed.' Sharon flashed her warrant card. 'Yes I thought it would be something like that.' She turned to Amy and said, 'I can see you are going to be a difficult patient, and by the looks of it here comes another one.' She went towards the man carrying a huge bouquet of flowers and said, 'Mr Slingsby-Smythe, this patient has had a nasty shock to her system and needs rest.'

'It's OK, Sister, I spoke to Angus and he cleared it.'

Amy said, 'Theodore, the flowers are not necessary, I only fell over.'

Augustus said to Sharon, 'Perhaps I could treat you to a cup of tea in the volunteers' tea room.'

Amy said, 'There's no need to go,' but they ignored her and wandered off chatting to each other.

'I've brought a vase Mr Slingsby-Smythe.'

'Thank you nurse, very thoughtful of you.'

'Theodore?'

'Hush, the sister said you must rest. Angus tells me he is setting your wrist this afternoon.'

Amy nodded, but she could tell Theodore was far more in his medical focus. He was looking at her charts on the head of the bed and the bandaging. He gave a medical gaze into her eyes and, Amy presumed subconsciously, held her wrist and took her pulse. Finally he said, 'Nasty fall, it's not like you. You normally run very well and have good balance.' He couldn't possibly know anything, thought Amy, but it is a strange thing to say. As Amy had already guessed he had an easy bedside manner from his years in the medical profession, 'You didn't say your mother and father were doctors.'

'No, I didn't,' thought Amy, and with a sigh, and added to her thought, 'that it shouldn't make any difference.'

'You don't know them, do you? said Amy.

'I once attended a lecture during my training days about the role of the GP. It was your mother who gave it. Most fascinating.' Amy could never fault the camaraderie of those who trained in the medical profession together, but such reminisces weren't helpful at this point.

Theodore added, 'I've been a complete ass towards you, but now is not the time to tell you, as I must go because I'm operating in half an hour.' He kissed her on the forehead and strode off down the corridor. She was astounded at the difference in the man. What had changed him? She knew that the hospital was his home environment, but what a difference in his attitude.

There was a succession of medical staff, who had been sent by the consultant to do various checks and tests, along with an elaborate description of the alternative forms of anaesthetic that could be administered.

Amy after all that activity was feeling tired and wanted to rest. It was then that the Matron appeared and gave her a lecture on following the rules and she should make her guests follow them. She was a stern woman and Amy didn't take to her, but realised she was only doing her job. Amy finally said, 'Do you know my parents?'

'No, I don't think so'

'They are doctors.'

'No. I am sure I don't.'

'That's wonderful,' said Amy, 'I will have a sleep now.'

For the first time the Matron's stern face broke into a slight smile, 'You come from a medical family, I can see why there is all the attention. She tucked in Amy's pillows. Have a little rest now.'

Amy relaxed back as the Matron's pager when, 'I'll leave you to it.'

'Thanks,' said Amy as she closed her eyes.

In a few minutes she opened them again as she sensed a presence at the side of the bed. It was the Matron again, 'Sorry my dear, even I can't stop these. It's the hospital manager and he has with him, the Bishop and the Chief Constable.'

She fully opened her eyes and waited for them to come to the bedside and said, 'Bishop, Chief Constable so kind of you to come.'

Amy finally had her operation under a local anaesthetic and she was feeling much better by late afternoon, when the Matron appeared this time with a smile, 'It would have been easier to have the Queen staying.'

'Sorry,' said Amy with a meek smile.

'It's OK my dear, it's just that you are obviously so popular.' Amy found it very hard to believe it especially after yesterday evening, when everyone seemed to want her to leave the village. The Matron giggled, and Amy knew this wasn't something that she normally did on duty.

'What's so funny?' said Amy catching the infectious giggle.

'We turned down many requests to come in to see you, but

I had one, the like of which I have never had in thirty years of nursing.'

'Go on, tell me,' said Amy conspiratorially.

'It was the landlord of the *Brace of Pheasants*, who said that he had heard that hospital food wasn't up to much and should he send one of his lads down with a rabbit stew for you.' They laughed together, but agreed it was a very sincere offer. The Matron said, 'I told most of them that you were progressing well and would leave us tomorrow, but there were two who asked to come down.'

'Which two?' said Amy.

'One was a man who said he was in the woods at the time of your accident, and saw you in such pain, that he just wanted to come and check on you, so that he could assure himself. If you were settled and calm, then he would go home and sleep tonight. I wasn't sure and won't let him in if you say not.'

'He will be fine, I'd like to see him. He's a good man.'

'OK, I'll let him through, the other was a young lady, who said her name was Anna.'

'Yes, she was the one who found me.'

'She explained to me that it had been the first time she had arrived at an accident before anyone else and hoped she did the right things. She was worried because you were in so much pain, but she said that she wanted to see you, so she could tell you something. It wouldn't take long.'

Ged arrived and was very nervous, but he brightened when he saw that she was sitting up and talking. He looked embarrassed and wouldn't stay even though he was asked. She wanted to talk to him but he wouldn't say anything, he just smiled.

Amy thanked Anna when she came and that made her go bright red. Anna then fussed over Amy and made her lie back. But Amy was fully awake when she said, 'As I was dialling 999, and speaking to the operator, I saw a movement near the tree. It was near to where you tripped. There was definitely someone in the undergrowth.'

'It could have been Ged,' said Amy, 'he was in the woods at the same time.'

'Yes, I know, as after I finished the call, I shouted for Mr Rudd, that's Ged. I knew he would be around and he came from the path on the opposite side.'

After Anna had gone Amy looked through a number of telephone messages that had been left at the nurses desk for her. There was a very formal message from Lady and Colonel Crimpton, regretting her accident, and trusting she was not too badly hurt. There was also a cursory note from Damien, which just read get well soon. Amy had mixed feelings about all of the people, who had sent messages. She had to admit that it did show the friendliness and togetherness of the village, even if it was to an outsider. But on the other hand, if there was a trip wire one of them did it!

Chapter Twelve

Amy arrived home the next day and her every need was met by Mrs Battersby and her granddaughter, who fussed over her, making sure she was conformable. Whilst her legs and arms were sore, from the heavy grazing they had taken from the path, she felt fine. Her plastered wrist was in a sling and the pain killers were doing a good job. She had looked in a mirror before she left hospital and her face wasn't a pretty sight. There was long graze along her forehead, a black eye, and a swollen cut chin. She decided to avoid mirrors for a few days!

The more she thought about the trip wire the more she convinced herself that her mind was playing tricks. She expected it to be sinister, and in the accident, her subconscious imagination had placed the glistening wire for her to see. Sharon had been to the scene and had seen nothing unusual to warrant further investigation. The movement in the bushes spotted by Anna could easily have been an animal. Anna was sure that it was a person, but Amy had remembered both Jack and Ged talking about deer in that part of the woods. They were quiet and secretive animals and could easily have caused what Anna had seen.

She was with Augustus in the afternoon and they chatted away, but had come up with no further information about Bernadette. Whilst everyone had been kind, when they realised she had been in an accident, she still remembered the night before. Theodore had criticised her, and Ged said that the village would be better without her. She knew from Lorraine and Damien there would be no further contact, and she wouldn't be welcome at the visitor's centre.

Amy knew that Colonel and Lady Crimpton would never speak to her again and that would make it difficult for Augustus. Her resolve to leave Nether Crimpton had resurfaced and she went down to Gus's study. She told him she was going to leave.

Whilst he said that he would love her to stay, she clearly wasn't going to be happy and that he would, of course, give her his blessing and wish her well.

She then went and rested for a couple of hours. It was the end of the afternoon, by the time she awoke, and it was bright, sunny and warm. Her brother had gone to the church to help organise the forthcoming flower festival. Despite her stiffness, and a limp, she decided to have a walk in the sunshine. She would go over to see Jack and Anna to thank them personally for their help. As she was going to leave the following day she would also say goodbye.

Amy's parents would be pleased to see her so that they could personally check out her injuries. They already had a detailed operation report on the resetting of her wrist from Angus.

She decided to go along to the end of the track and then down the lane. It would be an easy walk and less hilly that going through the woods which added quite a bit to the distance. She knocked on the door of the cottage and Anna answered in no time at all.

'Hello, Miss Andrews, come in. Mum and Dad will be so pleased to see you.' Amy assured them, that apart from being a little scratched and sore, she was now feeling fine. She thought she wouldn't mention about leaving Nether Crimpton, until she was about to leave.

Shirley said, 'Jack, you'd better take Amy and show her what you found,' and she continued, 'while I've been at work, Jack has been up in the woods, as he often does. I was coming round a little later, to see if you were fit enough to join him up the track.'

Jack looked serious as he wheeled his way out of the house.

'Can you make it up the track, only I can't push very well,' said Amy

'Yes, I've been up here many times. My old friends in the forestry business see that many of the paths are kept flat and smooth for my wheelchair. Even though it was the woods that crippled me, I can't be without the air and trees.' Jack, Anna and Amy made slow progress up the track, and Amy guessed where they were going. As they neared the bend Jack said, 'This is where you fell?'

'Yes,' said Amy and her whole body shivered as it remembered the impact. She looked down at the scuff marks in the gravel. It was where her trainers had gouged into the surface.

Jack said, 'I've seen you run, when you have gone past the house. You come down this track and take the lane.'

'It's a lovely run, I've really liked it.'

'I also know that from your other sports you are nimble and agile, so I thought I would come to see what caused you to fall. I was expecting a sand pot hole. They occur in this tracks quite often. The hole is created by the frost and water, but feet, wheels and the wind force sand into it. It looks like a normal surface, but would easily collapse when it is trodden on.'

Amy said, 'I nearly fell the other day and it was just like you describe.'

Jack carried on, 'No doubt your ankle turned slightly, but you recovered your balance. If you had fallen then with your agility, I would have expected you to only have superficial damage, because of your ability to land well when off balance.'

Amy replied, 'That's what has always happened before when I have fallen. I was surprised that it was such an impact yesterday.'

Anna said, 'The police sergeant came here and examined the trees, I told Dad that she had said that there was nothing unusual.'

Jack looked up at Amy and said, 'She looked in the wrong place.' Amy hadn't told anyone about the trip wire, and she continued to give no hint that she had such thoughts. 'I explained about the track, but it is flat and even, and has no loose gravel on which to slip.'

'So how did I fall?' said Amy

'There were no logs or branches on the track because you would have seen them.' He paused and added, 'Someone deliberately tripped you.'

'How?' asked Amy.

Jack manoeuvred his wheelchair over to a bush with pendent branches hanging down. He forced his wheelchair towards the back of the bush and into the branches, which he pushed away. Anna held more of them out of his way. 'Look down there at the trunk about six inches above the floor, you can see the score

on the trunk. It's only a faint line, but it isn't on the other side.'
He crossed the path to a young sapling. He pulled away some of the plants that grew around it. 'Look it's the same this side.' He paused and then added solemnly 'It was a deliberate trip wire!'

Amy then explained to Jack and Anna about what she thought she had seen before losing consciousness. Jack asked Anna where she saw movement?

Anna made sure of her bearings and pointed to behind the sapling. Jack said, 'That's the village side of the track, so whoever it was, hoped to be able to make their way through the undergrowth and back to the village, without having to cross this track. At the edge of the wood they would be able to pick up the lower path and easily go in any direction.' He turned to his daughter and said, 'Are you going to try for real?'

Anna nodded, but Amy was puzzled. Anna then carefully stepped behind the sapling and looked around. 'The person went this way, I'll follow it as far as I can.'

'Good girl,' said Jack.

'How could they remove the wire so quickly?'

'The wire would be started from one side passed across the track round the bush and back across the track. It would then be twisted tight. I would guess it was very thin wire, so you wouldn't see it. After you tripped it would be a quick cut and pull the wire back. Luckily Anna was very close by and they only had time to cut and recover the wire when she appeared.' He paused and said, 'She might be a little while. She's trying to follow the trail. It's been a delight to teach her all my skills in the woods and she loves them as much as I do. We come out here together in all weathers.'

'Got it!' shouted a distance voice.

'Well done, Anna,' called out her father.

In a few minutes she returned with her news. 'I found the wire, it had caught in a bush and whoever it was had tugged at it, but it was firmly caught. I also found several footprints, which I moved around so as not to disturb them. My guess is that it was a tall and quite heavy man.'

'How do you know?' said Amy

'There is one full footprint. It looks like a large trainer, which is much bigger than women wear, and the imprint of the pattern of the sole is really noticeable, so I assume the person is quite heavy. I left everything as it was for the police.'

Amy wasn't sure she wanted the police involved, but could think of no reason not to call them. She shuddered as she stood at the scene where someone tried very carefully and deliberately to hurt her. She gulped. Was it a warning or were they hoping she would be so badly injured that... Amy did not want to finish that line of thought. It was going to have to be the police, but perhaps their presence might put off whoever it was that wanted to frighten her.

Now that this discovery had been made and Amy couldn't put it down to her imagination she felt very tired. After a quick conversation it was agreed that Anna would go back to the house and directly ring Sharon's number. Ten minutes later Anna returned and said that they were to wait here and that Sharon would be over in about twenty minutes. Amy and Anna sat on a log next to the track. It was beside a path that led up the hill to the car park. Jack's wheelchair was on the opposite side of the path. Amy was happy to let Jack talk about how he had taught Anna about the forest and the various skills that he knew.

Amy was tired and the realisation that someone disliked her enough to be violent gave her a cold shudder. It wouldn't be much longer now and the police would be here. Then she heard a loud dull thud. Amy knew it was somewhere behind her, but took no notice and didn't turn to see the cause of the noise. She was looking at Jack and suddenly his face showed terror. In a split second he shout, 'Jump!' and pointed. Amy and Anna turned quickly to see a load of logs cascading down the hill towards them.

Amy reacted first and tried to drag Anna with her good arm and they both went, as best they could, across the track to help Jack. He shouted, 'Get out the way!' and pushed them as hard as he could up the track, to get them out of the way of the logs. The force of the push and with the two women pulling he fell out of the wheelchair. They managed only a scrambled step, before the logs crashed and bounced past them. One of the logs caught the top of the wheelchair and sent it tumbling down the slope. Most of the logs came to rest in the trees and bushes past them. One had been checked by a tree and was now rolling gently down the track.

Anna was gasping for her breath, Amy was hurting, but Jack knew they were safe and said, 'Thank god you weren't hurt, and I'm only grazed.'

In the noise and chaos of the logs they had not heard the approaching police siren, but relief swept over all three of them as they saw the blue flashing light of the police Range Rover. All three were still lying on the track, and as soon as the driver saw them he accelerated hard up the track towards them. He had to stop when a log barred his way. Sharon and the driver both jumped from their car and raced to the assistance of the three lying on the floor.

Within twenty minutes, the forest was alive with police and the fire brigade, who secured the area and ensured that there was no further movement of any of the logs. An ambulance crew checked over Jack, Anna and Amy and pronounced them all unhurt, but shaken. They provided a wheelchair and assistance to get the three of them safely back to Jack's house. Anna was very shaken, but was also very determined not to give into the fright. It wasn't a time to think through what could have happened, particularly as Jack's wheelchair was crushed beyond repair.

Augustus arrived and helped to calm Shirley, who was thoroughly upset at the danger the three of them had been in. Having found the trip wire they all assumed the worse and that the logs were not an accident. They were just thinking how lucky they had been when Sharon arrived at the house.

Sharon said, 'It looks like the logs were an accident. I know it seems very unlikely to you, given what you found Amy, but let me explain what happened.' The three of them had been joined by Shirley and Augustus.

Before Sharon could start, Jack said, 'I'm always checking that log pile when I go that way, especially because it is at the top of the slope. It's convenient for the loggers to put them there, but it was perfectly secure the other day.'

Sharon said, 'But not when the pile has been hit by a car.

There is no reason to assume it was anything but an accident. Let me explain. A couple of visitors to the area had stopped at the car park to walk their dog. They have an old Ford Focus, which they parked on the far side of the car park, but the young man who was driving forgot to put on the hand brake and it wasn't in gear. It rolled down the car park, crashed into the logs. It was sufficiently heavy an impact to break the log restraints and so they rolled down the hill.'

'We've taken a detailed statement from the couple. The driver says he normally puts it into gear, but couldn't remember doing it. The dog was excited about his walk and they were keen to get going so he couldn't be sure.' Sharon looked around at the faces and said, 'The couple are being treated by paramedics, because when I said that there were people at the bottom of the slope, the woman collapsed and the man turned white and was sick. I'm convinced it is an accident.' She had another look round at the faces, 'I get very nervous when accidents occur, when we are investigating a crime, but this looks genuine, which is a relief all round.'

Amy wasn't sure, but as Sharon seemed to be convinced, she had no reason to doubt it. Sharon said, 'Now we have cleared that matter, I want to have a look at the trip wire.' She called in one of the other policemen, and said, 'Now Anna can you tell us exactly where you found the wire?'

Anna added, 'and the footprints.'

'Yes,' said Sharon, and the policeman smiled at Anna's insistence about the details.

'It's not on the path, it's in the thick of the wood and you might not find it very easily. Also you might accidentally tread in the wrong place and spoil the footprint, so I want to take you there and show you.'

Sharon said, 'That's very thoughtful of you, but you've had a nasty shock and are shaking a little. Your mother is concerned for you.'

'I don't feel weak. I can't stop shaking, but I'm not cold, dad, may I insist on going.'

'If you feel up to it.'

'I do!' said Anna standing up.

'OK,' said Sharon, 'You win, but take it slowly, you only have to show us and we will do the rest.' They prepared to go and Augustus was keen to take Amy home with the assurances that he would be with her all the time, until the police confirmed what actions they would recommend, if the trip wire proved correct.

Anna gave him a frown, as she knew it was correct, but didn't say anything.

Sharon said, 'We did find one person in the woods after the logs accident apart from the couple with their car.'

'Was he local?' said Jack.

'Yes,' said Sharon looking at her notebook, 'it was Gerald Rudd.'

Jack said, 'That's Ged, he's often in the woods.'

Anna immediately said, 'He was close by when Miss Andrews was tripped. I had seen him earlier and I called out and he came straight away.' The impact of what Anna said caused the group to go silent.

Sharon was the first to speak and she said to Anna, 'When he came to help after Amy had fallen, what was he like?'

Anna said, 'I don't really see what you mean.'

'Was he agitated?'

'I think he was a little, but so was I. We were frightened by the amount of pain Miss Andrews was in.'

'Anything else, Anna?'

'I think there was, but it was funny, because it was first thing in the morning.'

'What was it?' said Sharon full of concentration.

'I think he was drunk,' said Anna.

Amy heard Jack sigh, nobody else noticed. Amy glanced at Jack and could see in his face that he understood something. He shook his head very slightly and looked down.

Sharon turned to the policeman with her and said, 'I'll take Anna up into the woods. You go and pick up Gerald Rudd, I want a much longer word with him.'

After the police had gone, Shirley had walked up to meet Anna leaving Amy and Augustus alone with Jack. Amy said, 'There is something about Ged being drunk isn't there?'

'Yes, he's a very dear friend, but there are drunken moments, which we all try to keep as a secret. Fortunately they are rare, but when they do occur he often cannot remember, what he has done.'

Augustus nodded and said, 'One incident, that I know of, was when I was in the old church yard looking around just after I arrived in the village. I heard shots very nearby. I went to investigate and found Ged, with his rifles, doing shooting practice across his yard, only a few feet from the high street. He was so drunk he could hardly stand-up.'

Jack continued, 'The Reverend here took the guns from him and locked them away, and kept the key, until he sobered up. People in the village like Ged, and if we see him in that state, we all try to protect him from himself. The problem is that if we don't spot it, we don't know what he's done.'

Amy said, 'He seems very normal and only has a couple of beers.'

'Yes,' said Jack, 'he's not an alcoholic and most of the time he enjoys a few beers like anyone else. Sometimes he hits the whiskey at home and that's when the problem occurs.'

'What triggers it?' asked Amy

'It started when he was in the Army. It was the same regiment as the Colonel at the manor. He had a bad time, no one is sure why, because of the Official Secrets Act. When he was on leave, the tension was released and he was drunk for several days. In the end the Army said he was too big a risk for them.' He paused and thought for a moment, 'It seems to be an incident that affects him emotionally, but none of us really know. It's bad if he had one yesterday, because he also had one last week. Normally they are only about once a year.'

Amy just hoped Ged hadn't done anything wrong. They took their leave of Jack and returned to the vicarage. Amy was tired, but her mind was racing, so she didn't want to go to bed. She just wanted to feel safe in her brother's company. He made her a hot drink and brought it into the study. He went back to fetch the biscuits, but was gone a long time. Amy was just going to go find him as she could hear him moving around when he appeared and said, 'Someone's been in the house.'

Augustus explained that he had felt a draught and realised the cellar door was partly open. When he got down into the cellar he had seen that Bernadette's boxes had been disturbed. They both went down to see whether anything was missing. After checking all the boxes they went back to the study and rang Sharon, who answered almost immediately;

'Sharon, it's Augustus, there has been a theft from the vicarage, while we were out.' Amy guessed that Sharon had asked whether anything had been taken, and Augustus said, 'Yes, but only two things as far as we can tell. The first is the folder that Amy was given with the pictures of Bernadette. The second is the photograph of Bernadette and Mary that was in the cottage.'

Chapter Thirteen

Amy was up early the following morning. She was sore and her wrist hurt more that yesterday. Her mind was very uneasy about what happened in the woods with the log pile, and the theft from the vicarage last night, while they had been out. She knew that Ged had been taken into custody, and whilst she thought that he wouldn't want to harm her, there was that underlying doubt.

He had wanted to go out with Bernadette, who turned him down, and was murdered. Someone had tried to harm her the next day after she refused him. Jack knew about his drunken rages, as did most of the village and they kept it quiet, because he was one of their own. Undoubtedly, it was the drink, which seemed to combine with some form of mental blackout, and everyone worried whether he knew what he was doing at those times. At least the footprint in the woods, near where the wire was found, should be fairly conclusive.

She limped around the house until after breakfast, at which she agreed with Augustus, that she would still go home to Brighton. Her parents had suggested using a courier for her luggage, so that way she would only have to get herself onto the train. She had agreed to stay one more day to rest before taking on the journey. She thought through who she needed to say goodbye to and it was only really Jack, Shirley and Anna. However, she did feel obliged to go and thank Theodore for the flowers and ensuring she was well looked after in the hospital.

After speaking to Sharon on the phone last night about the break-in, no police had arrived and Amy knew it was better to leave it all to them. Perhaps they didn't think the break-in was significant.

It was the day of the meeting at the *Marquis* pub about the national footpath and cycle way. Amy had long since forgotten about it and wasn't going, until Augustus said would she mind popping into it. He wanted to know what happened, but had to be at a meeting of local churches in Sheffield. He said that the two landowners were totally opposed to it. Amy already knew of Lady Crimpton's views. Augustus told her that the other landowner for the path, where it passes near the station was Theodore.

Amy couldn't get any enthusiasm for the meeting, but said she would go for Augustus. It was time to have some fresh air. She would go for a walk around the village, and then pop into the meeting. First, she would go and thank Theodore. While he had been charming in hospital and she liked him like that, his remarks beforehand, and criticism of her, made her think it would never work out between them. She walked slowly up his drive, and glancing through the bushes she could see him in his garden by the side of the house.

He was laughing and joking with Justin. Amy turned round and walked back down the drive. He had criticised her for handling the teenagers badly, and said that Justin was leaving. He'd obviously forgiven him and had lied to Amy about it. Also he had still never given her an explanation about Bernadette. She walked around the long way and was coming past the visitor's centre when Anna came the other way.

After answering Anna's questions about her injuries, they stopped talking as they saw Lorraine, Damien, Clint and Mary come out from the centre. Amy noticed how, as soon as Mary saw them, she dropped to the back of the group. Lorraine went past first and completely ignored both of them. Damien stared at the ground, and Amy got the feeling that he was embarrassed by Lorraine's attitude. Clint had the usual scowl on his face, but looked at Amy and showed no reaction. As he glanced at Anna he gave the faintest of smiles and walked on.

Mary walked past them, and gave a little smile, but kept her eyes on her mother, who turned to check she was following. Mary suddenly stopped just past Amy and Anna and called out, 'Mum, my shoe has come undone,' and she bent down to do it up. She deliberately dropped a piece of paper behind her. 'Coming,' she called out again, as she stood up and trotted up to join the others.

Anna waited for them to go a good distance and then went and picked up the paper. She read it to Amy, 'Meet me tonight, 0900 at the station, Mary.' Anna continued, 'It is such a pity Mary's mother has banned us from talking. We used to be such good friends. '

'The station?' said Amy.

'For many years it was our secret meeting place. We would sit in the hut on the platform. There are so few trains and no one in the evening uses the shelter.' A very serious look crossed her face and she said, 'I'll ask mum and dad before I go, because they blame the family, especially Clint.'

'What do you think?' said Amy.

'Clint is lazy and doesn't get on well with adults, but to me he has been fine, you saw even after all the trouble, he still gave me a smile.'

'Yes, I noticed that,' said Amy. They chatted a little about what had happened and then Amy said, 'I'm going home tomorrow I will come and say goodbye to you and your parents before I go.'

'Oh dear, that's such a pity as I've really got to like you. First, Bernadette is killed and then you're going away.'

'Did you know Bernadette very well then?'

'Oh, yes. She was lovely. She worked with Mary as you know, but sometimes when they went out they would invite me as well. It was always great fun. We even went to London to do some shopping. It was great being with both of them.' Tears came into Anna's eyes. 'I've lost my best friend, Mary, and poor Bernadette was killed and now you're going too.'

Amy did feel a little guilty, but she comforted Anna, and gave her a hug, 'I'll come and see you before I go, but now I must go to this meeting for Augustus.' They said goodbye and Amy went into the meeting at the *Marquis*. While she had been talking to Anna, many of the people from the village had gone in for the meeting and so it was busy and the room was full by the time she arrived. She stood at the back near a corner. She preferred not to be seen and certainly wasn't going to speak.

The chair was the leader of the parish council, who said the purpose of the meeting was for everyone to have a chance of airing their views about the proposed national footpath and cycle way. He would summarise those views and send them off to the relevant authorities who were suggesting the path.

'Today we have three main speakers. I would ask everyone to listen to their views, as well as questions from the floor of the meeting. I am anticipating disagreement, but please can we be restrained and polite at all times.' Amy thought that the chair looked worried. He clearly wasn't sure what was going to happen, but he said, 'And the first speaker today is Lorraine Smith from the visitor's centre.' She had dressed very smartly for the occasion with a woman's red business style suit with matching red shoes and handbag. She had a full complement of dangling jewellery and her hair was immaculately presented.

After the usual courtesies at the beginning, Lorraine then went on to say, 'This is a great opportunity for the village,' and there were a few groans from the audience. She paused, gave them all a long smile and continued, 'Of course the extra visitors will benefit my business, but the extra numbers will be in the village overall, so it's better for the pubs, the excellent village shop, the crafts and local produce makers. And I recently gave agreement that the jam stall, as we affectionately all call it, will have a permanent and more prominent position in the centre. This will directly benefit many local initiatives, including the church restoration fund.'

There were a few questions, but no one was surprised by Lorraine as everyone expected her views. What Amy, along with many others, was interested to see, was exactly how Lorraine would respond to opposition and criticism of the centre. Amy could see in the face of the chair, he was worried about what was going to follow and he said, 'Our next speaker is Theodore Slingsby-Smythe, who lives at the Gentleman's Residence and owns the path from here to the station. The proposed pathway crosses his land.' Theodore was dressed casually in chinos and an open necked check shirt. Amy thought how handsome he looked. Whilst his hair was thinning a little on top, it gave him a distinguished look and his overall impression very much suited a highly skilled medical consultant.

'Thank you for the opportunity to address this meeting. My main concern was loss of revenue.' Amy knew that he wouldn't beat about the bush, but even she was surprised by his directness. He continued, 'I currently lease the fields to a local farmer and receive the income. At present, the footpath tends to only be used by local people going to the station, and therefore the cattle can graze at the same time as the path is in use.' Theodore was eloquent and never faltered. He was at ease standing on the platform and speaking. 'It is not planned to fence this portion of the path or to gravel it. The authorities believe it needs no work. The farmer has indicated that if it goes ahead, it will be too busy to put his cattle there and will not renew the annual agreement and therefore I shall lose money.'

There was some murmuring in the audience. Amy thought the same as many that were there. He is a rich man and the income from the field is trivial for him. But he held up his hand, 'I think we all want a thriving village, therefore I am prepared to forfeit the income from my field and support the national footpath and cycle way. There was a stunned silence in the room. The chair did a double take as Theodore sat down, he could hardly believe what he had just heard, and Amy was the same. The villagers didn't particularly like him and he always kept himself aloof from them. So why had there been the change of heart?'

The chair gathered himself again and said, 'Is our third speaker here, yet?' At that point the door at the back of the room opened and the Colonel walked down the gap between the rows of chairs and went up onto the stage. Amy thought that they had obviously not been able to browbeat anyone into speaking on their behalf and Lady Crimpton had sent her husband along in the end. He was introduced to the audience, but everyone knew him already.

He had a loud military voice, although there was a hint of shakiness in it. 'Lady Crimpton has asked me convey her compliments to this meeting. As many of you will know the proposed route crosses the estate land of the manor for several miles. Whilst we have a number of concerns about fences and gates, the manor has a tradition in supporting its estate village, Nether Crimpton. For that reason, and that reason only, Lady Crimpton and myself have agreed to support the proposed footpath and cycle way.

Amy replayed the Colonel's words to herself, but she knew

that he had said that he would support the footpath. The chair of the meeting was also harbouring doubts. The room was murmuring at the surprise of the announcement and the chair said, 'Colonel, can you just confirm that you support the proposed route?'

The Colonel didn't look pleased but said, 'That's what I said, for the benefit of the village.'

Amy was confused, why would both Theodore and the Colonel completely change their minds? She sighed as she was totally fed up with this village. Several people seemed to say one thing and then do the opposite.

As she left the meeting Amy answered a few people, who asked how she was feeling. She soon escaped their attention and went back to the vicarage. Sharon and Augustus both arrived at the same time as she did. They went in so that Sharon could update them on what had happened. Amy explained about the meeting and the complete change of tone from Theodore and the Colonel. Augustus was certainly surprised, but Sharon dismissed the U-turn and said there was almost certainly a developer involved somewhere along the line.

Sharon added, 'The developer offers an incentive to agree to the path. They are always legal, but not necessary in the interest of this village. It's not worth bothering about as it has no connection with the murder.'

She then asked Augustus to take her through the break-in last night, but in the end said, 'So the front door was unlocked and as far as you can tell only two things were taken, the Colonel's smutty pictures and the photograph of Bernadette and Mary. I wouldn't say it was significant, just an opportunity taken by the Colonel to get his pictures back. He could have easily come round to ask for them and walked in. Would he do that?'

Augustus said that before he had knocked on the door and opened it and called out.'

'There you are then,' said Sharon, 'he did the same last night and got no answer, so decided to help himself to his own property.'

'But...' said Amy, but she noticed the irritation come across

Sharon's face and stopped.

Sharon replied, 'Not really relevant. The pictures weren't forced were they?'

'No,' said Amy

'Even Lady Crimpton knew about the arrangement. I'm too busy to contact the tax people about it all. It's hard work on this murder enquiry and we are not getting very far at the moment. I might need to get the people at the manor, on my side to answer questions, when we have some leads, so I don't want to antagonise them yet.'

Amy sighed. It was definitely time to give up on this village and what was happening.

Augustus asked, 'How is the enquiry going?'

'Extremely slowly. We are going over witness statements again, to see whether we missed any movement in the village that evening. But it was thundery, very wet and foggy, so there were very few people out, and they were under umbrellas and hoods. Also, we are following up any unusual visitors to the village, but that is difficult with so many strange faces around all of the time.

'Any leads on her past life?' said Augustus.

'None. We are going through all the aspects we can find. We are hoping to get a link back to her past, but there are very few leads. Even the agency that she told the centre she worked for, went out of business a while ago and both the owners have since died. And before you ask, there was nothing suspicious about their deaths.'

Amy was going to speak, but changed her mind and sat there glumly.

Sharon said to her, 'We are taking the trip wire seriously, but it's a common type of wire, available at any local agricultural merchants. We need to have a suspect, before we can get their shoes for comparison.'

'What about Ged?' said Augustus.

'By the time we picked him up last night, he was seriously drunk. The police doctor said dangerously so, and therefore we have had to send him to hospital. We reviewed what we know about him and his movements. We now have learned that he's the local poacher. That accounts for why he would be in the woods a lot, but doesn't make him a murderer or a likely suspect for your trip wire.'

'Are you going to charge him for being a poacher?' said Amy irritably. The police seem to be doing very little and were getting no where with the major crimes.

'We know that he is taking game from the woods, much of it illegally, but we checked with the people at the manor. They have asked Ged to keep the rabbits down in the woods and as a payment he may take a few pheasants. So we don't really have a chance of a prosecution, especially as there are the old regimental loyalties between the Colonel and Ged.'

Amy could only think about poor Bernadette, but it was beyond her now as to how to help. Sharon looked annoyed with the lack of comments or help from Amy. Augustus walked Sharon to the front door to show her out. They chatted for a while, but Amy couldn't hear what was said. Finally Augustus came back into the room and said to Amy, 'It's all getting on top of you, isn't it?'

'Yes, it is, the police seem to be making no progress. I can also tell that the opinions of me, in the village, are going downhill. I really have had enough.'

'Don't fret yourself any more. Why don't you go and say goodbye to Jack and his family and then catch the train to Brighton? Or do you need to say goodbye to Theodore as well?'

'No,' came a terse reply from Amy. She was going to explain about this morning when she went to Theodore's house, but changed her mind. She said, 'Thanks, Gus, I think I will take your advice.'

Amy checked the railway timetable and in half an hour she was ready. She hugged her brother, who promised to send her clothes and shoes by courier. She cried as she left Gus as she was letting him down, but knew that he would never criticise her. It was a slow walk down to Jack's house and she said goodbye to him. Anna and Shirley were both out. She left her best wishes and wearily made her way to the station. The rickety old train finally arrived. She got on board with her only regret being the leaving of her brother. In the end it had been a difficult and frustrating time in the village. She had come to the conclusion that she didn't like Nether Crimpton, or most of the people in it.

Her spirits picked up slightly as she got on the train at Sheffield, which would take her to St Pancras. She was looking forward to being home. Her parents would fuss over her. She relaxed back in her seat and felt much easier now that the painkillers were working better. She took some time at St Pancras to go around the fashion shops. A new pair of pink Roman style sandals, with rows of beads across the toes caught her eye. They were soon bought and she made her way to catch the Brighton train.

At least the dirt and dust of the track, outside the vicarage, wouldn't cover her new sandals. The weather was much better by the time she got to Brighton station and her parents were there to meet her. They took her home, redressed her wounds, and chatted about Angus and the other doctors they knew. Amy gradually relaxed throughout the evening and enjoyed dinner with her parents and some of their friends. She went to bed, in a much better frame of mind, and slept soundly.

She was suddenly woken with a jolt as there was a banging on her bedroom door. Her father's voice called out, 'There's an urgent call for you.'

'Dad, it's six o'clock in the morning!'

'Yes, I know, but it's urgent.'

Amy pulled on her dressing gown, opened the door and took the cordless phone from her father. She shook her head to clear it of sleep and mumbled sleepily, 'Hello.'

'Amy, it's Jack I'm so sorry to bother you. I wouldn't normally, but it is so important.'

'What's happened?' asked Amy with increasing alarm.

'Anna's been knocked down, and she is in hospital.'

'Oh, no! Is she badly hurt?'

'Yes, she has multiple injuries and they have already operated. She is very incoherent, but keeps asking for you.'

'Then I will come as soon as I can, I shall leave at once.'

'Thank you, we will tell her that you will come today.'

'What happened?' said Amy.

Jack's stuttering voice at the other end said, 'We don't know, the driver didn't stop.'

After she put the phone down, she was furious, 'When is someone going to stop these accidents!'

Chapter Fourteen

Amy's fury didn't subside on the journey north. Just before she had left home, she had spoken to Augustus. He had only just found out himself when Jack had rung him to ask for Amy's number. It took several hours for her to get to Sheffield station, where she took a taxi straight to the Northern General Hospital. She was greeted by a very tearful Shirley. Jack had stayed at Anna's bedside in intensive care.

The nurse said she could only have a few minutes, and added that normally they would only let the parents in, but Anna had specifically been asking for her. Amy went to the bedside. Anna was very pale, her face and head were heavily bandaged, and she was linked up to many of the machines that stood by, and behind, the bed. Her breathing was erratic and she seemed in a disturbed sleep. Amy knew that she would have to wait for her, but she would stay at the hospital as long as was necessary. Amy gently caught hold of Anna's hand. For a few moments there was no response, but then she felt a squeeze and as she looked at Anna's face so her eyes half-opened.

'I'm here, said Amy, 'now close your eyes and rest please.'

Anna went as though she was going to speak, but no sound came.

'Rest now, Anna,' said Amy gently, 'I will be here later when you want to talk.'

She closed her eyes and Amy just hoped she would be calmer now. But there was another squeeze and her eyes opened again, and this time the frail little voice said, 'The car drove at me.'

'Don't distress yourself, Anna, we all want you better.'

But Anna hadn't finished, 'Someone stole the picture of Mary and Bernadette, from Mary's room. I took it with my camera.' With that she closed her eyes and went back to sleep. Amy was confused, but she stood up.

It was time to move from the bedside and leave it to Anna's parents. But why did she tell me that? She must have met Mary last night and they talked about the photograph. Amy wondered if it was the same one, which was stolen from the vicarage.

Augustus was waiting for her when she came out from seeing Anna. She hugged her brother and said in an uncompromising tone, 'It isn't good enough, Gus, I can't stand by and see a poor kid just knocked down by a hit-and-run driver!'

He took a deep breath and said, 'All these incidents must be related. I thought at first some might be coincidental, but now I am sure there is one or more people behind them.'

Amy said, 'As much as I like Sharon, she doesn't seem to be doing very much.'

'I spoke to her just now. She said that Anna was knocked down, late at night, on an unlit road near her home. They are doing all they can, but have no witnesses and no idea what type of car.'

'Well, we need to do something about it.'

'I admire your intentions, sis, but what do we do?'

Amy explained about Anna meeting Mary last night and the photo, she then said, 'Someone knows something. The photo of Mary and Bernadette seems important for some reason. I will go to the centre and speak to Mary.'

Augustus said, 'I thought...' but his voice trailed off when he saw the determination on Amy's face.

Amy had seen that Jack had come out from the room, while Shirley stayed by Anna's bed. She went over and said, 'Anna is talking about a picture that she took and was stolen from Mary.'

'I'm afraid I don't know anything about it?'

'I was thinking if Anna took it, then it might still be on her camera or computer. It might help to make her calmer, if we could print it and give Mary another copy.'

Jack nodded as he could see the logic on what Amy was saying, 'Here, these are the house keys, her room is upstairs on the right. If you wouldn't mind?'

'Thanks,' said Amy, 'That's what I was thinking as well.' Amy took the keys and said to Augustus, 'You will come with me, won't you?'

'Yes, of course, but we will have to go back on the train, I didn't come in the car today.'

They were lucky and managed to catch the train without a long wait. When they arrived in Nether Crimpton, Mavis Rudd was there and they decided to take a taxi to Anna's home.

Mavis said, 'Ged's being released from hospital this evening, the police don't want him any more.'

'It's all a great worry,' said Augustus.

Mavis didn't answer, but drove through the village at her usual high speed and then turned down the lane towards the cottage, where Anna lived with her family. The lane dipped down into a cutting with high banks on either side. As she rounded the bend she slowed down and stopped. Gus and Amy exchanged glances as they did not know why Mavis had come to a halt.

Amy could see the markings made by the police on the road after Anna's accident. Mavis said, 'The road widens here. I've come down here many a dark night, and it's easy to take this bend and see anyone walking along this road. You would always pick her up in your headlights. The bend is too sharp to take that quickly and she always wears a fluorescent jacket, when she is walking this lane. The village is saying its a terrible accident. It wasn't,' said Mavis with finality, 'it was attempted murder.'

Silence fell as neither Augustus nor Amy were quite sure what to say. Finally Mavis turned to them and said, 'My Ged would never dream of hurting you. He really likes you. They are trying to find someone to pin it on. He has his drink problems, so he's an easy target.'

Mavis took a deep breath, and there were tears in her eyes, 'He wouldn't do anything to harm you or Bernadette.' Her voice stuttered slightly and she said, 'The police are trying to find the evidence against him, instead of finding out who is causing all this violence. You are the only ones in the village who can solve it. Please help my Ged.'

It was said with a determined resolution. She then slowly pulled away and they were soon at the cottage. She refused a fare and drove off without saying another word.

They slowly and quietly went into the house, which was as silent as they expected. Amy and Augustus found Anna's neat and tidy room with ease. She was a well organised young lady and the computer sat alone on the desk. There was no password required. It only took Amy a minute to bring up the directories and files, which were all clearly labelled.

She immediately went to the directory, "photos". They quickly found the one they were looking for and printed it. It was a good photo of Bernadette and Mary, with each of them smiling broadly. They left everything neat and tidy. They then walked up the lane to the visitor's centre, where there were very unsure of their reception, but both Amy and Gus were in a determined mood.

Damien saw them as they crossed the central courtyard, Amy took a deep breath and awaited the confrontation. As he arrived in front of them, she looked into his face. It was drawn and he looked haggard. She guessed he hadn't slept for a long time. The old confident Damien was gone and he looked a shadow of his former self. The neat shirt and shorts, and his medallions that swayed around as he walked, were all gone. He had an old pair of muddy trousers on and a dirty tee shirt. There was no jewellery at all.

'What do you want?' he said, but there was no fire in the question. It looked like it was all he could do just to speak.

Amy asked in a steady and controlled, 'Can we speak with Mary?'

He looked her up and down and stared at her plastered wrist for a while. Then he concentrated on the grazes on her forehead. They waited and suddenly he seemed to remember he had been asked a question. 'She's gone away. After the accident to Anna, Lorraine said the village wasn't safe for her and has taken her to one of her relatives.'

'Is it a long way?'

'No idea,' he said in a monotone, 'they just went this morning, but didn't tell me where they were going.' He breathed deeply, 'That poor kid Anna. I've always liked her.' There was no animosity towards Amy, just a tired and defeated look. He stared at her wrist and then her face again.

It was a type of distant look that Amy found unnerving. She was just about to speak when he whispered, 'Your wrist, your face.' Damien then turned white, staggered and collapsed, before either Amy or Gus could catch him. It was a complete transformation in a few seconds and it had taken them by surprise as both were thinking about Mary.

It took a while before he was sitting on a chair and at least some of his colour had returned. The drink of water had helped, but he still looked very pale and tired. Clint appeared and asked his dad, if he was all right. Augustus explained what had happened and Clint thanked them in a normal manner. He helped his father upstairs to the flat where they lived, which was on the top floor of the old stable block.

'There's nothing else to do here,' said Amy to Gus.

'I'm not sure what we can do, but if you've got any ideas?'

'Let's go and look at the car park from where the logs fell. Sharon seemed convinced that nothing was amiss and that it was just an accident.'

'You don't seem to have a lot of faith in Sharon.'

'Think back to the hospital, Gus. Sharon came in and said that my fall was an accident, but Jack found out it wasn't.'

'That's true,' said Gus as they walked up the lane to the car park at the top of the woods. It was overcast and drizzling a little, and that combined with the late afternoon, meant there was only one car there. It was near where the pile of logs had been, and it was badly damaged at the front.

'That must have been the car that hit the logs,' said Amy, 'let's have a look at it.' Augustus went to explain his reservations, but chose to stay quiet. They walked all around it and looked at the slope, which led down to where Amy and the others had been sitting. Amy went back to the driver's door. It opened at her touch. She was standing there peering into the car when a voice shouted, 'Hey! What are you doing with our car!'

Amy immediately turned to face the couple, who were approaching her. They were in their mid twenties, very scruffy with old jeans and faded tee-shirts. The woman's hair was straggly and uncombed. The man's was black, but dishevelled. Amy thought quickly and stood up from bending and looking into the car.

Even in her flat sandals, she was considerably taller than both of them. Augustus had been looking down the slope, and on hearing someone shout, came quickly round the side of the logs that hadn't fallen. The man and woman stopped in their tracks at the site of this very large man. Augustus towered over them. He drew his shoulders up to his full height and came to stand next to Amy. His unkempt hair and his cassock swirled in a gust of wind.

The man, who had been shouting, gulped and whimpered, 'Bloody hell!'

Amy, took advantage of the moment and said, 'I'm sorry, but we were just looking around at the place, where the logs came from.'

'Why?' said the man feebly, as he continued to stare upwards at Augustus.

'I was down there, when they came down the hill.'

'Oh, my god!' said the woman, grabbing her partner, 'Look at her injuries. Our car did that.'

The man was shaking, so Augustus said, 'We mean you no harm whatsoever. We are not blaming you, are we Amy?'

'No, definitely not!'

They didn't look terribly convinced, but the woman said, 'Look at your injuries,' and she started to cry. The pair hugged each other.

Amy wasn't sure what to say, when the man said, 'Look inside if you want to, we don't mind. We arranged to meet the breakdown here, that's why we've come back.'

Augustus was intent on trying to calm them down as they were now very agitated, so he said, 'Amy didn't get those injuries from the log fall, she had an accident the day before.'

'Two accidents in two days, you're not a good women to be around,' the woman said taking several steps backwards, 'Look in the car, do. Oh, my god! It's horrible. I want to go!'

'Yes,' agreed the young man quickly, as he grabbed hold of his girlfriend, 'Look at the car for as long as you like. We're going!' and despite calls from Augustus and Amy they ran off.

Amy said, 'We didn't handle that well. Did we?'

Augustus replied in his quiet voice, 'No, we didn't. I'll get their details from Sharon and contact them to apologise.'

Amy said, 'As we're here we might as well have a good look at the car.'

'Do we know what we are looking for?'

'No,' said Amy, who shrugged her shoulders and smiled at her brother.

They looked as best as they could, without being sure what they were looking for, and confirmed that the hand brake didn't work. That had been expected. They were just going to give up, when Amy spotted something on the floor just in front of the driver's seat.

'What is it?' said Augustus as Amy picked up a small piece of bright, red, thick imitation leather.

'It's a piece that has snagged from a shoe.' She bent down and peered closely at the front of the driver's seat. The handle on the rachet, that slides the seat is broken, and its rough metal. It looks like it caught on a shoe and tore it off.'

'Doesn't look like the type of shoe that either of them would wear,' said Augustus.

'I'd agree with that, but I suppose they could have friends, who drive the car.' And with that she put the piece in her handbag. She closed the door of the car, stood looking at her brother and hoped he would have inspiration.

'Sorry, sis, I've no idea what to do next.'

'Neither have I,' replied Amy, 'but we are going to do something.' They began to walk back towards the village. Finally Amy said, 'The only one I can think of now, is Theodore. He seems to have changed his mind about his nephew. Also he was very awkward when I asked him simple questions before about Bernadette.'

'Are you sure?' said Augustus.

'Yes, definitely, it never got started with him, so there's no need to tread lightly.'

They walked through the village and up the lane. As they turned into the drive they saw Theodore coming out of his garage. He looked at them, but didn't smile. He nodded and muttered,

'Amy, Reverend. Come into the house.'

As they followed him they exchanged glances, because both suspected there was something wrong. 'Come through, come through,' said Theodore, but Amy could see he was anxious and frowning with worry.

'What's the matter, Theodore?' said Augustus.

'I've just rung the police.'

'Why?' said Amy, who now that the lights were on in the room could see his worry.

'It's Justin. He's suddenly left.'

Augustus said, 'Do you think that something has happened to him?'

'No, that's not my worry,' and he slumped into his chair. There was a long pause. He looked very agitated and finally said he'd better explain everything to them.

Now that he had decided to speak his voice was calm and strong as he said, 'His parents were delayed coming back to this country and so he had to stay on longer. I've been out all day and have just got back. One of my neighbours told me about Anna, but when I went to his room I could see that he didn't come home last night.'

Although Amy didn't like Justin, she tried to say lightly, 'He's a young man, they do stay out.'

But Augustus said, 'What's he got to do with Anna?'

Theodore took a deep breath, 'I know what I tell you will be confidential, as its a family secret.'

They both nodded. 'Justin has been convicted of assault before. He has a violent temper, which has got him expelled from two schools. He blamed Anna for all the trouble and for saying he was the supplier.'

Augustus said in his calm and authoritative voice, 'Temper is instantaneous. It flares up.'

'Not with Justin. On both previous occasions, it was revenge. The attacks were nasty and violent.'

Chapter Fifteen

The previous evening had brought Theodore's interesting revelation about Justin. After meeting with Theodore, Amy couldn't go for her usual evening run, because of her injuries, so she opted for a walk around the village to get some fresh air before bed. She had looked in to see whether Ged was back as she started her walk, but his workshop was closed. She had tried the door, but it was locked. At the end of walk she found that the workshop was still closed up and there was no sign of him. As she returned to the vicarage there was the sound of police sirens and she wondered if they had detained Justin.

She had used the time last night as she drifted through the village to think about Justin. Amy was convinced that the hit and run, that had badly injured Anna, was related to the murder of Bernadette. She tried to think about whether there was any possible connection between Bernadette and Justin.

Augustus's housekeeper had said that she had seen Bernadette at Theodore's house on many occasions. It therefore figured that Bernadette would have known Justin in some way, but could there be a link strong enough for murder? She hadn't had the opportunity to ask Theodore about Bernadette, because he was so concerned about Justin. It wasn't long after they arrived at Theodore's last night, that the police came.

All that was last night and Amy was now thinking through the possibilities for the day ahead. The hospital had said that Anna was still seriously ill, but she was stable. Amy's pain from her injuries was fading, and it was mainly stiffness that was causing her discomfort. Her plastered wrist also felt more comfortable. She decided there were several things to do today, but her intentions came with some reluctance and wariness.

She was back in Nether Crimpton and wanted to do something to help Anna. Her plans were made. She felt obliged to go and see

Theodore to find out if there was any news of Justin. After that, she would go on to Ged's, who should be home by now. He was clearly at the centre of things and he must just have some piece of information, which might help.

As she rounded the corner to go to Theodore's, so she had to walk past several police cars which were at Ged's. There was no sign of him, but there was a lot of police activity, with many officers around the barns and workshops. She drew in a deep breath.

Her intuition told her that she felt sorry for Ged, but the continual police pressure on him, didn't look good from his perspective. As she turned into Theodore's drive, a policeman appeared from the side of his garage. Amy guessed that Justin hadn't been found and he was there in case the teenager turned up. He allowed her to go to the door. The conversation had been heard by Theodore, who opened the front door to let Amy in. He looked tired and worried. She could see, by his appearance, that he hadn't slept hardly at all. She asked whether there was any news of Justin. He shook his head and fell silent. Amy updated him about the condition of Anna.

Then to Amy's surprise, Theodore said with a sigh, 'Come in and sit down. I need to tell you about Bernadette.' Amy assumed that, because of the pressure that was caused by Justin, he wanted to talk.

He took a deep breath and said quietly, 'You asked me about Bernadette before.' Amy nodded. 'And I told you to mind your own business. But with everything that has happened I need to explain and at least I can hope you will be on my side.'

Amy thought that it was a strange thing to say. Was he expecting everyone to be against him?

'As you probably already know I don't mix a lot in the village. I have an occasional drink or meal, but it can go many months, before I meet anyone. I recognise faces from events, such as the garden competition, but I don't know names.'

Amy was wondering where this was leading. 'About six months ago the hospital operating theatre schedule changed and I had the early slot on a Thursday. This meant that I would be on the first train in the morning, which went at seven o'clock. There was normally only one other passenger at the station. As she was friendly, we started to chat and travelled into Sheffield together.'

Amy didn't know that Bernadette went to Sheffield regularly on Thursday mornings, no one seemed to have noticed. 'As you know she was a good looking woman, a little younger than me, but she wasn't married and didn't appear to have a boyfriend. So, as I enjoyed her company on the way to Sheffield, I asked her out.'

'She refused?' said Amy.

'Yes, I tried to persuade her, but she wouldn't give a reason. We met each week at the station and, on one occasion when the train was cancelled, I came back home to get my car and gave her a lift in.' Amy just wondered why he had been so defensive, unless he was vain about being refused.

It all seemed very strange as she didn't think it likely that many single, available women would refuse Theodore. He was frowning and looked down at the carpet and continued, 'As I said I didn't really know people in the village and only knew her name to be Bernadette. Well, one morning I had a new patient. The nurse showed her in, and it was Bernadette.'

'Did you not recognise the name?'

Theodore didn't seem to mind being asked questions, and he said, 'I only knew her first name, and on the sheet I was given, it said Mary Bernadette Murphy.'

'I assume that she came to you through the NHS.'

'No, I thought it strange, but she was a private patient. She had been referred by a GP in private practice. It didn't seem to add up, as she said she worked as a waitress at the visitor's centre, but she said it was only a temporary job.'

Amy said, 'She had worked there for over two years.'

Theodore just shrugged his shoulders, and said, 'She chatted very well about the news and articles in the papers, but said very little about herself.'

'Did you treat her?'

'I didn't want to because I knew her personally and I said that I would pass her on to one of my colleagues. That was the only time she seemed to get irritable and said that passing me on would take time and she wanted it done soon and no more delays.'

'Did she know what treatment was necessary?' asked Amy, who paused and then added, 'I don't want to break any confidentiality.'

'Now that you mention it, she did seem to have some type of medical background, because she knew about the procedure and how long it would take. It was a non-invasive simple method that needed some follow up, but nothing specialist.'

'So she insisted.'

'Yes, I did the procedure that morning.'

'Did she come back for the follow ups.'

'She was due to, but never turned up for some reason. But then she came round here in the evening to apologise. And after that she accepted some invitations to come round, even though they were not medical.'

'Did you ever go to her cottage?'

'Yes, on two occasions. I took some tablets around for her.'

'You must have liked her to go through all that bother for her,' said Amy, as she thought it out of character for Theodore.

'Yes, I did, but clouding the lines between my profession and private life had to stop. I just didn't invite her any more and she stopped getting the early morning train on Thursday, so it just fizzled out.'

Amy couldn't help thinking that the usually very confident Theodore looked very nervous as he explained the relationship with Bernadette. Amy wondered whether he had given her an edited view of what had happened and it went further than he said.

'So why would Bernadette come and see you here and yet not go out with you? Any idea?' Amy said lightly.

Theodore managed a brief smile, 'So you think there was more to it than just coming to see me?'

'I just wondered,' said Amy meekly.

'Nothing I can think of,' stated Theodore emphatically.

That did look genuine thought Amy, but she was convinced there must be something and so she said, 'Did she know Justin?'

'Not very well,' he said rather absentmindedly, 'but he was here a couple of times when she came round.' But then a flash of recognition came across his face, 'I think he went round to her cottage, a couple of times, when he went out with Mary from the visitors' centre.'

He looked thoughtful and then added, 'I believe Mary was friends with Bernadette and often went there.' Amy now realised that the links between Bernadette and Theodore were much greater than he led her to believe. Justin's involvement with Mary made it more complicated. Theodore stood up, and Amy gathered he had said all that he was going to say. As he showed her out he said, 'It's hard just waiting for news of Justin, but I shall just have to be patient.'

Amy left him with his worried look, which had returned, after he had seemed to relax when he was speaking to her. She thought to herself that money keeps coming up with regard to Bernadette.

Private medical treatment is expensive, but she seemed to have enough money for that? Where did she get it from? Other questions buzzed through Amy's mind as she walked down the drive. Was it just coincidence that she went to Theodore for treatment? Why did she say her job was temporary?

Amy turned towards the high street. The police were still at Ged's and there was no sign of him, so she walked down the road towards the visitors' centre. She was surprised to see the whole centre cordoned off by even more police. Something had obviously happened. She said good morning to the landlord of the *Brace of Pheasants* as he came the opposite way with his dogs. He said, pointing to the centre, 'Someone has been shot.'

'Do you know who?'

'No, the police aren't saying anything,' and with that he passed by. Amy walked towards the centre and turned down the lane, which would take her to the manor house.

The Colonel opened the door and said without any surprise, 'Oh, it's you. You'd better come in.'

Lady Crimpton frowned at Amy, but invited her to sit and she said, 'I believe there has been a shooting at the visitor's centre.'

'Yes,' said Amy, 'that's the rumour in the village, but I don't know whether it is true or not. It might just be the usual village gossip.' She was trying to dismiss the topic.

'Why have you come?' said Lady Crimpton in a haughty voice.

'To ask the Colonel whether he came into the vicarage and took back the pictures of Bernadette.' He shuffled in his seat and said nothing.

Amy said, 'When we spoke to the police they said that as the front door was open, and that the photos were your property, they were not interested.'

'No, I didn't go to the vicarage,' he said without deviating his eyes from Amy

She thought he seemed fairly convincing and hadn't shown any nervousness in his reply to her. That gave Amy another problem. He didn't show any surprise that they had gone from the vicarage, so who had taken them? She thought that coming to the manor wasn't going to be profitable, but it could have been worth a try.

Lady Crimpton said, 'Someone had left them on the step outside of the front door. We assumed it was you.'

'No, it definitely wasn't me,' said Amy, but she didn't believe that was what had happened. Amy decided to change the subject. 'Why did you change your mind about the footpath and cycle way? When you wanted me to speak on your behalf you were adamant you were going to oppose it.'

Lady Crimpton said spitefully, 'We would certainly have picked a poor advocate if we had used you, as you seem just to want to cause anguish in this house. We changed our mind and have absolutely no intention of explaining it to you. Now, get out of my house!' It was delivered with venom and spitefulness, but it was what Amy had expected.

Amy had got nowhere with Lady Crimpton and the Colonel, and as there was no point in arguing, she got up and left. However, she knew that he had the photos of Bernadette back and they were up to something. She didn't know what and why they had the sudden change of heart over the footpath.

The next part of her plan was to go back to the vicarage and put the photo of Bernadette and Mary into a frame. She would then take it to Anna, in the hope that it would calm her a little. She walked back along the track and saw a police car outside of the vicarage. She hoped it would be Sharon, who had come to update them and give them some further information about either the murder or the hit and run.

She went straight to the study where Sharon and Augustus were waiting.

Augustus said with a deep sigh and worried look, 'Sharon wants to talk to you.'

Sharon looked very downcast and serious. 'Any news?' said Amy catching the seriousness of the faces and therefore choosing not to smile.

Sharon said, 'The only reason I am still on the case is the lack of manpower we've got. There are so many things that have happened and we are not keeping track of them. They will be bringing in help from Scotland Yard soon. But that's not why I've come.'

Both Sharon and Augustus were looking hard at Amy as Sharon said, 'After you and Augustus came back from Mr Slingsby-Smythe's house, last night, what did you do?' Amy now knew she was being questioned about something? But what? She did not know.

'I went for a walk around the village. It would have normally been a run, but I'm still too sore. I do like some fresh air before I go to bed. Do you want to know where I went?'

Sharon nodded.

'I went round to Ged's, to see if he was back?'

'And was he?'

'No, he was nowhere to be seen. There were no lights on in the buildings and the door to the workshop was locked.'

'Go on,' said Sharon.

'Then I walked along the High Street and took the lane out of the village. Then I came back by the footpath behind the centre and that led to the entrance to the manor.'

'Did you see anyone?'

'No, I don't think so, but I was pondering about Theodore, so I didn't really notice whether there was anyone outside the pubs.'

'Did you come straight back?'

'No. I went up to the high street and back to Ged's, but there was still no one there.'

'The walk must have taken about half and hour,' said Sharon.

'No. It would have been much longer by the time I got back to the vicarage.'

'Why?'

'I sat on the bench along the track, the same one as we sat on that day when we chatted.'

'How long?'

'About thirty minutes. The fresh air was pleasant and I was trying to think what to do next.'

Sharon said, 'The times correspond with what Augustus told me just before you got here.' Then she took a deep breath, 'and you saw no-one? And no one saw you?'

'Not that I know of,' said Amy, 'and now are you going to tell me what all this is about?'

'Before I do that, did you go to Intake Cottage yesterday? That is where Anna's lives.'

'Yes, I know that,' said Amy who was getting irritated with Sharon, 'Gus and I went there straight from the hospital.'

'But did you go back there later on when you went for your walk?'

'No, I did not.'

'Do you know Clint Smith?'

'Yes, you know I do, he was the one I caught vandalising the gardens.'

Sharon said in a slow and calm voice, 'The inspector that arrested you last time, has now been placed on sick leave because of the stress of this operation. We want to ensure that we do not make the same mistake twice.'

'I don't see what you mean.'

Sharon continued, 'So I said that I would come to the vicarage and try and clear up the matter.' She took a deep breath and said, 'but I'm left with no alternative.'

Sharon stood up and said, 'Amy Andrews I am arresting you for the attempted murder of Clint Smith. You do not have to say anything, but it may harm your defence, if you do not mention when questioned something, which you later rely on in court.

Anything you say may be given in evidence. I will now take you to Sheffield Police Station.'

Amy and Augustus just looked at Sharon in disbelief.

Chapter Sixteen

The tall slightly balding man entered the room. He was wearing a dark suit, white shirt and grey tie.

He spoke in a deadpan voice, 'I am Superintendent Hargreaves from London. I have just taken responsibility for this series of cases, which have been complex and at the moment show no signs of abating.'

They then went through the formalities for the interview recording with the tape recorder.

Finally Amy said, 'Why can't my brother be with me? Can you tell me what I am supposed to have done?'

'Miss Andrews,' said the superintendent, 'there has been enough evidence to arrest you in connection with the attempted murder of Clint Smith, at the visitors centre last night. I would also say that your brother is also being questioned about activities in Nether Crimpton last night.' He looked down at his paper work. Since her superior officer had entered the room, Sharon had not said a word and just sat opposite Amy. The superintendent continued, 'I note from the custody sergeant that you have refused to have a solicitor present.'

'That is correct. I do not need a solicitor, although I may consult one afterwards.'

'Afterwards?' said the superintendent.

'Yes, this is the second time that you have arrested me, and I would wish to consult a solicitor about suing you for wrongful arrest. Of course, I am not sure of the exact legal terminology, but it does seem like harassment to me.'

The police officers took their time considering what Amy had said and then the superintendent said, 'Given that I have only just joined the case, I am going to ask the sergeant to conduct this interview.' Amy glanced at Sharon, whose face showed that it was a job she did not want.

Sharon said, 'Miss Andrews I shall take you through exactly the same questions, as I asked you at the vicarage. Your answers will then be recorded.' Amy gave exactly the same answers as before.

The superintendent then jumped in with a question so quickly that both Amy and Sharon jumped, 'When was the last time you saw Clint Smith?'

'It was yesterday afternoon at the visitor's centre. One of the staff called him to help his father, who had collapsed. Clint then assisted his father up the stairs to where they live.'

'Did we know about that?' said the Superintendent.

Sharon just bluntly said, 'No.'

Amy then had to explain what she was doing there. She began by saying she had visited Anna.

Again the superintendent jumped in, 'Did Anna's parents let you see her. I thought she was in intensive care. How do you get past the police officer?'

'What police officer?' snapped Amy.

The superintendent said in an exasperated manner, 'The one who is with Anna.'

Sharon said, 'We haven't put one there.'

The superintendent looked at his sergeant in disbelief.

Amy said very firmly, 'Jack, Anna's father, rang me in Brighton, when I was at my parents' home, and they asked me to come as Anna had asked for me.'

'Sergeant, can I speak to you outside please?' Amy gave a loud and deliberate sigh. He turned sharply and said, 'We are investigating a murder, a hit and run, as well as a break-in, and that's in addition to this attempted murder. So we will conduct the interview when and how we decide to. Your irritability is not helping.'

Amy stared at him and said in a loud and direct voice, 'Why aren't you investigating the assault on me using a trip wire? Unless of course you think that all these injuries were self-inflicted.'

The detectives did not reply as they left the room. Amy could hear a heated exchange between them, but couldn't quite make out what was said. The constable who was left standing in the room raised his eyebrows at the argument in the corridor.

Amy only heard the very last remark as they opened the door to come back into the room, 'Very well sergeant, you do it your way! But you may expect severe consequences if you are wrong!'

Sharon replied shortly and sharply over her shoulder as she came into the room, 'I am right, there is no doubt.'

They came back to the table, and Sharon said, 'We are still recording.'

Amy answered, 'Yes, that is fine by me.'

'Have you ever handled and shot the rifles belonging to Gerald Rudd?' asked Sharon.

'Yes. I fired a shot from one of his rifles in the woods when I met Ged. I aimed at, and hit, a knot in a dead tree. I can show you if you wish.' Sharon went to say something, but Amy held up her hand. 'The previous day, I had handled the second of the rifles, when I visited Ged in his workshop, and there was a witness.'

'Gerald Rudd?' said Sharon.

'Yes, him of course. Also Lorraine Smith from the centre. She came in to ask about Ged doing a small joinery job.'

'I believe you are an expert shot,' said Sharon.

Amy said, 'It is public knowledge with hundreds of witnesses, including yourself, that I scored the most in the clay pigeon shooting. So if that makes me an expert, then I am one.'

'Did you hear a shot last night when you were out walking?'

'No, I did not, and I also did not see any activities suspicious or otherwise at the visitors' centre.' There was a long pause and then Amy said, 'Has Clint been hurt?'

The Superintendent snapped, 'No.'

'Am I right in assuming that Clint was shot at with Ged's rifle?' asked Amy

'Yes, but it couldn't have been him, as he was in custody at the time.'

'Do you have a key to Gerald Rudd's workshop?' The police were not pleased that Amy was taking this interview so calmly and had started to ask questions.

'No, I do not,' said Amy

'We have not searched you or your handbag yet.'

Amy picked up her bag and slid it across the table, 'Help yourself.'

Sharon emptied the contents and asked about the key that was in the bag. Amy explained that it was to Anna's house. It had been given to her by Jack. She then explained to the police as to why she went to the cottage where Anna lived.

'So you went to the house to print the picture?'

'Yes, this one,' and Amy took the picture from the plastic folder.

Sharon said, glancing at the tape recorder, 'It is a photograph of the murdered woman Bernadette Murphy. In the picture is also Mary Smith, who is the daughter of the owners of the visitors' centre.' Both of the police officers looked at the picture and then handed it back to Amy, who put it back into her bag.

Sharon turned to her superior officer and said, 'Well?' he nodded, and then she continued, 'you'd better say it.'

He glared at Sharon, but turned to Amy and gave her a half hearted smile, 'We seem to have done it again. Despite your close proximity to the attempted murder and the fact that your fingerprints are on the weapons, all the information that we have corroborates your account. So we will detain you no longer, but will you remain in Nether Crimpton?'

Amy looked squarely at him, she was in no mood to be conciliatory. 'No.' He glared and Sharon looked surprised, Amy continued, 'I had left the village, because I had had enough of all these crimes and I had gone home to where my parents live. I only came back for the express purpose of seeing Anna. As soon as I assure myself that Anna is calm, then I shall return home.'

Sharon said, 'Last night, at about the same time as the shooting, someone broke into Intake cottage and wrecked the computer in Anna's room. They tried to set fire to the building, but there was only minor damage as the fire didn't catch. Whilst much of the computer was completely destroyed, we found your fingerprints in the room. There was also another pair so far unidentified.'

'They belong to Augustus.'

'Yes, I've guessed that,' said Sharon.

Amy met Augustus at reception and he was still wiping the

ink from his fingers. She knew him well and, being questioned in a police station, would bring the slightest of smiles to his face. She just loved his character. It was completely unflappable and, of course, he was guilty of absolutely nothing.

He sensed the tension in Amy's face and knew that she would have had a difficult time. Augustus decided that it was time to diffuse the tension and make her smile. He raised himself to his full height, and stepped towards the unsuspecting constable who was finishing the formalities. Augustus towered above him, looked down and said, 'May I have another tissue to wipe the ink from my fingers.'

It made Amy smile with contentment at her brother, 'Yes, sir, Reverend,' came the stuttered reply. Amy could see under his calm exterior, he was not impressed with what had happened, especially to his little sister.

He said in a quiet manner addressing the desk sergeant, 'You said I may make a phone call, and I...' and at this point he flapped at his cassock, 'do not carry a mobile phone.'

'Yes, of course, I will find you a room for privacy.'

'That won't be necessary,' said Augustus, 'the call is not private and quite short,' as he peered at the phone on the desk.

'Please use that one,' said the desk sergeant, who was joined at that time by the superintendent and Sharon, 'Do you need me to get a number for you?'

'No, thank you,' said Augustus and gave the slightest of winks to his sister, who couldn't resist a smile despite all the tension. Augustus slowly dialled the number. Everyone pretended to be busy, so that they didn't listen to the conversation. In a slow, loud voice Augustus said, 'Good day, Bishop, I am at Sheffield Police Station, and I am glad to tell you that, despite being fingerprinted, I am being released without charge, although I was questioned '

Amy looked at the faces around the room and it was only the superintendent who showed no reaction.

The desk sergeant, who was a long service officer, said quietly, 'Thank you Reverend, I think that we have probably deserved that.'

'Do you wish to make a complaint?' snapped the superintend-

181

ent.

But before Augustus could reply the desk sergeant said, 'I think I can speak on behalf of the Reverend. He wouldn't dream of making a complaint.'

'Thank you, sergeant. Now shall we go Amy?' She glanced round and saw Sharon smiling behind the superintendent.

As they got outside Amy said, 'That was a bit naughty of you, Augustus, you know what will happen now?'

'I have no complaint against the desk sergeant, and especially Sharon. I was very unhappy with the treatment I received, and you were not treated well. It was the new officers from London that caused the difficulty.' He thought for a few minutes and then said, 'I believe that Sharon will take what I said in the context that it was meant, and not against her. From my limited understanding of police matters, the desk sergeant is responsible for many matters. I shall pop in to apologise in person, but from his comments it was clear he was unhappy with what was happening.'

Amy said with a smile, 'You know what will happen, don't you?'

The smile was returned by her brother who nodded and said, 'The Bishop and the Chief Constables are very good friends.'

After a police car had dropped them off at the vicarage and they were sitting in Gus's study, Amy said, 'The police don't seem to be getting anywhere near finding out the explanation for all these crimes. Even we must have missed something in the village. Someone must know something about Bernadette, which would be a clue to everything falling into place. The one who is likely to know the most is Mary, but she is not here. In fact, the only two that are around that might know something are Theodore and Damien.'

The phone went and Augustus had a short conversation. After he put the phone down he said, 'The bishop wants to see me.'

'You go, Gus, I shall be OK.' She said good-bye to her brother and rang the hospital to receive the news that Anna had had another operation and was still critically ill, but she was stable.

Amy said a silent prayer for her. The poor kid did not deserve that. She resolved to find out more from Theodore. He must know something, and that could be the vital clue in solving these crimes. Amy was convinced they were all linked and that none of them were accidents. She wasn't going to make a very good impression on Theodore, but she couldn't help that, as she was going to demand more information.

As she slowly walked through the village, she thought about who had murdered Bernadette. She shivered, but it wasn't that horrific taking of life, that she felt very uneasy about. A single murder of an anonymous person living in a village could be the result of her past life. But the subsequent events meant that it was much closer to home. Bernadette had a limited circle of friends and acquaintances in the village. Was it one of them? If it was, then she knew the murderer and it was that which made her shiver.

The chain of events from the murder had finished at the near killing of Anna, and someone trying to kill another youngster, Clint. While she didn't have much time for him, there was no way it was right that he should be shot. Her annoyance at the police arresting her had now passed. Augustus had charmed her around. She could easily turn her back on Nether Crimpton, but she knew she couldn't after she had seen Anna laying in intensive care. Her short walk had made her very uneasy, but she was determined. She had to start with someone who knew Bernadette as much as anyone in the village.

He must have seen her coming up the drive of his house, because Theodore opened the door by the time she had arrived. The policeman had looked around the corner of the garage, but had not moved because he recognised Amy. She studied Theodore as they went through to the lounge. He seemed a little less anxious than before, but he was far from his usual calm and sophisticated self.

'Any news about Justin?' she said in a quiet and calm manner.

'He very briefly rang me to tell me not to worry, he was safe, but not coming home.'

'Did he say where he was?'

'No, that was the only thing he said, and then he hung up.'

'So you are no nearer to knowing whether he was involved?'

'No, and, of course, his parents are distraught by the news. I had to tell them the full story. When he is found, he will be arrested and questioned by the police.' He poured himself a large whiskey and offered one to Amy who declined.

'Anna has had another operation,' said Amy.

'Yes, I know, I spoke to the surgeon this morning. Completely unprofessional, I know, but I was desperate to know. The only good thing was that it wasn't the result of an emergency. When she came in the other night she had to go to theatre. They would only do what was immediate at the time. They decided to leave something else to be fixed later.' He took another swig of the whiskey, 'But she is critically ill.' She could see that he was struggling to cope with the thought that his nephew might have tried to kill Anna.

'Augustus and I have just got back from the police station, I was arrested again, this time for attempted murder.'

'What? Who is it you are supposed to have tried to kill?'

'Clint Smith.'

'Was that the shooting at the centre last night?'

'Yes, and I'm getting really fed up with all of this. All of what is happening is connected somehow. I'm sure of it.'

'The police do not seem to be making any progress.'

'Have they interviewed you about Bernadette yet?'

'No.' He studied Amy for some time before he said, 'You obviously have not told them about Bernadette and me.'

'No, I've tried to retain some loyalty to you, Theodore, but I'm afraid...'

He stared hard at her, which she found disconcerting, and then he said, 'You don't think I told you the truth do you?'

Amy remained expressionless. She didn't want to accuse him of lying because what he said might be true, and that would put the final nail in their relationship that never got started. He was thinking through what he was going to say. All of his usual composure had gone and he looked vulnerable and unable to cope with the pressure.

A tear came to Amy's eye, she felt so sorry for him. He was already struggling with his own thoughts. She wondered whether there was a lot more to it than Justin. Amy couldn't press him further she didn't have the heart to do it.

Finally he said, 'I suppose I must go to the police and tell them what I know, but it will be the end of my career.' So there was more to what he had previously told her, and she guessed by mentioning the end of his career it would be a professional misconduct charge.

She had sympathy for him, but what was she going to do now? He said very slowly, 'I should never had let her come in the house. She was a patient of mine and I should have kept her at arm's length, but I didn't.'

Amy said, 'It's very sad that Bernadette is dead, but that doesn't mean you have to ruin your own career.' He looked up at her, and she said, 'Hear me out before you do anything drastic.'

'Go on,' he said, but there seemed little confidence in his voice.

'The police know nothing about the background of Bernadette. We liked her, and people in the village liked her, but she was an imposter. It wasn't her real name. She had done everything possible to hide her background.'

He said, 'I assumed the police would have traced everything by now.'

'No, they haven't, they are no further forward now, than they were the day she was killed. She had no credit cards or a mobile phone. All her payments she did in cash. She had plenty of money, far more that a waitress would earn. She was a mystery.'

'I don't see what we can do?'

'We must find something from among the people who knew her here. She must have had some link with her past life. You are one of the key people who can help. That doesn't mean you have to jeopardise your career if we do it right.'

'I thought you wanted me to go to the police,' said Theodore.

'There would be one serious complication with that.'

'You mean my career?'

'No, but what you have just told me, the police could easily interpret as a motive for murder.' Amy could see his mind racing, then he staggered and grabbed the side of the armchair and gently slid into it.

'I have no alibi for when the murder took place.' Amy had an instant concern that his passion for his job had driven him over the edge, but she dismissed the thought. She was convinced he didn't do it. He said, 'Do you really think that they will consider me as a murderer? I shall explain to them.'

Amy knew that she had to convince him to do it her way, 'Bernadette had the capability of ruining your career. You have no alibi, and did not come forward with evidence. If they take your fingerprints, will they be able to match them somewhere in her house?'

'Oh, my God.'

'Let's look at this sensibly, Theodore. We know you didn't do it, but we need to find out some clue to her background, because I'm sure that is the key to finding the killer.'

'What do you suggest?' he said recovering himself a little. Amy knew he was fragile when she had arrived. Now he was very pale and looked like he was going to collapse at any time.'

'Bernadette must have registered with your office and you said she used the name Mary Bernadette Murphy.'

'Yes.'

'But what about other information on her form.'

Theodore was now thinking about it. He picked up the phone and rang his administrator in the hospital. Amy waited. Finally he put the phone down, 'She put very little on the form and the woman in the office had circled some things that didn't check out and was going to ask her next time she came in.'

Amy decided on a different tack, 'What about her medical history?'

Theodore said, 'The patients fill in their own history, so it's never very reliable at the best of times.' He sat down and was obviously trying to think.

'Was there anything when you examined her?'

'No not really. Nothing out of the ordinary.' He suddenly stopped talking as though he had just remembered something. Amy waited and then he continued, 'Bernadette said to me she had never been married, but I could tell she had given birth a long time ago.'

Amy said, 'Did you ask her about it?'

'Yes, she said it was a long time ago and the baby died. That was all, I'm afraid there's nothing else.'

'When you gave her a lift into Sheffield, where did you drop her off?'

'Yes, I thought that a little strange. I expected her to say the shopping centre, but she insisted on the station.'

'Perhaps, she travelled on somewhere else, but even if we found out that wouldn't be a lot of help.'

Amy was running out of ideas, 'Can you remember what she said when she turned you down?'

Theodore said, 'Normally she just said no, but once I remembered she said "not yet" I asked her if there was someone else and she said that there definitely wasn't.' Amy stood up, there seemed no point in continuing this conversation. She still hadn't discovered anything that could be useful either to her or to the police.

'Sorry, that wasn't too helpful was it?' asked Theodore.

'Never mind,' replied Amy, 'but do try to think of something.'

'Yes, I will,' but Amy could see that he looked very nervous. He didn't speak again until Amy was near the front door and he said in a quiet voice, 'Amy?'

She turned and faced him and he said, 'Are you going to tell the police about me?'

Amy looked at his distraught face, and gave a gentle smile, 'No, I'm not.' She stepped forward kissed him on the cheek and left him standing there. She opened the door to leave. As she turned to say goodbye, a smart new Jaguar swung into the drive. The policeman on duty came out from by the garage and went straight to the car. The man, who was driving the car, looked very much like Theodore. He stepped from his car. He looked sternly at the policeman, who immediately noticed his army uniform. The policeman saluted and said, 'Good evening, sir.'

'Good evening, constable.'

While this was going on Amy watched. Theodore stepped to her side and whispered, 'Please don't go, it's my brother and his wife, Justin's parents.' Amy gulped. Should she make a quick exit? Theodore hadn't said they were coming, and its a family matter. He reiterated, 'Don't go,' and caught her hand and gave it a quick squeeze. She didn't want to stay but, for no specific reason she could think of, she didn't want to leave Theodore.

The man said in a firm and deep voice, 'Good evening, Theodore,'

He nodded to his brother, and said, 'Let me introduce, Amy Andrews.'

Amy said in a calm and unhurried way, 'Good evening, Brigadier.'

Theodore led the way into the house. The Brigadier declined refreshments, as he wanted an update of what had happened and the location of Justin. All four went into the lounge. Amy noticed the immaculate dress sense of his wife, Ruth, but she could see the sadness in her eyes. She winced slightly as Justin's name was mentioned. Amy sympathised for a distraught parent. Theodore gave them a quick update about Justin and how he had disappeared. Ruth said, 'You've had a murder in the village as well, didn't you say you knew the woman, Theodore?'

'Only, incidentally, we used to be the only two passengers on the early train on Thursdays.' Amy noticed that he didn't even glance at her. The next question from her got quickly to the point, 'Did Justin know her?' And Theodore explained about Mary and Bernadette being close friends and that, for a while, Justin went out with Mary.

The Brigadier kept glancing at Amy but she said nothing to add to Theodore's explanation. Finally, Theodore picked up the message from his brother's glances, and said, 'I asked Amy to stay because it was her that found Justin and the others smoking the drugs.'

Amy was now sure she was going to be interrogated. She had no thanks for Theodore now he had landed her with this. The Brigadier said with intensity, 'If I understand it correctly, you stepped from the dark of the night into a room, with an unknown group of teenagers in a deserted place, to restrain them from taking drugs.'

'Yes, Brigadier.'

He said with emphasis, 'My name is Jeremy.' Amy just nodded and waited for him to speak. 'Then you are either very brave or very foolish.'

Amy knew she would be confident in her reply, 'It was neither, I recognised two of the voices and knew they held little threat, and I am highly capable of defending myself.'

Theodore said, 'Amy wanted to give one of the girls that she knew a chance, it was Mary. She went out with Justin for a while, but at the time he was with Anna.'

Jeremy snapped, 'Always thinks he's a lady's man. But that's irrelevant.' And then he turned back to Amy, 'What was Justin doing and how did he react to you?'

Amy took a deep breath, 'Slightly aggressively when I first went into the room, but he soon calmed down. I told them I was not going to the police, but would speak to their parents and so I came to see Theodore.'

Ruth said, 'Thank you for trying to help Justin.' Amy had a great deal of sympathy for her, as she obviously just wanted her son back, even if he had faults.

Jeremy said, 'I do appreciate what you have done, but I think you are being evasive about what happened in that room.'

'I promised them it would go no further.'

'And that includes the parents?'

'Yes, it was the drugs that was the issue, as far as I was concerned, and I didn't want young lives spoilt.'

Theodore said to Amy, 'I think many people know what happened. I closely cross-examined Justin as you asked me to Jeremy. He told me what had happened with Clint.'

Amy knew that it might well become common knowledge and Theodore would tell the version given by Justin so she had to do her best to stifle the matter. 'If it goes outside of this room I shall deny it.' It was said with as much steel in her voice as she could manage. Jeremy didn't say anything, so Amy pressed him, 'Do you agree. It does not go outside this room?'

'You have my word.'

'The other lad, who was there drew a knife on me.' Ruth gasped. 'I was concerned that in a small room, the others could be hurt in the fall out, but I disarmed him.'

Jeremy's comment was sharp and to the point, 'What did

Justin do?'

Amy thought long and hard and said, 'He stood up initially, but I told him to sit back on the floor and that's what he did.' It was to her a fair reflection of what happened, but she saw Jeremy's face gradually go redder and redder with rage. She feared what he was going to do.

Ruth said, 'Jeremy, please calm yourself, please my dear.'

He shouted, 'How can I when a thug with a knife threatens a unarmed woman, and Justin bloody sits down. He's a coward. We have bred a coward in the family!'

Theodore said, 'Calm down, Jeremy! Calm down you are upsetting Ruth.

Amy said in a cool and measured tone, 'I am sure I was much better trained at dealing with the situation than Justin.'

But he snapped back, 'The army these days isn't about gung-ho and tackling him. It was his friend, he should have stood between the two of you, and persuaded him to put down his knife. No heroics, just common sense.'

Amy sensed that Ruth was not as much in the background as she had so far appeared to be, as she said, 'Theodore, I notice your whisky bottle is open, perhaps you would prepare Jeremy a drink.

Amy saw the look on Theodore's face that he knew he had to do something. He quickly put together two drinks and suggested to his brother that they walk in the garden together and leave the ladies in the lounge. Jeremy acquiesced. Amy wanted to leave the house, but knew that she would have to wait for them to return, but she said to Ruth, with a smile, 'You go and join Jeremy and make sure he is all right.' She accepted Amy's offer, who could see in her face that she wanted to be with her husband.

The room was now empty and she sat thinking while the others talked in the garden. Suddenly a train of thought hit her. After the visitors' centre and Theodore, the person who probably knew Bernadette the best, was Justin. He had met her here at this house, and he had been going out with Mary, who went to see Bernadette. What happens if he took a fancy to an older woman. It wasn't unheard of, and his father said he was a lady's man.

She started to put it to the back of her mind, when she remembered Theodore talking about Justin's vengeance. It perhaps would have only needed Bernadette to belittle him and he could have argued and sought revenge. She shuddered at the thought. Amy slumped into the chair. The talking tonight about the drugs incident brought back the focus on the group of four.

Anna was critically ill in hospital, and Clint had been shot at. I have fallen badly on a trip wire and Anna and me were at the bottom of the log pile. Her skin turned to goose-pimples. This whole situation was very serious. She went even colder, when she realised he could return to finish the business with her, because he hadn't succeeded very well in the first two attempts. What about Mary? She had gone away with her mother, it was a sensible thing to do. Perhaps Lorraine suspected something. But if Justin couldn't be found, was he looking for Mary to extract his revenge?

Amy was getting agitated and not just for her own safety. What about Mary? She tried to calm herself down, why would he want to come to the vicarage to steal the pictures? No reason at all, thought Amy as she tried to calm her fears. She pondered the reasons why he might be the killer. If he was, as his father suspected, a coward, all of the attacks would have been in keeping, as they were non-confrontational.

She kept coming back to the theft from the vicarage of the Colonel's pictures and Justin wasn't the army type so he probably couldn't shoot. Eventually the other three came back into the room. Jeremy's temper had calmed, but should Amy reveal her thoughts or was this far best left to the police? She knew she could give Sharon a call as soon as she left, but there again while Sharon seemed to be on her side, she hadn't had time to follow-up anything that she didn't think was helpful.

Jeremy thanked her for her bravery and loyalty to his son, which thoroughly embarrassed her. She decided to change the topic away from her, so she said in a light manner, 'So it's not a military life for Justin, then?'

Jeremy said, 'No he's never shown any interest in it at all.'

Ruth added, 'He did join the Air Cadets.'

'I think that was at a time when he wanted to humour me,' said Jeremy, 'although he was a damn good shot.' Amy's heart sank, what was she going to do? She had to move the conversation on, 'Of course, we have an army man in the village, at the manor.'

Jeremy smiled for the first time, 'Ah yes, the Colonel, grand old soldier he was, I served under him in Hong Kong. First rate leader of men.'

She now knew she had to ask the question, 'Did Justin know the Colonel?'

Jeremy replied, 'I have to say at least one good thing about Justin, and it was how he would always meet and talk with old soldiers. He got on very well with the Colonel.' Amy's mind was now made up. She had to act. Theodore wouldn't thank her for not telling him and Jeremy, but it had to be. She would make her excuses to leave and ring Sharon.

The opportunity came a little later, when Amy declined a dinner invitation and said her goodbyes and left Theodore's house with her mind buzzing. She found a quiet spot further up the lane where there was a mobile phone signal and dialled Sharon's number. She had worked out what to say, but the phone went through to the answer machine. She decided not to try to explain and left a quick message to ask Sharon to ring her and it was very urgent.

She would have preferred to have Augustus's wisdom as to how to phrase her conclusions, but he would be busy all this evening and she knew that it couldn't wait. Her mind kept going over the facts, as she knew them, and how Justin could have been involved. She was thinking hard as she walked back down the lane to the high street. She hardly noticed what was going on around her, but she glanced up, and saw Ged looking at her from the other side of the road.

Amy said, 'Hello, Ged,' and she crossed the street to talk to him.

He looked pale and drawn and Amy noticed that his hand was shaking. He was in a poor way. The episode of events in the village had really got to him. She felt sorry for him as she quite liked him. 'I didn't think you wanted to speak to me, and were going to walk past and ignore me.'

'Why, would I do something like that?' She would have preferred to go back to the vicarage and wait for Gus to come back, or for Sharon to ring. But she felt that she should make the effort to help him out of the downer he was in.

'Well, with everything that has happened and the hassle you have been given.'

'Come on Ged, we both like the fresh air let's walk and have a chat.'

'Would you prefer to come into the workshop, that way you won't be seen around the village with me.' Amy could see that all of his confidence had gone. She guessed he was partly ashamed about his drinking and wondered whether people would think him guilty.'

'Don't be so ridiculous, Ged, of course, I am happy to be seen walking through the village with you,' and she deliberately turned so that they would walk the length of the high street. Amy had guessed that he wanted to talk to someone. Normally he would have turned to Jack and Shirley, but they were permanently at the hospital.

He didn't begin to walk along side her so Amy stopped and turned to see why. He looked her up and down, and while the graze across her forehead was much better, it was still a mixture of scars and bruises, and the plaster on her wrist was very evident, as was the sling. He was trembling as he said, 'Oh, my God, I just hope it wasn't me.'

Amy said, 'Why would you think it was you? You would never do anything to hurt me would you?'

He shook his head violently and Amy could see the distress he was in. He needed more medical help rather than just a chat with her, 'Of course, I would never want to hurt you, but when I get drunk, and go on one of the benders, I never know what I'd done when I have recovered my senses.'

'Do you think that you get violent? I don't think any one in the village does.'

'You don't know the background.' It was said with finality.

'Then tell me,' said Amy gently.

He was silent for a while, but began to walk alongside of her. 'It was in the army. I was on a mission, it doesn't matter what, and it went all wrong. We were under siege for a while and my friends were all killed. Eventually, I was captured, but soon the rescue teams came and I was released. It was traumatic for me. I was injured and spent some time in hospital, but the doctors said I would never return to action.' His voice was shaking, and his walk was uneven, but Amy didn't speak. She believed that he wasn't finished. 'The long recuperation was boring and I started to drink. Most of the time it was fine, just a couple of beers to relax. But occasionally I switched to whiskey and then I had a period where I couldn't remember what had happened.'

Amy said quietly, 'Just because you can't remember, doesn't mean you were violent.'

'I haven't finished yet,' he said abruptly. 'One of the first times it happened, I beat up my best friend, he was in hospital for three weeks.'

'Have you had any help?'

'Yes, lots over the years. The incidents have got less and become shorter. The doctors have said that I'm not an alcoholic, but that stress can bring it on as a panic attack and that's why I turn to the heavy drink. And I really can't live with myself knowing that I have probably committed some of these dreadful things.'

'Why do you think you've done them?'

'I've had several spells of the drink just recently, and they all occurred when something has happened.'

'When did they start this time?'

'That's the worrying thing, I spoke to Bernadette the day she was killed. It was later that afternoon, I tried again to get her to go out with me, but she wouldn't. I was hopeful, but after she refused, I felt really down and started to drink.'

'But it can't have been you. After all you were digging a grave the next morning because you found us in the church yard just after the police arrived.'

'I only vaguely remember that ...' and his voice trailed off.

'The night that Clint was shot at, you were in custody.'

'Yes, I know that, but they think as you were my friend and we were in collusion, haven't the police spoken to you?'

'Yes, they arrested me, earlier, because someone had taken your rifles and my fingerprints were on them.' As Amy spoke about the rifles, she started to think through who would know about them, and be able to take and replace them without being seen.

'Ged, do you know, Justin, Theodore's nephew?'

'Yes, he has been in the village a few times over the years, during the holidays, as his father is in the army. Justin has been with me to the woods shooting on several occasions, he's a good shot.'

'Has he been in your workshop?'

'Yes, he must have been, as I've spoken with him on many occasions.'

Amy was now convinced that it must be Justin. She wondered if he was about the same afternoon that she handled the guns. It provided a good way to get revenge on Clint and me at the same time.'

'You really do need some professional help, Ged.'

'Yes, I know and even the police recognised that. They had to dry me out the other day. Then they passed me on to the mental health unit, who have given me some tablets, but they want to do further tests. I think that is the only reason I'm not in a police cell.'

Ged jumped visibly as the sound of police sirens were heard further down the high street. The two police cars with blue flashing lights and sirens blaring were coming down the street at highspeed. People walking along the pavements stopped to watch them go by. The noise was deafening as they came towards Amy and Ged. The driver of the first car suddenly seemed to see the pair of them and swerved across the road and screeched to a halt. The second car did the same.

Four policemen and the superintendent leapt from the car. Two grabbed hold of Ged, and held him while the superintendent approached and said, 'Gerald Rudd, I am arresting you for the murder of Bernadette Murphy. You do not have to say anything, but it may harm your defence if you do not mention when questioned something which you later rely on in court. Anything you say may be given in evidence.' The policemen handcuffed him and then he was bundled into the leading police car. The superintendent came straight up to Amy, 'Unless I have your immediate assurance you will not leave the village, I shall arrest you too.'

Amy was angry at the heavy handed approach of the police. Ged was clearly not going to run away as all of his spirit had drained from him, so she snapped back, 'On what charge?'

She received a very aggressive reply, 'Perverting the course of justice by interfering with a murder investigation.'

She snapped again, 'I will not leave the village until my solicitor informs you of any intentions I may have. Now go away, I will not be bullied by you!' The superintendent clearly did not expect her to be so aggressive and was weighing up his options of arresting her again. In the end he said nothing, got back in the car, and both the police cars drove off at high speed.

Amy continued her walk slowly along the high street. She was worried about Ged, but more concerned that Sharon had not rung her back. It now seemed to her that it was a low police priority to find Justin.

She was feeling vulnerable and frightened. The thought of Justin's name made her shiver. No one knew where he was. That was what was worrying her.

Amy had a few minor injuries from her trip wire, but he might decide to come and finish her off as well. She shivered and looked around nervously. Another police car came cruising down the street. There had been a very steep rise in the number of police officers on the ground in Nether Crimpton. Some were investigating the previous incidents, while others were in the village and visitors' centre just to exert a presence.

She desperately wanted to speak to Sharon, so she tried again, but she still had to leave a message on the answer phone. The police have arrested Ged, presumably because they have found some evidence. I must speak with Gus as he will know how to ensure that Ged has a solicitor, because he desperately needs one. She was now convinced that it wasn't Ged, but it was Justin. It all fitted together so well. Theodore had raised his doubts about the attempted murder of Anna. It was the same time as Justin had disappeared. She resolved there would be no walk in the dark tonight. She would return to the vicarage and wait for her brother.

Amy was feeling tired with the nervous exhaustion of the day so a bit of peace and quiet would be welcome. She turned her steps up the lane and along the track to the vicarage. It was the middle of the evening, but it was still light. It would give her a chance to secure the house before dark. She went in and was surprised that Desmond didn't bounce out to meet her. The dog was a persistent nuisance at times. Gus must have taken him along for the ride to the Bishop, who loved dogs, and was particularly fond of Desmond.

The old house always seemed so draughty and cold even in the hot weather, but that was just the nature of the thick stoned building. Her movements were silent as her sandals made no noise on the hall floor. She went to ring Sharon to let her know that she was back at the vicarage.

Suddenly there was a creaking noise that made her jump. Also there was a much more pronounced draft in the hall. She went to dismiss it as a draughty old building creaking, when the noise came again. She stood perfectly still and listened. She tried to apply a rational explanation, but she didn't feel happy about any form of logic as she was frightened.

Where was the noise coming from? The door from the hall, which led down to the cellar was slightly open and she listened at the gap. There was nothing and she relaxed a little. She moved up and down the hall, but could hear no noise at all. The creaking of an old door had gone silent, but a new noise sounded and it was a slight scraping.

Amy quickly skipped round the hall to determine the direction of the noise. There was no doubt it was coming from the cellar. What to do? She could hardly ring the police? If anyone had come in why would they want to go down to the cellar?

Perhaps it was Desmond and he was hurt. She couldn't just leave the house, if he was hurt. He could easily have got into the cellar and boxes had fallen on him. She had to go down. It was just a fanciful imagination that was getting the better of her.

She stepped lightly down the stone steps to the cellar. Just in case, she took off her sling. The rest of her limbs were working normally and her confidence in her defence training returned as she moved the arm that had been restricted. The plaster cast was a weapon in itself. There was no noise, but the cellar door was open and there was no light on inside. She turned it on and there was still no noise.

Amy prepared herself for someone behind the door, but the attack came from the other side as a tea chest, on top of the pile, was pushed towards her with a lot of force. She heard the considerable grunt from the energy put into the effort to propel the box forwards.

Her aching limbs responded, but not quickly enough. The tea chest crashed into her, knocking her to the floor. A large trainer aimed a kick at her as she lay slightly dazed on the floor, but it landed on her thigh. She yelped in pain, but it wasn't enough to stop her mind racing.

She was on the floor and her assailant was standing. He pushed another box towards her as she went to get up and it knocked her to the floor again. This time the man leap on top of her. She was face down and he shoved her face against the hard stone floor. She went to scream, but her attempt to draw in a breath meant that a large hand closed over her mouth. She wriggled as best she could from the heavy weight that was on her.

Her injuries were hurting her. The blood pumping through her system gave an excruciating pain in her plastered wrist. She could feel the blackness descend as she was going to pass out, but she fought it and managed a breath of air which caused the darkness to recede. She knew she was fighting for her life with Justin. Her hair was grabbed, but then she felt a lightening of the weight and she responded with all her energy to unseat him from her back. He must have been half pushed off by Amy's movement and half jumped. He turned and rushed for the steps. He pulled cases and objects down on to her to help his escape. The flying objects knocked the bulb out of the socket and the cellar went dark, but she could see his silhouette begin to take the stairs. She got past the pile of crates and leap up the steps after him, she wanted to make sure that he was really going and not going to try to kill her.

He grabbed her bag as he went towards the front door. Even in her injured state she was quicker than him. She tripped at the top of the stairs. He was going to get away, but she managed to crash her plaster against his trailing ankle and he fell heavily into the door. He tried to rise at the same time as Amy and both were on their knees and he lunged at her, but her instincts came to her in the end.

The fierce and accurate karate punch hit him across the bridge of the nose. Amy yelped with the pain in her hand, but the impact was true and sure. He folded into a semi-conscious crumbled heap on the carpet, with blood streaming from his nose. Amy's adrenalin was flowing and she leapt to her feet and stood over him in her karate position.

'Don't hit me again!,' he screamed and cowered away from her. But Amy wasn't going to drop her guard, 'You've broken my nose,' he shouted and moved his hand to the pocket of his jacket. Amy kicked at the hand with force. 'Ah! Came the yelp of pain, 'I want a handkerchief to stem the blood.'

'Don't move at all, or I shall hit you again.' The threat seemed to work and he stayed slumped motionless against the wall. She eased back a little so that he couldn't grab her, and suddenly realised, as she did so, that he was too big for Justin. She looked at the bloodied face and couldn't help exclaiming, 'Damien!'

'Oh, god,' he said, and closed his eyes.

'Don't attempt to move, or I shall hit you even harder!' she considered tying him up, but at the moment the threat of violence against him seemed to stop him moving. 'Lie flat on your face with your arms and legs outstretched!'

He went to protest, but Amy took one step towards him and raised her arms, and he did as he was told.

'Don't move, I'm going to ring the police!'

'Please don't! please don't! I just want this to all end, it's a nightmare!'

'Do you know where Justin is?'

'Justin! Why the bloody hell would I know where he is?' It seemed genuine, but he was clearly getting over the punch and returning to full consciousness as he said, 'Let me get up I'm breathing in my own blood.'

'Tough,' shouted Amy, 'you should have thought about that before you attacked me. What are you doing here?'

'Lorraine made me...'

'You don't expect me to believe that do you? A grown man does breaking, entering and assault, just because your wife tells you. What were you looking for?'

Damien didn't reply.

'OK, you have it your way, you can explain to the police.'

'No, I was after that photo of Bernadette and Mary.'

'What photo? The one that was stolen from here last week?'

'No, I've already got that one. It's the one you printed at Anna's.'

'How did you know about that? Never mind! Why do you want it?' He started to move on the carpet. 'Don't move and turn you head away from me.' He hesitated and Amy jabbed her foot down on the back of his neck, 'Do as I say!'

'You're a bloody maniac, you're going to kill me in the end.'

'Stop being so melodramatic. Now keep your face down. What's so special about the photo?' said Amy who was coming down from the adrenalin high. He was middle-aged and very overweight and certainly wasn't a sportsman, so he won't be able to get up quickly from there. I've got enough time to deal with him. 'Why do you want a picture of Bernadette? She was only your employee?'

'I didn't kill her!' came the cry from Damien.

Amy immediately thought, why would anyone think that he was involved with her death? So she decided to take a guess, 'You were having an affair with her weren't you, so when she rejected you, you killed her.' It certainly sounded plausible, as it rushed through Amy's mind.

She could hear a mixture of crying and coughing as he tried to explain, 'I know you started to become friends and I guessed she must have told you. I was having an affair, but I didn't kill her and I don't know who did.' Amy didn't believe him.

'Did you trash Anna's bedroom to destroy the photos.'

There was only the noise of crying and coughing, until he said, 'I'm bleeding to death here.'

'There's no ambulance until you answer the question.' She felt this could all go terribly wrong, she just hoped that it was only a bad nose bleed.

'Yes, it was me, and I had an affair with Bernadette, she was lovely,' he croaked, 'but I didn't kill her.'

'You were hoping to find the picture down in the cellar, weren't you? And then, when you couldn't, you tried to snatch my bag on the way out.'

'Yes, but I didn't murder her.'

'What's in this photograph, that so important?'

'I don't know, and to be bloody honest I don't care. I've had enough of all this.'

Amy took the photo from her bag and looked at it, 'I can't see what's so special about this photo.'

'I must destroy it, I must,' and he went to roll over, but Amy was ready for him and her foot came down squarely on the back of his neck.'

As she did so, her glance at the photo seemed as though she was looking at it with fresh eyes. There was no doubt in her mind. The photo of Bernadette and Mary looked very much like a picture of a mother and her daughter. She felt the wriggling under her foot and jammed her heel into the back of his neck and he let out a tremendous yelp of pain, as his face and more particular his nose was jammed into the carpet.

At that point, the front door opened. Augustus and Sharon walked in. They looked at a very hot and bothered Amy. Their eyes then went down to Damien, who was writhing in agony in a pool of blood.

Chapter Seventeen

Amy had enjoyed her good night's sleep. She now felt relaxed and had finished her breakfast with Augustus. The previous evening's tussle with Damien had reawakened some of her injuries, but generally she felt bright and good. The door bell rang. Augustus, went to answer it, and brought Sharon into the study, where Amy and her brother had been chatting over the events.

Sharon said, 'I've been released from the investigation to come over and thank you for all that you have done.'

'Has Damien confessed to murdering Bernadette yet? Presumably he will have done it in one of his fits of temper,' said Amy

Sharon answered, 'We haven't talked to him as he spent most of the night under guard at the hospital, while they fixed his injuries. So we have had to wait. But he has admitted having an affair with Bernadette, as well as three counts of breaking and entering. Two of which were here and the other one was when he smashed up Anna's computer. He had also said that he set up the trip wire, which caused you to fall. He was careless, because he was wearing the same trainers when we arrested him, and so we had a match.'

Amy thought that Sharon looked so much more relaxed this morning, and Augustus said, 'There must be a lot of relief at the police station, now that you have caught him.'

Sharon gave Augustus a beaming smile, 'Yes the Chief Constable has sent the superintendent back to London, so we are back with the old team who are all relieved that it is over.'

'What about the photo?' said Amy.

'You were right about Bernadette and Mary being mother and daughter, once you gave us that lead it was easy to confirm the details. We rang social services in Lewisham, which is where Damien and Lorraine came from. They gave us the name of the natural mother of Mary. The social worker, who was involved with Mary's mother confirmed that the picture was her. Last night you said about Bernadette's Thursday morning trips. That is when she linked back with her old name and life. Once we had her name it was easy to get mobile phone information and bank withdrawals.'

'Did she go on further from Sheffield?'

'Yes, about another thirty minute journey to Derby. She left all her cards and phone in station lockers and left luggage. She would pick up messages when she was there. Social services, who were responsible for Mary, were talking to Bernadette regularly about whether Mary had agreed to meet her mother. We don't believe that Mary knows yet, and her social worker is travelling up from London later today to explain to Mary about her mother.'

'Do you know why she decided after all these years that she wanted to see her daughter?'

Sharon replied to Amy, 'You were right about something at the beginning of the enquiry, but we never got anywhere with our investigation into the agency that she used for her employment. All that we found out was that it closed down three years ago.'

'Why was it relevant?' asked Augustus.

'Bernadette, whose real name was Catherine Patrick, had a bad time when she was young. At sixteen, she ran away to London from Ireland. It was in the capital that she got involved in the sex and drugs scene. It was during that time, that she got pregnant and the baby was taken away from her.'

Amy said, 'That probably accounts for why she would pose for the Colonel to make her cottage rent free.'

'Yes,' said Sharon, 'she had spent several years during that period of her life as a stripper in Soho.'

'She must have been able to get away from that life,' said Augustus.

'Yes, it is not clear how. The guess is that the trigger was the baby being taken away. She seemed to disappear for a while, but then trained as a nurse.' Amy thought that is why Theodore found out that she had medical knowledge. But she didn't want to mention him, just in case the police still hadn't picked up his involvement, with Bernadette. It wouldn't need to come out now.

Sharon continued, 'She became a successful nurse and then it got interesting.'

'Why?'

'She left nursing to join an agency that supplied temporary staff, including nurses. The owners were getting old and they made her a partner. When they finally retired, she ran it for a short period on her own, and then closed it down.'

'Is that why she had money?'

'Exactly, and because she was dealing with all forms of identity, she got to understand how her deception could be done.'

'But how did she find Mary?' said Augustus.

Sharon replied, 'That bit is speculation at the moment, but when she was a nurse she worked at the hospital in Greenwich, which was the closest to where Lorraine and Damien lived in London. We are still investigating, but the agency supplied a lot of temporary staff for Social Services in the London area. We guess that Bernadette was determined to find out the adoptive parents.'

'But what made her follow them up here?'

'She probably had known about Mary for a while and was going through the formal channels of being able to meet her at last. Social Services told us that the parents, Lorraine and Damien were completely against it. Therefore it would have to wait until her eighteenth birthday.'

'But when I spoke to Mary,' said Amy, 'she was very undecided, but Bernadette had tried to persuade her to meet her natural mother. I still don't know what she decided in the end.'

'Bernadette would no doubt have been able to see Mary at a distance. In London, because it is such a busy place, no one would notice a person who was often around her and watching her. But it all changed when Lorraine and Damien decided to throw up their life in London and move to the quiet and secluded Nether Crimpton. She would know that she would stand out, so she developed the plan of Bernadette Murphy, and set up a fictitious identity.'

'Was it a real identity?'

'A stolen one as far as we can work out, its probably a young

Irish nurse like herself who went to London to start a career, but after a few years returned to Ireland. Catherine could then have taken her details, such as National Insurance and used those if she was desperate, but it appeared she led this two-fold life very successfully.'

Amy asked, 'What happens to Damien now?'

'He has admitted the break-ins, also we will charge him with grievous bodily harm with the trip wire that he set for you. He will appear in front of the magistrates today and be remanded in custody. We can then put together the whole case of the incidents and we will go through them in detail with him. At the moment he won't admit the murder, or the attempted killing of Anna, but that isn't unusual. Both crimes could mean a life sentence, where as the other offences will be a few years.'

Amy said, 'Do you know when he found out about Bernadette being the mother of Mary?'

Sharon replied, 'He was as talkative as anything about what he had admitted to, but kept denying the major offences. Then he asked about the photograph and we showed it to him. He then went silent and hasn't spoken since.'

From Amy's point of view the matter was now all over and it was time to return to a normal life again. She had re-affirmed last night that Nether Crimpton was not the place for her and she had told her brother. But she had said that she was in no hurry to go and wanted to remember the little village as a happy and friendly place. She had decided to go and see Theodore.

Amy was surprised how quickly yesterday evening, after the arrest of Damien, that her mind cleared and she became relaxed. Scotland now seemed a long time ago, and she had begun to pass it to the back of her mind. She liked Theodore, but was in no hurry for a man. She thought that she would get a good job first and then consider looking for a man.

She thanked Sharon and left her talking to Augustus, and slowly walked the long way round through the village and finally turned up the drive towards Theodore's house. To her surprise it was Ruth, his sister-in-law who opened the door, and said that the men were in the garden chatting and to come through.

Amy raised her eyebrows as she stepped through the french doors into the garden. Theodore immediately stood up, and so did Jeremy, but Justin just sat there with a look of terror on his face.

Ruth snapped at him, 'Justin, a lady has arrived,' and he dragged himself to his feet, but the look of terror on his face at seeing Amy never left him. Theodore came over and surprised Amy by kissing her on the cheek. Jeremy shook hands and said, 'From the rumours that I have heard you have been brave and courageous yet again.' Amy passed the compliment off with a smile.

'Good morning, Justin. I see you are now back, which I am sure is a great relief to your mother and father,' said Amy as she studied the young man and shook her head slightly. It was less than twenty-four hours ago that she was convinced he was the murderer and responsible for all the other incidents in the village. He now looked very timid and frightened. She had pieced together in her own mind as to why he had run away, but she wasn't going to mention it.

He glanced at his mother and father, and said in a quiet voice, 'Good morning, Miss Andrews.'

Theodore said, 'It's a great relief that Justin turned up late last night. After he had briefly spoken with the police, they no longer wanted him.'

Jeremy said, 'It's good to know that he didn't commit any of the offences, but he showed he was a coward again by running away.' Amy had worked out that Justin thought that someone was getting back at those in the room with the drugs. First, there had been Amy's own two accidents and when Anna was hurt, he decided to keep out of the way for a while. After he found out that Clint had been shot at, he left the area.'

Justin said slowly, 'I went to Scarborough and came back when I heard they had arrested Mary's father.'

Jeremy added, 'We haven't dealt with the drug taking yet, but in ten days it will be his eighteenth birthday. He can then tell me what he intends to do with his life. Then I will decide whether I will continue to give him any money or not.'

Amy guessed that Jeremy was a hard task master so she

glanced at Ruth, who had a pitying look for her son, and she said, 'Jeremy is right in many ways. Justin needs to make some decisions about his life.' There is nothing to disagree with there thought Amy.

They chatted a little while about matters in general, but none of the group wished to discuss the recent events and they would all be happy for it to be a book that had been closed, and would always remain so.

When Amy came to take her leave, Theodore walked her back to the front door and said, 'You have been magnificent in this whole catalogue of events, whilst I have let myself down rather badly, and I am deeply grateful to you.' He smiled, kissed her on the cheek and opened the door to let her out. Amy thought that he was going to speak again, but he didn't. He called out a gentle goodbye and closed the door behind her. She had at least expected the dinner invitation to be renewed.

As she walked down the drive she didn't know whether she would have accepted or not. But she wasn't asked and now she couldn't decide whether she was pleased or upset. As she arrived at the bottom of the lane she saw the battered old taxi of Mavis Rudd pull into the yard outside of the barns. Mavis got out first and opened the door for her son, who wearily stepped down from the taxi and the pair of them went into workshop.

Amy hesitated she didn't know whether to go in or not. She wasn't sure why she hesitated, she liked Ged. He hadn't done anything wrong. He was badly ill, and needed help and support, not being ignored. She crossed the yard and lightly tapped on the door of the workshop. It was opened by his mother who said, 'Come in, dear, you are most welcome, come through. She went into the main part of the workshop and was surprised to see Ged with his joiner's apron on.

'It's Amy, dear,' said Mavis. Amy was pleased at the smile she received and there, at least, looked a little more brightness in his eyes today. His mother continued, 'I have just brought him back from the hospital. He's seen a new doctor and that has cheered Ged up by telling him that his illness is completely manageable and will disappear over the years.

Ged came over and said, 'It's such a relief to meet a doctor that understands and to know they have arrested someone else for the crimes.' Amy thought that it wasn't necessarily all over, but she wouldn't mention that to Ged.

'Were the police very heavy with you?' asked Amy, 'I feared they might be after they arrested you in such a dramatic fashion.'

Ged said, 'I think I was lucky, because when I was bundled into the police station, the desk sergeant was very kind.'

'What did he do?'

'He told the men to take off my handcuffs and to take me straight to hospital and that I was in no fit state to be in a police station.'

'That couldn't have pleased the superintendent.'

'No, it didn't. They argued in front of us all, but the sergeant said he was the custody officer and that he refused to accept me because of my medical condition. He won the argument and the superintendent stormed off and I was taken to the hospital.'

'I see you have your apron on.'

'Yes, when I told the doctor what I did, he said that was fine and just to do that for a few days and he would see me again.'

'I'm so pleased to see you are on the mend, Ged.'

'And it's all down to you,' said Mavis.

'I didn't really solve anything, I just happened to get lucky.'

'That not what I meant, my dear.' Amy gave a quizzical face that Mavis noticed, 'It was when you walked through the village with Ged yesterday. There have been several nasty people, who have either ignored us or have been outright hostile, but not you. It made a difference to Ged and he was much calmer as a result.'

Ged nodded and said, 'Yes thanks, it made me feel much better to be able to talk to you and to know that you didn't think I had committed any of those crimes.'

Mavis added, 'And I shall make it a quiet few days, because there are only three people who are welcome here. It's you, and, of course, your brother, the Reverend. And the Colonel.'

'The Colonel,' said Amy with some surprise.

'You know that he is far from our style of living, in the big posh house like that, but he has always been supportive to Ged and has helped him a number of times. He even called into the hospital last night after I had given him the news.'

'Will you manage to stay with Ged for the next few days?' asked Amy.

'Oh, yes, many of the villagers haven't been helpful and they can ring me if they want a taxi. If they are one of the ones who have been spreading nasty rumours, then I shall tell them to bugger off!'

The expression and determination of Ged's mother brought a smile to Amy lips and she said, 'The Colonel will be pleased that he is back home.' Amy just hoped that the relationship between the Colonel and Ged wouldn't break-up in the future, if the pictures of naked Bernadette are part of any trial.

'I was going to pop and tell him that Ged is at home, I'm sure he will want to drop in later and we can talk to him then, as I don't like going to that big old house.'

Amy thought for a moment and knew that she had to go and smooth the water with the Colonel and Lady Crimpton and there was no better time than now so she said, 'I'm just going up to the manor, would you like me to pass the message on for you, then you can stay with Ged. '

'That's very kind of you my dear, I would much appreciate that. You are a great benefit to this village and I hope you will stay.'

Amy just smiled and took her leave of Ged and his mother with a promise that she would pop in regularly. She left the workshop barns and began to walk down the high street towards the manor, when a voice called out, 'Hi Amy, have you got a minute?' It was the landlord of the *Brace of Pheasants*.

She didn't really want to talk to him, but she crossed the road and followed him into the pub. 'We're not open yet, but I wanted to thank you. I speak for many in the village, for all you have done to sort out the ghastly things that have happened.' Amy was embarrassed, but managed a smile and nod. He continued, 'I banned talking about it in the bar in recent days, none of us know the facts, so it just doesn't help.' Amy thought that he was a strange man. His taciturn and abrupt nature were not welcoming, but he often seemed to make a lot of sense. 'Hopefully it's all over now, although I don't think we will every return to the normal we used to know. It must be so hard for Lorraine.'

'Yes, it must,' said Amy who hadn't thought much about her at all. She wondered if she had picked up something from Damien and that was why she took Mary away from the village.

The landlord wasn't a man for small talk so she started to leave and he said, 'You know you are always most welcome. I've brought in some good quality wine for the ladies,' and he showed her a bottle, which Amy acknowledged was good wine. 'You can always bring your brother, I am told that about once a year, he can be persuaded to have a small sherry,' he said holding up a bottle.

Amy laughed and waved goodbye. She walked up the High Street where she received a number of compliments, which she passed off with a smile. She knew that seeing the Colonel and Lady Crimpton was the last difficult thing to do. She decided that she couldn't cope with everyone praising her and that she would go back to Brighton and let it all blow over. Augustus would understand, and she could always volunteer to come back and do her churchwarden duties over the busy Christmas time. That role brought a smile to her face as she passed on the lane in front of the visitor centre. It was closed and police were both outside and inside.

She had now planned the next steps in her mind. This afternoon she would go into the hospital and see Anna for a short while, and then spend the evening with Gus. She would travel back to Brighton in the morning. She had just gone past the visitors centre, when she again heard a voice call out to her, 'Not another one,' she said to herself. But when Amy turned she immediately smiled, as she saw Mary walking towards her. Amy was pleased to see her again, but became concerned about how she would react to her father being arrested.

'Hi, Mary.'

'Hi, Amy, it's lovely to see you again.'

Whilst Amy was pleased to see her, she remembered that she had been told to stay away from Clint and Mary. Whether that still applied she didn't know, but as Lorraine wasn't around she would have a quick chat. Mary explained that her mother had taken her away because of the danger. She didn't feel threatened or frightened, but her mother had insisted. They had both come back this morning after the police called, and her mother had gone into Sheffield to speak to the police, but mainly to see her husband.

Mary just started to speak as though nothing had ever happened, 'I've decided to take your advice and see my mother as a one-off and then decide whether I want to see her again.' That comment made Amy shudder. The poor kid would learn later today, who Bernadette was.

Amy couldn't understand just how someone would break such news, and then have to deal with the reaction. Amy nodded, 'I don't know the full details yet about Dad, but is he really going to be charged with murdering Bernadette?'

'Yes, I think so, but I'm sure someone will come and explain it all to you.'

'Yes,' said Mary thoughtfully, and then added, 'are you going for a walk? And can I join you?' To Amy's ears that little request sounded like a small girl, but within weeks she would be an adult, who would have to sort out her own life.

'Yes, of course, but I must quickly pop in and see the Colonel first, it won't take long.' Amy decided it was better to walk with Mary and just give the message about Ged. She could come back at another time and make her peace with Lady Crimpton and the Colonel.

Mary had made a face when she mentioned the Colonel, and she said, 'He's a bit creepy, but I'm happy if I'm with you.'

Amy smiled at her young friend, 'Yes, he is isn't he?'

The little old car had gone and they wondered whether anyone was at home, but Amy knew that Lady Crimpton often went out on her own, so they still went up to the house, to find that the front door was wide open. Amy knocked, and called out, but there was no reply.

'He must be here, but hasn't heard us. Let's just go down to the end of the corridor to check if we can find him. If he is not here, I will write a note and then we can shut the door on the way out.' There was no one in the living room, and so it was a bit of a mystery as to why the front door was wide open. Amy took a pen and a scrap of paper and left a note about Ged. They had just come out of the room, where she had left the note, when there was a distinct scraping noise from further down the corridor.

'This is a really scary place,' said Mary with a shiver.

'Yes, it is. Come on let's go, I've left the note.' It was then that they heard a large groan. Both froze where they were and Mary grabbed Amy's arm, who wasn't sure what to do. 'We'll leave it to the police,' said Amy, 'this is not the place for you.'

'No,' whispered Mary, 'it was a definite groan someone is hurt, and they are not far away.'

In a very low voice, Amy said, 'You go back to the front door and wait outside, while I go and have a look.'

'No, I'm not going through this house on my own, let's go together to find out who groaned,'

Amy put her fingers to her lips, not so much for the reason they had to be quiet, but she wanted to see if she could hear where any noise was coming from. They crept along the corridor together. They had just reached the second door when there was a loud crash and a woman's voice said, 'Damn!'

'That's mum's voice,' said Mary straight away and went towards the door, 'she might be hurt.' Amy knew she had to get to the door first, but they arrived at the same time and they quickly opened the door and went in.

The scene in the room shocked them both. Mary screamed and Amy grabbed her to hide her from the grim reality of the Colonel's body slumped under the window.

He was motionless and a lot of blood was coming from his stomach. The sudden surprise of the door bursting open caused Lorraine, who was on the far side of the room to spin round, and face them. Amy looked at her face and saw evil in it. Her attention then transferred to the gun, that was in Lorraine's hand, and was pointed at her.

'Mum, mum, what's happened?' shouted Mary, 'why have you got that gun? But she didn't let go of her grasp of Amy. Mary then realised what had happened, 'You've shot him! You've shot him!'

'It was an accident! It was an accident! He drew a gun on me and I struggled with him and it went off.'

'Put the gun down, Lorraine,' said Amy in as calm a voice as she could manage.

'Come over here, my darling, Mary.' Mary went to let go of her grip on Amy's arm, when Lorraine spoke again, 'He was a nasty man and tried to blackmail me and hurt you. It was an accident when I shot him.' Amy felt Mary relax a little, but she stayed fully alert.

Mary said, 'Put the gun down mum, it's frightening me and Amy.' Mary released the grip on Amy and stepped slightly away, 'Why won't you put it down, mum?'

'Come over here, my darling, we can't trust her, she will make up some lies about what happened and we don't want that.' Lorraine tried to point the gun more accurately at Amy.

'Mary, step to the side out of the way of the gun,' said Amy, 'it's only me she wants to aim at.'

'What!' said Mary but she didn't move. 'I'm not moving until you put the gun down.

'I've done it all for you and now come over here quickly,' and Amy could hear that there was menace in her voice.

Mary looked quickly back and forth between her mother and Amy, who looked around the room to see whether there was anything that might help her get out of here. It was the room where the Colonel had taken his pictures of Bernadette. There were two cameras on tripods and several lights with reflective screens. Mary was still torn as to what she should do and Amy could see it on her face.

Lorraine moved to try to get a better aim at Amy, and to avoid Mary, but as she moved her heel caught a tripod and sent the camera crashing to the floor. She dropped the folder she was carrying and, the photos that were in it, spread all over the floor

Amy knew it was too far across the room to attempt to tackle Lorraine, who regained her balance and composure quickly, and still pointed the gun directly at her. Mary was still not away from the line of sight. Amy saw her glance at the photos on the floor and she went to bend down to pick one up when Lorraine shouted, 'Don't! Please don't touch them! Don't even look at them!'

Amy admired the bravery of Mary as she continued to bend down. She picked up one photograph. Lorraine began to cry, and so did Mary, who said in a low voice, 'This is you.' Amy had already seen they were naked photos, but thought they were the ones of Bernadette.

'He made me do it! He made me do it! He blackmailed me.'

'I don't understand about the photos, and I don't know why you won't put the gun down.'

'She'll tell lies about us and then we'll be separated. She was part of the plot with that dirty old man there.'

'I wasn't Mary, I wasn't part of any plot.'

'Be quiet! Be quiet! Or I shall shoot you.'

It was that threat that Amy could see had the effect on Mary, who shouted, 'You're not going to shoot my friend,' and she rushed back into Amy's arms, who wasn't prepared for that movement by the brave young girl.

'Leave me, Mary, stand out of the way, your mother is dangerous, but she won't hurt you.'

'No, I'm not moving, until mum puts down that gun.'

Lorraine was now shaking with rage. Amy was convinced she would shoot, if she got the chance. Mary said, 'Amy, why won't she put the gun down. Why has she allowed those pictures to be taken, tell me, tell me,' she sobbed.

'It was all for you darling.'

Mary looked at her and said, 'I wouldn't want you to do any of this for me. You shouldn't have undressed so that man could take pictures of you,' Amy felt her shiver as she looked at the body slumped by the window, 'You can't say you did it for me. Why did you do it? Why did you do it?'

Amy could see that it had a devastating effect on Lorraine, who moved the gun carelessly and restlessly between her hands, but she didn't say anything.

Amy said, 'Put down the gun Lorraine and I'll leave you alone with Mary so you can explain to her. You know it's best that it comes from you.'

'Shut up! Shut up!'

'You know that you wouldn't shoot Mary, even if you shoot

me. Mary will be a witness and you will never get her to lie.'

'You're not going to shoot Amy,' said Mary and stepped in front of Amy.

'Get out of the way, you don't understand.' Lorraine wanted to frighten her daughter out of the way and so she fired twice at the windows, which shattered with a resounding crash. The ploy didn't work and Mary turned and caught hold of Amy even tighter.

'What does she have to explain?' said Mary.

'The police know Lorraine. Social services are on their way here this afternoon. Give me the gun and have some time with Mary. Damien went along with your ideas, but Mary won't.' Amy was hoping she hadn't gone too far, she didn't want Lorraine to think the only way out was to kill all three of them.

She was that unstable anything could happen. Why Amy looked down she wasn't sure, but she focused on Lorraine's red shoes and could see that a piece of the material had torn off by the heel. It all became clear, it was Lorraine that had released the brake on the car that started the log roll. Amy also now knew that Damien had been right. He had only done a few things at Lorraine's beck and call. It was her that had found out about Bernadette being the mother of Mary, perhaps she got it from the picture. It was even worse when she found that her husband was having an affair with her. It was Bernadette's way of ensuring she could get close to Mary.

It was Lorraine that had murdered Bernadette and tried to kill Anna. Lorraine's movement brought her back to the reality of how she was going to get out of this. Mary was still staring at the pictures on the floor, Amy said, 'They were nothing to do with it were they?'

But Lorraine didn't answer. Amy knew that her best hope was to keep her talking, 'Mary, your mother was desperate to improve the business and wanted the footpath and cycle way, so it was a way of getting the Colonel's support, the pictures are not that bad. She came here this afternoon to get back the pictures, but she didn't mean to shoot him.'

It didn't seem to pacify either of them, but then the tension was broken by a policeman's face at the window. Lorraine fired and missed. Mary grabbed Amy even tighter. Amy heard the police shouting into his radio, 'One person shot, two hostages taken, and fugitive still armed! Call the armed units and a negotiator!'

'It's over Lorraine,' said Amy, who now concentrated on trying to get all three of them out of there alive, but she showed no reaction. There was movement outside of the room and Lorraine shouted, 'Stay away, I have a hostage!'

There was a general knock on the door and Amy immediately recognised her brother's voice who said, 'This is the Reverend Andrews, I am going to come in, please do not fire. I am unarmed and there are no tricks.'

'Stay there, Gus, Lorraine is just going to put the gun down. Mary and I are quite safe.'

'I will come in slowly,' said her brother, 'there are no police with me.'

The door slowly opened and gradually Gus stepped into the room. Amy was amazed how calm he looked. His eyes searched around the room as though he was going into any ordinary room and expected to be offered a cup of tea.

'Hello, Lorraine,' he said, 'I don't want you to shoot anyone else, so will you give me the gun and he took a few steps towards her.'

Even with all the tension Amy though it was bizarre that another gentle knock came at the door. The voice which was unmistakably Ged's said, 'Who ever you are with the gun, this is Ged.'

'This is Amy, Ged, Lorraine has a gun and is just going to give it to Gus,' but Lorraine just waved it around.

'Lorraine, you will recognise my voice. I have no gun and have no interest in you. But I'm coming in slowly and deliberately to get the Colonel. Amy was convinced he was dead, but didn't speak.

The door slowly opened and Ged came in and said, 'The police are back down the end of the corridor. I've come for the Colonel.'

'I'll shoot you if you cross the room.'

'Then you are going to have to shoot, I'm taking the Colonel and he slowly moved across and picked up the old man's body and carried it from the room.'

'Mum, I can't stand any more of this, give me the gun. You mustn't shoot the vicar and Amy, I don't know what's happened, but you can't shoot them,' and she walked up to her mother, but didn't take the gun, she threw her arms around her neck. Augustus was close enough to step forward and take the gun from her, so that she could hug her daughter. And that happened just as they heard the sound of the police helicopter landing and the distant sirens.

Amy hugged her brother, and then called out, 'It's over' and opened the door and went into the corridor. She could see armed police at the end of the corridor and they raised their guns. Ged, who was tending to the Colonel, with two paramedics said, 'Put your guns down, she said it's all over.'

Amy said, 'My brother, the vicar has the gun, and Lorraine is going to be brought out by her daughter.' Amy saw Theodore rushed forward to help with the Colonel, and behind the line of police was the Brigadier who had obviously just arrived and he barked out his orders, 'Shoulder arms, policewomen to the fore. I know this woman get her help immediately.'

Two of the woman police officers came straight down the corridor to meet Amy, who turned to see Mary with her arm around Lorraine leading her towards them. They were followed by Gus, who held the gun down by his side.

'Place the gun on the floor please sir.' Augustus did as he was expected. He continued to follow Mary and Lorraine. By the time they had reached the sitting room the place was swarming with police and paramedics.

Sharon arrived with local senior officers, who were keen to ensure everyone was checked over by the medical teams, before they were asked to give an account of what had happened.

Amy explained to Sharon that it was her belief that Lorraine killed Bernadette and attempted to kill Anna. She had also shot the Colonel with his own gun, when he had tried to blackmail her into more pictures. Sharon said that it would fit exactly with what Damien would admit to, and she passed the information on to the inspector. Amy was so relieved it was all over now, but she felt piteously sorry for Mary, and the social worker who would have to tell her the whole story. The medical checks and the initial questions took some time.

Lady Crimpton, who was in Sheffield, was told that her husband had been shot and died from his injuries. Various rooms in the house were turned into use for sections of the police operation. Lorraine had been arrested, and taken away, and another doctor who had arrived, was checking over Mary.

The old house was now quietening down. One policeman, who came in said that most of the village already knew that the vicar and Ged had been the heroes, which pleased Amy. She also knew it would embarrass both of them. But she felt calm and easy, and she moved to the main room where Sharon and Gus were laughing together. She went over and said, 'What's so funny?'

They both glanced at each other, and Sharon nodded to Gus.

Amy said, 'Go on, tell me, what are you two up to?'

'We were going to keep it a secret, but that has only lasted about five minutes,' said Gus,

Sharon said, 'We are going out on Friday together.'

'That's wonderful news,' said Amy as she gave them both a hug.

'Don't get too carried away, its only a day out together.'

'It's still wonderful news.'

They walked off with Sharon going back to her work, and Augustus going to see if his parishioners needed him. Theodore came up to say goodbye. He said to Amy,'You truly are a remarkable woman.'

Amy decided that she wasn't going to let him get away with just that, life was too short, so she said with a smile, 'If I am that remarkable, you can take me out to dinner tomorrow.'

He gave a wonderful smile back and said, 'It will be a pleasure,' and he left with his face beaming.

'That felt good,' she said to herself. She had one last duty and that was to say goodbye to Mary, and then she would go and see Anna.

Amy looked across the large room and saw some of the police

officers, including Sharon, talking to a woman who, Amy didn't know. She saw Sharon and the others nod and the woman walked across to Amy.

'I am the Head of Social Services and I have come up to talk to Mary about the complex case of her natural mother, which I believe you know all about, according to the officers.'

'Yes,' said Amy, 'could I help in any way?'

She looked Amy up and down and said, 'Yes, you can. Mary does not want to speak to me. She is adamant on that. She wants to know about her natural mother and why have her adopted mother and father been arrested.'

'Yes,' said Amy warily.

'And she said that she wants you to explain it, because you understand it all. The officers have agreed, here is the file.'

Amy's immediate reaction was that she couldn't do it, but knew she had to. She took the folder and went along the corridor to the room where Mary was waiting, she took a very deep breath and opened the door.

'Hello, Mary, I've come to explain...'

She never got any further as Mary threw her arms around Amy's neck and sobbed.

Books from The Creative Peak - Fiction

Weaving a Tangled Web - Terry Melvin
(Paperback and e-book)
ISBN 978-1-910236-01-7 (Paperback)

Accusations! They dominate Daz Faulkner's life. He also has talent and is driven to succeed. Daz is planning to get to the top in the computer industry, but faces immediate problems because he is down on his luck and financial hardships are beginning to bite.

The constant bickering with his long-term girlfriend means the relationship is going nowhere. He is desperate for some quick money to turn his life around. But how can he get some when everything seems stacked up against him? He knows there is no turning back, he must press on, but dare he risk running close to the law.

Then three new intriguing women come into his life, but are they what they seem to be? Daz struggles to deal with their competing demands. He is forced into some murky deals. The web of intrigue and deception deepens, especially as the police always seem to looking over his shoulder. Can he get his life back on track and rebuild his relationship?

Will He Come Back? - T A Cherry
(Paperback and e-book)
ISBN 978-1-910236-02-4 (Paperback)

Fashion was Jessica's entire life before she fell in love. She loved the drama at being at the cutting edge of the fashion world. She worked hard and played into the night in the high spots of London, Rome and Paris.

Then she met Justin. He was a City high flier, with a salary to match. It was love at first sight and she never looked back. They married and two children quickly followed. She became a proud mum at home, and dedicated herself to her husband and kids.

She is now in her late thirties and on impulse Justin has recently bought a farm in a remote part of the Peak District and moved his family there. But with her daughter at boarding school and her son starting university, she is getting lonely and longs for the high life again. And then Justin leaves as usual one Monday morning, but it wasn't for work, he was going to another woman.

**For all books please visit the website
www. thecreativepeak.com**

Model for Murder - Mel Cope
(Paperback and e-book)
ISBN 978-1-910236-00-0 (Paperback)

Andrea is an international supermodel married to Martin, the UK's youngest Police Superintendent. They become a celebrity couple after Martin is praised on the front pages of newspapers for his courage. Whilst she is drawn away to the fashion houses of the world, and Martin dedicates himself to the hard and gruelling work of his job, they are the epitome of a happily married couple.

Suddenly things start to go wrong. Martin's reputation is on-the-line when he fails to make progress in solving an armed robbery near where they both live. The stress is heaped on him when one of Andrea's friends is killed. He tries to protect his wife from the horror of violence and death, but she is at the centre of the events. Andrea wants to help her husband but has to deal with Martin's contrary inspector, who wants her out of harm's way.

The memory of her dead friend means she desperately wants to help. As the case deepens, she becomes frightened, but will not give it as she knows she must give it her all. The fashion catwalks beckon her to return to normal, but will she be safe?

The Elusive Quest - T M Elvey
(Paperback and e-book)
ISBN 978-1-910236-04-8 (Paperback)

The past meant she now had no friends, little money and an ailing father. She feared starting a relationship. The dark days couldn't be blanked from her mind. She had tried many times, but had never succeeded. All she wanted was to go back to the happy times. Would the long summer days bring the peace of mind and tranquillity that she earnestly desired?

Her own boldness frightened her when she decided to meet five strangers. In a rash moment she had decided that a walking holiday in the Peak District would bring her out of her shell, but could she go through with it?

The profiles she received gave her anticipation and fear. She only wanted one friend. Was that too much to ask?
The businessman is a rich widower. Should she dare to think of him as a potential......
Perhaps it would be the other man in the group, he was a slick salesman, and was very good- looking......
Friendship was more important to her than a relationship so perhaps one of the woman could become her friend.
The police officer, now she looked a steady sort.
Or the woman in her forties, she was old enough to have views on life, but young enough to understand.
But it would be the farm worker who was nearest to her age.

She wondered why they all wanted to join her on a holiday.

For all books please visit the website
www. thecreativepeak.com

Books from The Creative Peak - Non-Fiction
The Literary Way - Terry Goble
(Paperback and e-book)
ISBN - 978-1-910236-05-5
Ellastone to Hayfield

"*Twenty-one circular walks combine to form a fascinating long-distance route exploring the writers and landscape of the Peak District*"

Writers on the route include:
Samuel Johnson, George Eliot, Alexandre Dumas, Mary Shelley, Lord Byron, Daniel Defoe, Sir Walter Scott, Jean-Jacques Rousseau, D H Lawrence, Agatha Christie, George Bernard Shaw, E M

Forster, Ben Jonson, Robert Louis Stephenson, William Wordsworth, Alison Uttley & many more
www.theliteraryway.com

Food for Countryside Moods - Terry Goble
(Paperback and e-book)
ISBN - 978-1-910236-06-2

"Recipes inspired by the weather, season and the countryside"

The Countryside Awakes
Lazy Hazy Days
The Fires of Autumn
Grey Days
Crisp and Even

The fresh air and ambience of the delightful countryside of the Peak District builds our appetites as we cross the hills, valleys and moors of one of England's premier areas of natural beauty. The different moods of the landscape, whether it is the dark grey days of heavy mist, or the scintillating brightness of a fresh spring, engender the desire for food that responds to those moods.

The recipes drawn their originality from the countryside moods combined with the international flavours and tastes that are so much part of our modern cuisine. We present of fusion of cookery created from readily available fresh ingredients. The healthiness of walking the countryside is complemented by the carefully considered cooking methods which use tasty ingredients cooked in a light and nutritious way.

www.foodforcountrysidemoods.com

For all books please visit the website
www. thecreativepeak.com